Freeman Wills Crofts was born i
died in 1957. He worked for a
company as an engineer until 19 [illegible] to
detective fiction.

His plots reveal his mathematical training and he specialised in the seemingly unbreakable alibi and the intricacies of railway timetables. He also loved ships and trains and they feature in many of his stories.

Crofts' best-known character is Inspector Joseph French. French appears for the first time in *Inspector French's Greatest Case*. He is a detective who achieves his results through dogged persistence.

Raymond Chandler praised Crofts' plots, calling him 'the soundest builder of them all'.

BY THE SAME AUTHOR
ALL PUBLISHED BY HOUSE OF STRATUS

THE 12.30 FROM CROYDON
ANTIDOTE TO VENOM
ANYTHING TO DECLARE
THE BOX OFFICE MURDERS
THE CASK
CRIME AT GUILDFORD
DEATH OF A TRAIN
DEATH ON THE WAY
ENEMY UNSEEN
THE END OF ANDREW HARRISON
FATAL VENTURE
FEAR COMES TO CHALFONT
FRENCH STRIKES OIL
GOLDEN ASHES
THE GROOTE PARK MURDER
THE HOG'S BACK MYSTERY
INSPECTOR FRENCH AND THE CHEYNE MYSTERY
INSPECTOR FRENCH AND THE STARVEL TRAGEDY
INSPECTOR FRENCH'S GREATEST CASE
JAMES TARRANT, ADVENTURER
THE LOSING GAME
THE LOSS OF THE JANE VOSPER
MAN OVERBOARD!
MANY A SLIP
MYSTERY IN THE CHANNEL
MURDERERS MAKE MISTAKES
MYSTERY OF THE SLEEPING CAR EXPRESS
MYSTERY ON SOUTHAMPTON WATER
THE PIT-PROP SYNDICATE
THE PONSON CASE
THE SEA MYSTERY
SILENCE FOR THE MURDERER
SIR JOHN MAGILL'S LAST JOURNEY
SUDDEN DEATH

FREEMAN WILLS CROFTS

Found Floating

This edition published in 2000 by House of Stratus, an imprint of Stratus Holdings plc, 24c Old Burlington Street, London, W1X 1RL, UK.

www.houseofstratus.com

Typeset, printed and bound by House of Stratus.

A catalogue record for this book is available from the British Library.

ISBN 1-84232-392-X

For the sake of verisimilitude the scenes of this story have been laid in real places. All the characters introduced, however, are wholly imaginary, and if the name of any living person has been used, this has been done inadvertently and no reference to such person is intended.

CONTENTS

AUTHOR'S NOTE. This book was written before the Spanish War broke out. It is to be understood therefore that the Carringtons' Olympic cruise took place before the start of that unhappy conflict.

– 1 –

THE INDISPOSITION OF WILLIAM

It was the look she surprised on Jim Musgrave's face that first revealed to Katherine Shirley depths in her cousin's mind which she had never before imagined could exist. For it was a very terrible look that had shone momentarily in the blue eyes and twisted the good-looking features into an evil and repulsive mask. A look of hate, of baffled rage, of desire to destroy. The vision amazed and horrified Katherine. For the first time in her life she saw murder stamped on a man's face.

She had always liked her Cousin Jim. He really was a good fellow at heart, and up till now she would have said he was not the enemy of anyone in the world. He was tolerant and easy going: a lot too much so for his own good. In business indeed he was actually slack, slack enough, Katherine knew, to have injured his prospects of advancement. But though irritating in business, that slackness made him a pleasant companion socially. He was easy to get on with, remained unruffled in the minor adversities of everyday life, and never took offence at trifles.

This easy-going quality was what had made the revelation of his hidden passion so surprising and horrifying to Katherine. She feared that when a man like Jim looked as he had looked, he would stop at nothing to gratify his hate.

It was not against herself that his animosity was directed. When she had learnt Jim's secret he was unaware of her presence. He had called one evening to see Mant on business, and when he was leaving, Mant had himself shown him to the door. Katherine had heard them in the hall and had come out of the sitting room to ask Jim to stay for a drink. As she opened the door they had bid each other good night, and it was when Jim was turning away that she had seen his face. Her invitation remained stillborn on her lips. After a glance at Mant she had pulled herself together. Obviously he had noticed nothing.

"I was going to ask Jim to come in," she said, trying not to speak tremulously, "but he seems in a hurry."

"You can ask him another night," Mant had answered carelessly, passing down the hall to his study.

Thus Katherine had learnt that Jim Musgrave hated Mant Carrington with a deadly hatred. In the fact lay possibilities which might shatter the pleasant and happy lives of all of them. As she turned back to the sitting room Katherine shivered with dismay and foreboding.

She could not get the episode out of her mind, and picking up her sewing again, she let her thoughts run back over their family history, wondering what could have so incensed Jim.

They were cousins, these three, Jim Musgrave, Mant Carrington, and herself. She and Jim were also lifelong friends, having been brought up together in the district in which they were still living. But Mant was a newcomer. Born in Australia, he had lived there until some six months earlier, when he had come to join the others in England.

The head of the family, now long deceased, was Thomas Carrington. Katherine remembered him as a tall emaciated man with a beard, like the pictures she afterwards saw of

Abraham Lincoln. He had a habit of substituting "this little girl" for the personal pronoun in speaking to her, saying, "Would this little girl like an apple?" or, "What has this little girl been doing today?" But in spite of his peculiarities and his portentously solemn manner, she had liked him. He had always been kind, and in her child's mind she felt sure he meant well.

Old Thomas Carrington had flourished in the closing decades of the last century. "Flourished" was indeed the word to apply to him. He had started, so Katherine had learnt, as message boy in the small St Elmo Electric Supply Works at Bromsley in the outskirts of Birmingham, and had ended up by owning the whole place; and not only the place as it was when he entered, but a vastly larger and more important concern.

Thomas had four children, two sons and two daughters, of whom the youngest was Katherine's mother. The sons – her uncles – had early qualified in engineering – George in electric and William in civil – and had entered the works under their father. The firm not only supplied electric equipment, but erected it, and it was old Thomas's custom to send his two sons as engineers-in-charge of the larger jobs. William superintended the erection of the buildings and the putting in of foundations for the machinery, while George saw to the assembly of the machines themselves.

A good many of their jobs were carried out abroad, and in the early years of the present century they reached their till then high-water mark with an order for a complete electrical installation for the town of Akkondi on the Gold Coast. The two young men were sent out, but during the work there occurred between them some disagreement, and after the job was finished they separated, George leaving the firm and going to Australia, while William returned home to his father. William made good in the works, and when his father died in 1910 he inherited them, with half the old man's money to run them on.

George did not break entirely with his family. At long intervals letters were exchanged, by which those at home knew that he was married in Australia and had a son, the Mant who afterwards came to England. But George was not referred to with enthusiasm at Thomas's residence, the Grey House, it being tacitly held that he had acted badly in leaving the firm. All this Katherine had picked up at various times as she grew older.

Her own mother, Edith Carrington that was, had married a solicitor called Shirley, and she had been an only child. Her aunt, Maude Carrington, had also married – an accountant named Musgrave. Both of these latter were dead, their son, Jim Musgrave, being the cousin about whom Katherine was now so distressed.

William Carrington before the coming of Mant was a fine upstanding figure of a man in the late fifties. He had indeed always been something of an athlete. In his study were various trophies, cups and goblets mostly, for swimming, for the longer events in running, and for fencing. He had also been a skilful boxer, and as a young man had cleared 5 feet 4 inches with a running start. Though naturally he had long since given up these sports, he was in the habit of doing daily exercises and remained remarkably fit for a man of his years. Often he surprised Katherine by his strength and endurance. He dug in the garden with vastly more vigour than the man he hired for the work, and on their occasional works excursions to the moors or to North Wales he easily out-distanced all but the very young and energetic.

Mentally William was equally robust. To Katherine's own knowledge he was extraordinarily resourceful in dealing with the small emergencies which arose about the house, and she believed he was equally ingenious in his engineering management, as well as tactful in dealing with men. He was quick to make up his mind, and a decision once reached, he put it into effect with an energy which at times approached ruthlessness. He had the reputation of being honest with his public and fair to his staff, and he was generally respected, though by no means universally beloved.

William had never married, and Katherine kept house for him. Though she might not have admitted it herself, she was a quiet, rather retiring young woman of some three and thirty, whose chief interest in life was water-colour sketching. She was imaginative and artistic, but a blow she had had some ten years earlier had thrown her in on herself and robbed her of a good deal of her vitality. She had become engaged to the son of a Yorkshire mill owner, a pleasant young fellow with excellent prospects. The engagement had been announced and all was going well. Katherine was happier than she could have believed possible and the date of the wedding was being discussed. Then tragedy had intervened. The young man was driving his car through a village when suddenly a child ran out of a side road just in front of him. He swerved, collided with a lorry coming in the opposite direction, and was instantly killed.

For a time Katherine was inconsolable, then the death of her father and mother within a short time of each other added to her trouble and broke up her home. She had nowhere to go and her zest in life for the time being was dead. It was then that William had offered her a home in his bachelor establishment.

Gradually a curious kind of unemotional friendship developed between uncle and niece. William began to talk to her about the business. Finding she was responsive and could keep her own counsel, he grew more and more to confide in her, till gradually there was little about the inner working of the concern that she didn't know.

But recently a new and more normal interest had come into Katherine's life. A Birmingham doctor, a middle-aged man, had bought a practice in Bromsley. Katherine had met him at a friend's house. She had felt attracted to him, and to her surprise – she was in that frame of mind – he had appeared equally interested in her. They had had several other meetings, mostly, she noticed, through his contriving. Nothing had been said on either side, but she had come to believe that he loved her. The thought brought fresh life to her. She grew more like her old self, blossoming out as if her development, arrested during that dark ten years, had resumed its normal evolution. When she imagined what Dr Jellicoe might soon say to her, she smiled dreamily.

But now as she sat over her needlework her thoughts were far from happy. All was not well in her immediate circle. That revelation of Jim's inmost feelings had left her dismayed, if not actually frightened. She looked towards the future with foreboding.

Jim Musgrave occupied a comparatively minor position in the works. There was unhappily not the same cordial feeling between uncle and nephew as there was between uncle and niece. Jim was too slack, too casual: lazy, in fact. William's decisive and energetic mind chafed at Jim's easy-going methods. And William seldom hid his opinions. His comment on Jim's proceedings took some such form as, "Hang it all, man! Can't you wake up and get a move on?"

while Jim's reaction was: "What the blazes is the hurry? The thing can't go till tomorrow, anyway."

So it was that Jim's standing in the works was satisfactory neither to himself nor his uncle. He was technically Assistant Works Manager. Actually he had little power and was trusted only with comparatively small jobs. Jim felt it. He couldn't see why his handling of business, if less showy, was less efficient than William's own, and he felt his position humiliated him before the workers. He had a grievance, in fact, and he would have liked nothing better than to leave the works and look for a job elsewhere. But here again his easy-going character operated. He lacked the initiative to make the move.

But in spite of this business friction, Jim's personal relations with his uncle were normally good. He was a welcome visitor at the Grey House whenever he chose to put in an appearance, and he was asked to dine quite often. There was something likeable about Jim, in spite of his rather careless ways. Katherine, indeed, was sincerely attached to him.

So life had progressed up till about six months before Katherine had learnt the terrible secret of Jim's hatred for Mant. But during that intervening period events took place which were to have a deep significance for the family.

First came William's breakdown in health.

It was one evening on his return from the works that Katherine first noticed the change. The moment he entered the house she saw that something was wrong. He was preoccupied and depressed, ate practically nothing for supper, and scarcely spoke a word. When Katherine asked what was the matter he seemed annoyed and answered shortly that there was nothing. At first she imagined the trouble was mental: that he had received some shock or bad news. But afterwards she heard that he had had a kind of seizure at the works and had sent out urgently for brandy. She pressed him to have the doctor, but he refused quite brusquely. She felt she had come within measurable distance of being told to mind her own business.

A week later he had occasion to go up to London and when he returned she saw that he was considerably worse. He now admitted to feeling ill, and after some questioning she learnt that in the train on the way back he had had another attack similar to the first. At once the thought of the athlete's strained heart occurred to her, and she insisted on his seeing a doctor. He had been so healthy all his life that he had no regular medical man, and the question of selection therefore arose. In spite of Katherine's anxiety it was with a thrill that she heard him say: "I can't stand that old ass, Ponting. We'll have the new man, Jellicoe."

Dr Jellicoe came and was extraordinarily professional. But he was not extraordinarily illuminating. He sounded the old man and asked him questions. He took his blood pressure. He looked grave and very profound. Then he gave judgment.

"I'm glad to tell you, Mr Carrington, that there's nothing organic the matter with you. It looked at first, I admit, a little like your heart, but you'll be pleased to know that your heart is perfectly sound. It seems to me you've been overworking and you've just got the resultant breakdown."

"Nothing of the kind," William answered helpfully. "I never overwork."

But Dr Jellicoe was not to be beaten. He called Katherine.

"Tell me, Miss Shirley," he asked innocently, "how long is it since your uncle has had a holiday?"

Katherine shook her head. "It's ages," she declared. "Years! No proper holiday last year, though last February he did go out to Toulon on an Olympic cruise. But that was partly business: he wanted to see about contracts in Spain. However, it meant about a fortnight out of the office."

Jellicoe looked severely at his patient, yet with a kind of triumph in his eye. "What did I tell you, Mr Carrington? Now you've got to drop work for at least a month. Go off to Madeira or somewhere of that kind and put business out of your mind. If you don't," the doctor held up his finger and spoke as an oracle, "if you don't, it may become a year's job."

But William did not take a holiday – not then. He worked on for some days longer, growing gradually more irritable, more silent, more depressed. Katherine called in Jellicoe again, and once more the doctor urged him to take some action. But still he would do nothing. Then one day he amazed and rather shocked Katherine.

"I've cabled to Mant," he said, "offering him my place. He to do the work: I to act as consultant. I find the doctor is right. I can't go on. I must have a rest to shake off this – this illness."

Katherine stared. "Mant!" she exclaimed helplessly.

"Yes, Mant," he repeated testily. "Who else?"

"But you don't know Mant," she protested.

"I know about him. I've made very careful enquiries. He's an able fellow, and what's more, he's a worker."

The words were a hint to her not to make the suggestion he evidently saw in her mind; But she made it all the same. "What about Jim? Don't you think that with your supervision he could do it? And after all" – she paused at a slight loss – "after all Jim's here and he's – he's a good fellow," she ended lamely.

"He's a very good fellow, I grant," William admitted, "but you know as well as I do he's no businessman. In Jim's hands the works would be down and out in a twelvemonth. No, I've cabled to Mant and I'll be surprised if he doesn't come."

Katherine knew her uncle too well to protest further, but she saw at once that this would be a dreadful blow to Jim. She was sorry for Jim, but she did not see what more she could do in the matter.

Both William's elder brother George, who had gone to Australia from the Gold Coast job, and his wife, had died, and at this time their son Mant was a man of some five and thirty, unmarried and alone in the world. Odd phrases in his occasional letters had thrown some light on his career. That he had been through college and had taken a degree in engineering was known, also that he had a fairly good job in an electricity supplies firm in Sydney. What William's further information amounted to Katherine did not know. He volunteered no more, and she didn't ask.

For three days William made no reference to the matter, then on his return from the works he told Katherine that he had had a reply from Mant. "He's leaving his job at once and coming home by air. It'll take him a few days to square things up in Sydney, but he should be here in less than a month. Then I'll take all the holiday you want." He paused, then went on with an unusual hesitation: "I'm sorry about Jim, but what could I do? After all Mant is my nephew too, and the son of my elder brother. If my father had been alive it is what he would have done. Your Uncle George was a good fellow, and though we had a row about a girl long ago, it never developed into a real quarrel, and I should like to do what I could for his son."

This was the first time Katherine had ever heard her uncle refer to that unpleasantness which had taken place on the Gold Coast so many years before. She wondered what exactly had happened, but even with the opening he had given her, she did not like to ask him. He was very close, was her Uncle William, and he could never be drawn.

Mant's acceptance of his invitation seemed to gratify William. He settled down to await his nephew's arrival in a more contented frame of mind. He was taking things at the works more easily, Katherine knew, both from his frequent early arrivals home, and also from various things Jim told her. He seemed slightly better in himself also, and so far as she knew, had no further attacks. But even so, he had lost much of his former efficiency and energy. Indeed, at times she could not but see that he had been severely shaken, and was but little more than the wreck of his former self.

On his return one evening he told Katherine he had heard from Mant. "He's arrived in London," he explained, "and he'll be down here tomorrow for lunch."

"Here?" Katherine asked.

"Yes." For the second time William hesitated in a way utterly unlike himself. "As a matter of fact, Katherine, I've asked him to stay with us, at least for the present. I hope you won't mind?"

"Mind?" Katherine repeated. "Oh no. Why should I?"

If Mant proved agreeable it would, she thought, be pleasant rather than otherwise to have him. Often she found their way of life lonely; just the two of them in the house with the maid. And William after all was not much of a companion. He talked to her about the business, it was true, but she sometimes got tired of the business, and they had little else in common. Of course she was her own mistress. She could come or go at her pleasure and invite her friends to the house as she chose. But this last was usually for lunch. William did not object in so many words to visitors for dinner, but she could see he didn't like it. For one thing, it meant dressing, and he preferred his rather disreputable old smoking jacket; for another it gave him the trouble of making polite conversation, which he disliked extremely.

Katherine had often thought of leaving the Grey House and going abroad, perhaps to Italy, where she could sketch and get among painting people. She could have afforded it. Her grandfather, old Thomas Carrington, had, as has been said, left half his money to William, as necessary capital for the running of the works. The other half he had divided between his son George in Australia, and his daughters, the mothers of Katherine and Jim respectively. George had got a quarter of the whole, and Katherine and Jim, and Eva, Jim's sister, through their mothers, one twelfth apiece. These twelfths, invested, brought each in some £200 a year. In addition William allowed Katherine another £200 a year with, of course, board and lodging, for keeping house for him and acting as his hostess. Of her £400 she never spent more than about a quarter, so she had a tidy nest egg in the bank to draw on in case of emergency.

Katherine had committed the terrible mistake of allowing her triple loss in the deaths of her lover, father and mother to rob her of her energy and initiative. When these blows had fallen she had felt it was no longer worthwhile making any exertion. And when she recovered from the shock she found she had formed a habit – the habit of living at the Grey House, and she had not made the effort necessary to break it. There was in fact a little more in it than that. She feared that if once she left the Grey House, say for a winter in Italy, her uncle would make different arrangements – perhaps marry – and though his house would doubtless still remain open to her, she would not care to stay in it otherwise than as its mistress.

So she remained on in what were after all very comfortable circumstances. She had, during the ten years of her residence there, formed many contacts outside the house. Though not specially good at games, she belonged both to the tennis and badminton clubs. What gave her more pleasure was her membership of the local dramatic society. She was no actress and got only small walking-on parts, but she painted with enthusiasm the sets which the society required for their various productions. She belonged also to the Bromsley Literary and Debating Society, though here her interest was but half hearted.

On the whole then the coming of Mant was a pleasant rather than a disagreeable prospect, and she looked forward to meeting him with quite considerable eagerness.

– 2 –

THE RECEPTION OF MANT

Next day shortly before lunch William drove up to the Grey House with Mant beside him in the car. Katherine heard the crunching of the wheels and went out to meet them. The arrival of this new cousin from the opposite side of the world would affect all their lives, and she was anxious to see what he was like.

Her first impression was of his height. He was a tall man, a full inch taller than William, though William was all of six feet. Mant was also, so far as appearance went, every inch a Carrington. There was the same broad forehead, the same strongly marked features, the same heavy chin as appeared in the portraits of old Thomas, and which William also had inherited. And yet in spite of these, he did not give the same impression of force. Some little weakness about the mouth, a slightly shifty look in the eyes, robbed the face of its strength. His colouring also was different. While the elder men at his age had been swarthy of face and black of hair, Mant approached the albino type. His complexion was pale, his eyes light blue, and his hair the palest of straw.

As the car stopped he got out, and without waiting for an introduction, took off his hat and bowed low over Katherine's hand.

"I expect you're Aunt Edith's daughter," he said slowly, and with what seemed to her rather an American accent. "I'm pleased to meet my Cousin Katherine."

It seemed a somewhat formal greeting, but Katherine was not to be outdone. "I'm pleased to meet my Cousin Mant," she assured him, adding largely, "welcome to England."

"Now that's very good of you," he declared as he shot little questioning glances at her. "I think I should have recognised you. You're like the pictures of your mother."

His movements and speech were slow and deliberate, and Katherine sensed a sort of hesitation in his manner, as if he were not sure of himself or of his welcome. And yet there was no humility in his attitude. He gave her the impression that he could hold his own as well as anybody. He was well dressed, she noticed, English clothes, she was sure, and from a good tailor.

William now approached, followed by the gardener-chauffeur, carrying two suitcases. Mant turned to the latter.

"Thank you," he said. "I'll have them now." He took them out of the man's hands, then went on to Katherine. "Our uncle has been good enough to say I may stay here. I hope that is in order from your point of view?"

"Of course," Katherine said reassuringly. "Your room's all ready for you."

"Thank you," he said again. "Then if I may I'll take these grips up and get them out of the way."

"It's the blue room, uncle," Katherine directed. "Will you show Cousin Mant the way?"

As the two men went upstairs there had already arisen in Katherine's mind a faint feeling of disappointment. Mant was no doubt "all right"; he seemed quiet and competent, and was probably quite decent. But somehow she didn't take to him. He hadn't looked her straight in the face for one thing, and for another there was a quality in the looks he had given her which she instinctively disliked.

But for the moment Katherine had no time to assess her impressions. Household affairs demanded her attention. William had decided that it would be courteous to Mant to have a sort of family reunion at his first meal, and Jim therefore had been asked to lunch, as well as Eva Dugdale and her husband Luke. Eva, as has been said, was Jim's sister, and Luke was accountant and cashier of the St Elmo firm. That meant a meal for six instead of their usual two: an affair requiring thought and much personal supervision. By the time Katherine had satisfied herself that all was well she heard the others' ring at the door.

"Well?" said Jim in his sharp staccato way when she went out. "New boss arrived? What's he like?"

"He'll hear you," Katherine smiled, though she was sorry for the bitterness in Jim's tone. "He's in the room just above."

"Then he has come. What's he like?"

Jim was a complete contrast to the other men of the Carrington family, in fact both in temperament and appearance he was a Musgrave, not a Carrington. Of medium height, fair, and wearing a small reddish moustache, he looked out on the world through grey heavy-lidded eyes, as if he saw in it something whimsical and rather humorous, if not altogether freakish. His attitude was detached. He seemed to be sitting back and watching, in the kindliest way, his fellow creatures as they laboured and strove for futilities.

And yet Jim was neither superior nor a fool. In his own way he was extremely able. Quite as ingenious as William, he had yet less to show for his powers, as they were usually applied incidentally rather than to practical improvements in the business. And he was capable of carrying through difficult jobs also, against opposition if necessary. But the essential for such success was interest. He had to be interested in what he was doing or his work became second-rate. And his trouble was that he was not interested in the works. He was musical. He conducted an orchestral society in Birmingham, and right well he did it. His technique was first class, and his tact in dealing with inferior players of social standing was admirable. Also he was one of the best bridge players in the district.

Eva was a young woman of both charm and good looks. Why the beautiful Miss Musgrave had chosen to marry a comparative nonentity like Luke Dugdale, none of her friends could imagine. But she had married him and she never appeared to regret it. She made him an excellent wife. While not intellectual, she was thoroughly competent, as well as genuinely unselfish and kind. She had a large circle of acquaintances in the district, where indeed she was a general favourite.

Her husband, Luke, was of the type known as heavy. Heavy in appearance, with his large features and bulldog expression, heavy in society, with his pompous manner and platitudinous conversation. But he was a shrewd man of business, and the prosperity of the St Elmo firm was not a little due to his financial acumen.

"Well?" Jim went on as Katherine ushered them into the sitting room. "Haven't answered my question. What's the great man like?"

"Jim, you mustn't talk of him like that. He's simply your cousin," broke in Eva.

"Very much your cousin," Katherine declared. "He's just grandfather over again. He's the image of that portrait over the dining-room chimney-piece, only with lighter colouring."

"Lord!" Jim exclaimed. "Abominable type! Another Uncle William, eh? Only worse?"

"Don't mind him, Katherine," Eva begged. "He's in one of his bad twists today. Got out of the wrong side of his bed this morning, I'm sure."

"Well? Is he not?" from Jim.

"You'll see for yourself in a moment. There they are coming down."

Steps on the stairs preceded the entry of the two men. Once again Mant waited for no introduction. "Ah," he said, holding out his hand to Jim, who was just by the door, "you're Jim. Very pleased to meet you, I'm sure. And this is Cousin Eva?" He crossed the room. "How are you, Cousin Eva? And your husband? Very pleased to meet you, too. It's a pleasure to be met in so friendly a way on one's first visit home."

"You still call this country home?" said Eva, shaking hands.

"I guess we have that habit, though whether it's justified, I don't know."

"Not justified. No. Not at all," declared Jim with a slight sharpness in his tones. "Country a man has lived in is his home."

"How are you?" Luke broke in impressively, shaking hands in his turn. "I can see that you're a Carrington, wherever your home is."

"Find my contention justified," Jim went on, "when Australia starts a slogan, 'Australia for the Australians'."

Mant looked at him slowly, as if he were summing up the pros and cons of the question. "You may be right," he presently admitted. "It's a matter I've not fully considered."

"You came by air?" Katherine said hurriedly, feeling that the conversation was not developing as it should.

"Part of the way by air, yes, I did. But I came across France by rail. I wanted to see some people on the way through."

They discussed the safe subject of air travel until presently lunch was announced.

Before the meal was over Katherine's first impression was definitely confirmed: she did not like Cousin Mant. It was not that there was anything tangible against him on which she could lay hold. He was polite and he was obviously trying to please. But there was something about him which jarred upon her susceptibilities. And she could see that he was having the same effect on the others. Jim indeed took very little trouble to hide it. Katherine became annoyed with Jim. Why couldn't he have a little more sense? For his own sake it was most unwise to antagonise, quite gratuitously, the man who was going to be his boss. And that Mant noticed Jim's manner, Katherine had no doubt. He showed no consciousness of it, but Katherine already believed that there was little which happened that he missed. Luke also was not at his best and was distinctly patronising. Even William appeared slightly disappointed to Katherine, who knew him so well, though she didn't think Mant had noticed that. Eva was the most at ease of them all. Though Mant allowed his vaguely unpleasant glance to rest on her more frequently and for longer periods than there was apparent need, she chatted on lightly and Katherine felt that most of the success of the lunch was due to her.

After sitting for some time over coffee and cigars, the four men left to show Mant the works. Eva, evidently bursting for confidences, waited behind.

"Oh, my dear," she said as soon as she and Katherine were alone, "it's not going to work. I wish to goodness he had stayed at home."

Katherine felt that she must defend William's plan. "Oh, Eva, don't say that. Why should you think so?"

"I know it. I could see it. Jim and he'll never get on."

"They'll get on as well as Jim got on with Uncle William."

"No, they won't. They'll have a row. I can see it coming – already. Jim wasn't pleasant to him at lunch."

"He's disappointed about Mant being brought here."

"Of course, but it was more than that. Already he doesn't like him."

"Jim's not very wise, you know, Eva," Katherine went on. "If he did feel like that, he shouldn't have shown it."

Eva pulled in closer to the fire and lit another cigarette. "I'm not worrying about that. Mant wouldn't notice, or he'd think it was just Jim's manner. What I'm afraid of is afterwards: when they begin to work together. They won't pull. I can see it now. Their whole outlook will be different."

In her secret mind Katherine could not but agree, yet as in a sense the representative of her uncle, she still felt she must uphold his judgment.

"You don't know that, Eva dear. I think Mant was trying to be friendly at lunch."

"Jim, you see, is differently made," Eva went on pursuing her own line of thought. "He took after my father's family, not the Carringtons. As I often say, he's a Musgrave. The Musgraves were a dreamy lot, fond of music and art and all that, and hating business like poison. I wish he could get another job."

"Do you think he couldn't?"

Eva looked at her thoughtfully. "I don't know; it wouldn't be easy. Another commercial job would be no improvement, and I don't know what else he could do."

"Something musical?"

"Ah, yes, I dare say. But there's no money in music." Eva paused, then once again reverted to her own line of thought. "You know, he frightens me at times, Jim does. He can be so terribly violent. Or violent's not quite the word. Reckless would be better. It takes a lot to rouse him, but if he once gets roused I believe he'd stop at nothing. It's not what one would think about him with his quiet manner, but it's the fact."

Katherine shrugged. "I know. I've felt the same."

"I've been frightened sometimes when he and Uncle William have had a row, he gets so worked up. He ought to control himself. I wish you'd speak to him about it, Katherine. He minds you far more than he does me."

Katherine disclaimed any such influence over her cousin and changed the subject. Presently Eva said she was going out to tea and would have to run. With a half sigh at the turn events had taken, Katherine saw her to the door.

Such was the coming of Mant. Soon he fell into the ways of the Grey House, and settled down as if he intended to spend the rest of his life there. He gave but little trouble and was invariably polite to Katherine and the maid. But he was aloof and self-contained, remaining for long periods in his room and, except at meals, seldom joining the others.

For some time after his arrival things went on as usual. Then small changes began to occur. The first was that William gave up his study to Mant and moved to another room which had been called the breakfast room. Some of his furniture he took with him, and this Mant replaced with very much better and more expensive pieces. Katherine was not at all pleased. She thought that Mant might well have taken the breakfast room and furnished it to suit himself, without disturbing the older man. However, William didn't seem to mind, and after all, it was his business and not hers.

The next change, a very much more important one to Katherine, was that William began curtailing his visits to the works. This, which had been the whole object of bringing Mant over, did not please Katherine either. The old man so obviously felt giving up the reins of government that she was sorry for him and resentful against Mant for taking them out of his hands. She told herself she was being illogical, as indeed she was, but the realisation made no difference to her feelings.

But the old man's presence changed the whole routine of the house. Even though he sat for long periods alone in his room, the knowledge that he was there and might want companionship was ever with her. Indeed, she grew nearer to him than at any time before. As time passed, he seemed to depend on her more and more. She tried to interest him in some of her own undertakings, discussing viewpoints for sketches or the subject of the latest debate, but with indifferent success. He was too old to take up new ideas, and he had never been a man for hobbies.

He puzzled her, did her Uncle William. As the weeks drew into months she felt she was not wholly in his confidence, in fact that there was a whole side of his mind from which she was shut out. Also while he seemed on the one hand aged and broken, almost decrepit, on the other he was always betraying flashes of his old vitality and mental power. He was now rarely at the works and Mant apparently consulted him but little, yet he would not leave Bromsley for the long holiday Dr Jellicoe so urgently recommended. More and more he withdrew into himself, going out less, lunching less frequently at his club in Birmingham, seeing fewer callers. It was all wrong, Katherine told herself, yet he was his own master and she could do nothing about it.

Mant had completely settled down at the Grey House and nothing was said about his moving elsewhere. As time passed he thawed somewhat towards Katherine, and that in the very same way as had William. Slowly and hesitatingly he began to talk to her about the works. Whether she had that gift of sympathetic hearing which drew confidences, or whether Mant felt lonely and in need of feminine society, she didn't know. But gradually their strange intimacy increased, until soon he was obviously telling her more about what was going on than he told William.

It was during one of these confidences that she seized the opportunity of suggesting that he might perhaps please the old man by confiding a little more in him.

He looked at her slowly before replying, as was his habit. "Well," he said, "if you feel that way I doubt if you fully appreciate the situation. In the first place, I'm doing the very thing he asked me to come over from Australia to do: to take the worry and responsibility of the works off his shoulders. Next, I've found that he doesn't like to be told my plans, especially if they involve any little changes from his ways of work. The suggestion that his way wasn't perfect doesn't please him."

"I suppose that's natural. Still, a little talk about the works would tend to take him out of himself."

Mant this time hesitated for what was really a long time, even for him. "I think, Cousin Katherine," he said at last, "I must tell you something that's been worrying me ever since I came here." Again he paused. "It's not easy to do, but I can't help that. I don't think he's well. I don't mean in bodily health; it's worse than that. I've sometimes suspected his mind is touched. What do you think about it yourself?"

Katherine did not answer at once. She could not deny that this dreadful thought had also occurred to her. She was not sure. Sometimes she feared it must be so, at others that the breakdown was purely physical.

"I don't know," she said at last. "I confess I have sometimes feared it."

"What he wants," Mant went on, "is a change. A voyage. Why doesn't he go round the world and take you with him? He's got plenty of money. He'd come back a new man. Why not suggest it?"

"Suggest it? I have suggested it again and again. Not perhaps going round the world, but going away somewhere."

"And he won't?"

"Won't hear of it."

"That seems to me a sign of the trouble. However, if he won't, he won't. What about getting a mental specialist to have a look at him. I don't suppose Jellicoe is specially qualified in that direction?"

"He'd never allow it. Besides, it might do him harm if he were to know what is in our minds."

"I agree with that. But he wouldn't have to know. If we got someone, I would bring him in as a visitor to the works. These mental men do that sort of thing."

Katherine was not keen on the idea. It might, she thought, come to it later, but in the meantime it did not seem necessary.

One subject Mant sedulously avoided, until she herself raised it: his feeling towards Jim. She knew from Jim himself and from Eva that relations between the two men were not too happy. Jim naturally resented a man who was so little his senior in years, and a stranger at that, being placed over him at the works. And when he found that his junior position was to remain unaltered under the new management, his resentment only grew the deeper.

Katherine touched on the subject diffidently. She was sincerely attached to Jim, and her whole thought was whether she could say anything to ease the tension. But she was also terribly afraid of doing more harm than good.

Mant, however, was quite cool and businesslike on the subject. "Well, you see," he admitted, "I'll agree that we don't just hit it off. We're not made the same, and that's a fact. He's like so many of you people over here, if you don't mind my saying it. He doesn't like anything new. Because a thing's proved to be bad, that's no reason to a lot of English people for changing it. If a thing's been, it's just got to stay that way, no matter whether it serves its purpose or not. Now in Australia we're different. If we find a better way of doing anything, we think that's a reason for throwing out the old way and adopting the new. Now, it's been proved again and again that the first thing in overhauling a business is to get costs everywhere and see where your leaks are. That means putting down pretty accurate times of everything that's done, and some of these chaps don't like it. I've had to get rid of some men because they refused to do it. Nearly had the whole lot of them out over the head of it, though I got that stopped. Jim's one that dislikes time studies – and there you are."

It seemed reasonable to Katherine, so put. Still, she felt that there must be more in it than that. Greatly daring, she went on: "Do you not think that one cause of the trouble is that his position is too junior for a man of his years and standing? Do you not think that if he was more satisfied about that, things would be happier?"

Mant again delayed longer than usual in replying. "Well, Cousin Katherine, I didn't want to say it to you, but now you've forced me. The truth is, Jim's not worth it. He won't take enough trouble. His heart's not in the job, and that's a fact. I may tell you straight, if Jim wasn't a cousin, he wouldn't be there. He's not pulling his weight. He's a problem right enough, and I wish to goodness he'd get out of it."

Katherine sighed. The outlook certainly was not promising. It would be better, she agreed, if Jim could get something that suited his special gifts: something musical, for instance. And yet it seemed hard that here, in this works owned by his own family, he couldn't find a congenial job.

For a time after that conversation things seemed to go better. Jim appeared to have settled down and to have grown better friends with Mant. Then, some six months after the coming of Mant, occurred that dreadful incident when Katherine seemed to see down into the soul of Jim.

It was after dinner. Mant and William were in their studies, and she was by herself in the sitting room, sewing and reading. Often she deplored the family idiosyncrasy which made these two men retire so often into their respective lairs and leave her without company for the entire evening. She had however grown accustomed to it, and often she had her friends in and oftener still she went out herself. But this night she was alone. Not long after dinner Jim had come. She had not seen him arriving, and knew only that some caller had asked for Mant. But she heard his voice going out. Surprised and a little hurt that he should be in the house without coming to see her, she had opened the sitting-room door to invite him to stay. It was then she had seen his face. Murder was written upon it as clearly as if the letters had been painted. Murder! A murderous hate of Mant, almost maniacal in its intensity.

– 3 –

THE MINISTRATION OF KATHERINE

All the remainder of that evening and a good deal of that night, Katherine thought, horror-stricken, over the revelation she had surprised in Jim's face. She wasn't exactly frightened by it, for she felt that Jim was far too good and kindly a man ever actually to commit so dreadful a crime. But it was extremely disquieting to find that such passions existed in her immediate surroundings. And also hateful. Katherine was one of those who longed for everyone about her to be friendly and happy.

She believed Mant had noticed nothing, though with Mant you never could be sure. Often she had thought he had not seen things, and afterwards some chance word had revealed that he had observed every detail. But on this occasion he had at least given no sign. He had withdrawn again to his study after a commonplace word or two and his usual formal "good night".

First she had thought of following him and asking what was wrong. Then she decided that this might do more harm than good. But she felt she must find out what had happened, and then have a word with Jim in the hope of mending matters.

As it chanced when she came down next morning she found that Mant had already left for the works. She therefore racked her brains for an excuse to follow him to his office.

She found it in the case of a man who had been injured in the works a day or two previously. Owing to some unusual circumstance there was a doubt as to what his accident insurance would bring in. Katherine took a personal interest in such cases and a call to find out how the matter stood would, she thought, be unsuspicious.

So about eleven she set off. The works were quite close, in fact the Grey House stood on a corner of the works ground. The two were separated by a low hill covered with pines, through which ran a private path. She walked along the path and out on to the approach roadway to the works. A lorry loaded with the firm's products was just leaving.

Somehow the departure of these crates and cases always struck a responsive chord in Katherine's imagination. They represented as it were the consummation of all the activities and endeavour which had been poured into the concern. Old Thomas's foundation, William's building on it, her housekeeping, Mant's activities, Jim's, the workers' generally, those labourers who were opening a drain on the approach road, the message boy who trotted past with a bundle of envelopes, all these and a vast number more performed their daily tasks with the sole object that these cases and crates, packed with electrical machinery, might continue to pour out in a steady stream through the entrance gates. This stream represented a sort of focus or spinal cord which held together the whole complex organisation. The manifold activities of the works converged to form it. Then, having passed the gates, it diverged again into all the world, or nearly so, like radiations leaving a transmitter. Katherine loved in imagination to follow the units of the stream as they went to various parts of England, Scotland and Ireland, to certain countries on the continent of Europe, to Africa, to the West Indies, even on one memorable occasion, to Patagonia. She longed to travel with the machines and see them set up in their new surroundings, tended perhaps by men of strange colours who spoke incomprehensible tongues. Strangely enough the return current, infinitely more important to the welfare of the works, the money which poured in from all the world in payment for these machines, did not appeal to her imagination to anything like the same extent.

Five minutes later she was being shown into Mant's room. He rose when he saw her.

"Why, Katherine" – he was gradually dropping the Cousin – "this is a pleasant surprise. You don't often honour the works with your presence. I hope there's nothing wrong?"

"Nothing whatever. It's just that I thought I'd go down and see old Mrs Fletcher," and she put her question about the money.

"You're far too good to these people," he returned. "They misunderstand your motives and don't thank you for it. They think you're trying to put them off with soft words and get out of paying them money. It's a mistake."

Katherine smiled. "I don't believe it for a moment," she declared. "However we need scarcely start a discussion on the point. What about the money?"

"She'll get the money all right. There never was any real doubt of it. But she'll get it because she's entitled to it: not as charity."

"Of course. I'm with you there, Mant, absolutely. And I'm glad about the money. It means so much to these people."

Mant agreed, and for some moments they discussed the insurance point which had arisen. Then Katherine rose to go. "I mustn't keep you from your work," she declared, then added as if in an afterthought: "I was surprised Jim didn't call in to see me last night. I thought he looked annoyed. I hope there was no trouble?"

Mant shot a suspicious glance at her and she saw that he realised that here was the real cause of her visit.

"Did he look so very peeved?" he asked.

"He looked unhappy, and I hate to see him looking unhappy. He really is a good sort."

Mant agreed with an unconvinced air. Katherine saw that if she wanted information, she must ask the direct question. "Nothing was seriously wrong, I hope?"

"Just a little matter of business."

"A secret?"

"Not mine at all events." He paused, then went on a trifle sardonically. "I wasn't going to say anything about our little difference of opinion, but since you want to know, I'll tell you. And if you've any influence with Jim, I hope you'll use it."

"What do you mean?" she said sharply.

"I mean that unless there's a change in him, he'll soon be looking elsewhere for a job. I said I'd tell you and I will. Last night we had a row. Jim made a mistake in costing a certain article. A small relay it was, and he forgot to include the cast-iron box that contained it. It wasn't a big item in a way, only about six shillings per relay. But a serious error all the same."

"Six shillings? Nonsense, Mant, how can you say such a thing?"

"I didn't add that he was making up an estimate for 2,000 of them. His mistake has therefore cost us the small loss of £600."

Katherine was silent. If Jim had done this, it really was too bad of him. But she tried to make the best of it.

"Nonsense," she repeated. "The mistake remains only one of six shillings. And at all events, if it was such an important figure, why wasn't it checked?"

"It was checked," Mant returned grimly. "I'm dealing with that."

"But can you not say that a mistake has been discovered and put in a revised figure?"

"No. We got the tender because of the mistake."

"Then the mistake was an advantage to the firm."

Mant's grim look relaxed. "You should have been a lawyer," he said. Then his face hardened again. "No, unfortunately that's not correct. We stand to lose £600 over the transaction, and it's Jim's fault."

"What did you say to him?"

"What could I say? I pointed out the loss, which he admitted. I said that if anyone but the manager's cousin had made the mistake, he wouldn't have remained five minutes in the concern. He admitted that also. I said I couldn't make flesh of one and fowl of another, and that if he got off with this kind of thing, I should be unable to maintain any efficiency in the place at all."

"What did he say?"

"He was just a trifle offensive. He gave me to understand that the whole trouble was my having come over from Australia, and pointed out that English people could perfectly well manage their own business, without bringing colonials in. And you know," Mant gave a twisted smile, " 'colonial' is not the right word now that Australia's a self-governing country."

"Oh, Mant, he didn't mean it."

"No, he didn't stop to think. Then he asked me, did I want his notice? I said no, but that I wanted his work to be as careful as my own. He said that we all made mistakes at times. I said, 'Of this kind?' Then he looked at me as if he could have murdered me and cleared out. I haven't seen him since, but I propose to go on as if nothing had happened."

Katherine sighed. "All that distresses me very much," she declared. "I don't mean what you said or what Jim said or the mistake about the estimate. Those are all matters outside my range, so to speak. I mean it distresses me that there should be this personal feeling between you and Jim."

"Not on my side," Mant pointed out.

"Very well: on Jim's, if you like. I wish it hadn't arisen. But now that it has arisen I wish more than anything that it could be put right. What do you think about it, Mant? Can I do anything?"

Mant hesitated for a longer time than usual. "I have no personal feeling against Jim whatever," he said at last. "And if it takes two to make a quarrel there you are."

"Ah, but that's not enough. If Jim feels as he appears to do, there's some frightful misapprehension in his mind."

"Well, there's no doubt what that is, though whether or not it's a misapprehension I'm not going to say. He doesn't like my having come, and thinks he should have got the job. That's the trouble, and you know it as well as I. But he should remember that his grievance is not with me, but with Uncle William. If Uncle William hadn't asked me here, I shouldn't have come. And when he did ask me, it's up to me to do the best I can for the works."

"Yes, I realise all that." She paused, then went on: "Well, if I get a chance, I'll put in a word. Then you'll be meeting at the dinner shortly. Perhaps that will give an opportunity for a proper reconciliation."

Mant said he hoped so in a rather sceptical tone. Katherine decided she would see Jim at once. She had an almost pathetic faith in her own powers of persuasion and believed that what she had to say would clear the situation up. It scarcely occurred to her that she might make it a lot worse.

The dinner to which she had referred was a curious family survival. Ever since she could remember, on William's birthday a reunion had been held, at which small gifts were presented to him and his health was solemnly drunk. It took the place of the Christmas gathering common in other families. This year Katherine had given it more thought than ever before. Now that William had retired and was feeling ill and depressed, she was specially anxious that it should be a success. She did not want the old man to feel more forgotten and out of things than could be helped.

It happened that her intention of seeing Jim was fulfilled more quickly than she had expected. As she walked across the works approach road on her way out, she met him coming in. They stopped.

"Hullo, Jim," she greeted him. "What's the best news with you?"

He looked old and worried, but spoke normally enough. "Hullo," he answered. "What you doing here, eh? In the sacred precincts?"

"I came in to enquire about old Fletcher's money. I'm going down now to see Mrs Fletcher and I wanted to know how she stood."

"See the boss?" The words were lightly spoken, but there was a bitterness behind them that Katherine deplored.

"I saw Mant," she said. "He told me the money would be paid. Then I was coming to look for you. I have a crow to pluck with you because you didn't come in and see me last night."

"Last night? How did you know I was there?"

Katherine was discreetly amazed. "Well really, Jim! In my own house! I heard your voice in the hall, if you must know, but before I could come out and catch you, you had gone. What was the hurry?"

"Well really, Katherine, if you must know, I just called for a moment. Business with Mant. In a hurry to get back to finish up work. Another night I'd love to stop."

Once again the words were lightly spoken, but there was nothing casual about the eyes. Katherine felt warned off. It seemed, indeed, a new Jim who was standing there, with smiling lips and hard cold eyes. Quickly she changed the subject.

"We'll be looking out for you tomorrow fortnight. I'm so anxious that Uncle William should be pleased with his party this year. He seems so depressed by his illness and being so much out of things. It would never do if the evening fell flat."

Now there was relief in Jim's eyes. His expression grew more natural.

"Do all I can to help, of course," he declared, "but don't expect it'll be as pleasant as other years."

Feeling relieved, though slightly snubbed, Katherine decided that on her way home she would look in on Eva. Jim was very fond of his sister, and Eva, Katherine knew, would do everything in her power to prevent a breach occurring between him and Mant.

Having passed out through the gates of the works, Katherine therefore turned west, away from the city. The district was suburban, and so far it had escaped the devastation of the speculative builder. Luke and Eva lived in a small cottage cut off from its fellows by a belt of limes at one side, a copse at the other, and a couple of fields of grazing land behind. The house was low and long, with a thatched roof and a wooden porch, over which in summer rambler roses festooned in hanging masses of colour. Eva was a considerable gardener and she was very proud of her roses, not only at the porch, but in the long beds fringing the path to the gate. She managed to achieve what so many amateurs miss: the inclusion of plants which flower in rotation. It was seldom, therefore, that her garden was without bloom. The end of December was, of course, the worst time. Flowers had given up the struggle in despair, and the foliage, where any was left, was dark and drab.

Eva opened the door. She had no servant, but only a woman who came in each morning, and who had now gone home.

"Oh, my dear, how nice to see you," she greeted Katherine. "But I can't wait a moment. I'm just flying. One of those Haines' literary lunches, you know. Janet Young is going to speak, and I just love her books. Come in and talk while I finish dressing."

"I'm really not going in," Katherine answered. "It was just – "

"Of course you're coming in: if you don't mind my bedroom. What about joining me at the lunch?"

"No, I can't, I'm afraid. The Bevirs said they'd call this afternoon."

"Oh, my dear!" Eva threw up her hands in mock horror. "Poor you! Of all the absolute bores..."

"A bit heavy going," Katherine smiled. "But Uncle William likes John."

"John's a good solid plodding fellow. If Uncle William likes him, I'm glad you're having him."

They chatted on, Katherine lounging in the only armchair, Eva completing her adornment for the coming function. Eva looked charming at all times, but Katherine thought she had never seen her more ravishing than at the present moment, with her pleasant smile, her delicate features, her perfect complexion, her simple tastefully-cut clothes. How she had come to marry heavy bovine Luke, Katherine could not imagine. And the marriage had been a success. Both seemed happy and contented.

And yet this morning in spite of her good looks and vivacity and her happy marriage, Katherine somehow imagined that her cousin was ill at ease. Katherine had known her all her life and she could see beneath the bright surface manner in a way a stranger could not. She watched her as they chatted, and grew more and more convinced. Some worry was preying on Eva's mind.

But if Eva did not choose to give her confidence, it was no business of Katherine's. In any case, as it turned out, there was no time. As she was considering the matter Eva spoke. "There," she said, still dabbing with her lipstick, "I'm actually finished at last. Don't think me frightfully rude, Katherine, but this wretched lunch is at one. I shall have to fly. Sure you won't change your mind and come with me?"

Katherine stood up, and as she did so she glanced involuntarily at the dressing-table. One of the drawers was open and in it she noticed a fountain pen. In spite of herself she stared. It was very like Mant's, and Mant she knew had recently lost his. It was a special one that he was very fond of, and he had asked everyone at the Grey House if they had seen it.

At that moment Eva hurriedly slammed the drawer home. She was standing with her back to the room, and Katherine was sure she had not observed her glance. It looked almost as if she hadn't wished the pen to be seen. If so, what could that signify?

Katherine immediately grew ashamed of herself. The pen was like Mant's, but even if it were identical, it proved nothing. It was, of course, by no means unique: there must be thousands exactly similar in existence. For the moment it had seemed strange, but, of course, it must have been a coincidence.

A couple of minutes after leaving the bedroom she found herself parting from Eva at the latter's gate. She had intended to consult her on the Mant–Jim unpleasantness, and here she was leaving without having done so. Well, perhaps it was better so. The least said was undoubtedly the soonest mended. The affair would no doubt straighten itself out without her help.

Slightly relieved in her mind, Katherine continued on her way to the Fletchers' cottage.

– 4 –

THE CONGRATULATION OF WILLIAM

At length Friday evening came round, the night of the birthday party. It was a night which none of those who were present at the Grey House were ever likely to forget, for on it took place an incident which profoundly affected the future of each one of them.

It had been an unpleasant January day, dull, heavily overcast and with a raw dampness in the chill east wind; a day on which the smoke hung over towns and people felt dejected and nervy. Rain had not actually fallen, but the pavements were dark with moisture and everything looked its dingiest. Even the movements of the sparrows, grimy little balls of draggled feathers, seemed a protest against the depressing conditions.

For Katherine the day had been fully occupied. All the preparations for the evening festival devolved on her. The one maid that the establishment boasted, Sarah Stedman by name, was efficient enough in her way, but she was only the plainest of cooks, and Katherine had herself to do the lion's share of the work. She had called in Mrs Fisher, the wife of the chauffeur-gardener, to help in the kitchen, but she, like Sarah, was but a poor cook.

Katherine worked hard and by about seven was satisfied that Sarah and Mrs Fisher between them could serve the dinner. The meal was to be at half past seven and she had therefore half an hour to dress.

Before going upstairs she turned once more into the dining room to have a final look round.

It was a pleasant looking room enough, as Katherine saw it. Of moderate size, well proportioned and lofty, it was papered in cream with a dark dado. The furniture was old, solid and good, giving warm reflections from polished surfaces. Opposite the door was a French window, now closed and draped with curtains of greyish brown. A second door led to the service pantry.

The table in the centre of the room was of dark mahogany, oval shaped and without a cloth. It was lit by four electric candles, whose shaded tips were reflected in the polished surface. The light was very subdued, only these small candles and the flickering light from the brightly burning fire. So lit, the table looked extremely decorative. The *pièce de résistance* was the huge bowl of hothouse flowers in the centre. The shining silver and the white folded napkins stood out strongly against the dark wood, and the well-polished glasses scintillated with unexpected reflections. Katherine was pleased with her efforts.

She passed through the hall on her way upstairs. This was a long, irregular shaped chamber which straggled through the entire house from front to back. On entering from the porch there were doors on each side, on the left to a small cloak room and to the right to the main sitting room. Behind the cloak-room door in the left-hand wall was the dining-room door. Then came the stairs on the left, but beside the stairs the hall ran on back as a sort of narrower passage to William's sitting room, Mant's study, and the service rooms in the rear.

Katherine dressed quickly as she wished to look once again into the kitchen before the guests arrived. As she came down into the hall, William appeared from the dining room.

"Where are the cigars, do you know, Katherine?" he asked. "I thought they were on the chimney-piece in the dining room, but they're not."

"They were there," Katherine answered. "I saw them no later than yesterday. You're sure they've not got pushed behind the clock?"

"Well, look yourself."

She preceded him into the room. No, the box was not on the chimney-piece. She stood looking round.

"There they are," she said in a moment, "on the side table. Sarah must have moved them when she was tidying."

"That's all right. I wanted to know where they were for after dinner."

She watched him go out of the room, no longer the hale, upright figure he had been up till a few months earlier, but stooped and shuffling. A terrible change! And it was the same mentally. This matter of the cigars was symptomatic. A few months earlier he never would have asked a question like that. He would have seen the box at a glance. She sighed as she realised that his chances of recovery were gradually becoming smaller and smaller.

A couple of minutes in the kitchen showed Katherine that everything was in order and she went to the sitting room to be ready to greet the guests on their arrival. William was pottering restlessly about.

"They'll soon be here now," said Katherine. "It's twenty-five past."

"Yes. I'm glad that fellow Dugdale is coming. He's a dry stick, but he can tell a story. I remember – he told – I've forgotten exactly, but it was a good story." He passed his hand across his forehead. "I can't remember now – " His voice ceased and a baffled look came on to his face.

"Never mind, we'll get him to tell more stories tonight. He does it well, doesn't he?"

As she spoke the door opened and Mant came in. "Who does what well?" he asked as he crossed the room.

Mant was pre-eminently of those who look their worst in evening dress. The bull in the china shop was the simile which occurred to Katherine the first time she saw him so garbed. Somehow tonight he looked bigger and clumsier than ever.

As she glanced about her she was pleased with the result of her efforts in the sitting room also. It was a finely proportioned room, with a bow window to the front and a French window to the side. Here, as in the dining room, the furniture was old and good. Plain and dignified and comfortable. The room looked used, as it was. Though neither of the men sat much in it, Katherine occupied it all the time. It was a woman's room, with a work-basket and bits of sewing here and there, as well as plenty of books and magazines. The lighting was better than in the dining room. Besides the brightly blazing fire there were two standard electric reading lamps and a pendant centre light.

"There they are," said Katherine suddenly.

From without came the sound of car wheels on the gravel, followed by voices.

"I'll open the door," said Mant, and went out into the hall. Katherine followed him. Through the opening she dimly saw Jim's small Standard, and Eva and Luke getting out.

"Suppose I may leave her here?" called Jim. "Not expecting anyone else?"

"Leave her by all means," Mant answered. "She'll not be in the way."

"Oh my dear," cried Eva, bustling across, "let me get in out of this freezing night. It's simply bitter."

"Good evening, Eva. How are you, Luke?" from Mant.

"Have buttoned up her muff. Put a rug over her all the same," from Jim.

"We'll have skating if this frost goes on," from Luke.

With disjointed greetings they reached the hall and the door was shut.

"Come in to the fire for a moment before you take your things off," Katherine suggested to Eva.

"No, if you don't mind I'll do the thing in order and then get warm with a clear conscience," Eva returned. "Is it upstairs? Don't trouble to come up, Katherine. I can find my way."

"Of course I'll go up."

"That's right, Katherine," called Luke. "I shouldn't trust her with the family jewels unlocked."

Katherine led the way upstairs and the two women chatted while Eva was taking off her things. "There now," Eva said presently, "I've just to change my shoes. Don't wait, Katherine. I know you want to get down to see about dinner."

"Well, if you don't mind I'll just tell them to bring it in."

She went downstairs to the kitchen as the clock in the hall struck half past seven. "You may bring in dinner in about five minutes," she directed, knowing the little ceremony of the presentation of the birthday gifts would take place first in the sitting room. Then she walked back through the hall.

As she opened the sitting-room door, she saw a shadow move on the wall of the cloak room, whose door was partly opcn. Then she went in to find Jim and Mant chatting with William. It must therefore have been Luke who was in the cloak room and in a couple of minutes he came in, followed a moment later by Eva. There was bustling round the fire and warming of hands.

"Now that we're all here," said Mant, "I understand that the time has come for a small ceremony. As I am a newcomer, I propose with everyone's permission to leave the proceedings in the hands of Cousin Katherine."

Jim started up. "By Jove!" he said. "Left my offering in my coat pocket. Shan't be a moment."

A couple of minutes later he returned with a small parcel in his hand. Then the ceremony began. Katherine made it as informal and speedy as she could. She murmured a few words of congratulation and a wish that William would have many more birthdays in the future and that he would be speedily restored to complete health, and then each member of the little party advanced in turn and presented him with a small token of their remembrance and a short greeting. He thanked them all in a word, and the proceedings were over. At the same moment the gong sounded for dinner.

"Congratulations on your stage management," murmured Eva as they left the room. "It all goes to schedule, as Mant probably says."

"He does," Katherine agreed. "He uses lots of phrases that I thought were purely American."

They passed into the dining room and took their places round the table. "Eva between Uncle and Mant; Jim beside me, and you, Luke, between Jim and Mant," Katherine directed, and the others, knowing where the three members of the household sat, speedily found their places.

This matter of the seating, depending as it did on the positions usually occupied by herself, William and Mant, had at one time given Katherine a good deal of thought. When she and William had been living alone, she had invariably sat at the foot of the table, that is, at the narrow end of the oval facing the door. William had not sat opposite her at the head, but at the side at her left hand. He was a chilly mortal, in the winter preferring the fire at his back, and in the summer simply remaining in the same place. When Mant arrived the question arose where he was to sit. He had at once chosen the head of the table, on the grounds that, after living in a city all his life, he would prefer to be where he could see the garden out of the window. It was of course a matter of no importance, and yet to Katherine there seemed something of principle involved. Was Mant's taking the head of the table symbolic? Did it mean that he was going to rule the household, as he had been brought over to rule the works? She felt she was a fool to mind, but she did mind all the same. However, she couldn't very well insist on Mant's sitting elsewhere, and he acquired a sort of prescriptive right to the position, recognised by all members of the family.

A glance told Katherine that so far everything was well. The soup was excellent, and Sarah handed it round as if to the manner born. And yet the soup was little more than served when Katherine realised that things were hanging fire. Vigorously she began to talk, hoping that if once a good start were made, the atmosphere would brighten.

But her efforts scarcely met with the success they deserved. There was certainly something wrong. It was the first of these birthday dinners at which Mant had been present, and Katherine wondered if he were the wet blanket. He was never a very enlivening person socially, and tonight he was perhaps even more silent than usual.

It seemed indeed that no single member of the party was up to his or her usual form. William's deterioration due to his illness was very marked. Mant, as has been said, was no conversationalist, and Eva, between these two, was finding it hard to keep the ball rolling. Besides Eva herself seemed to have something on her mind. Her attention to what was going on was given with an obvious effort, and not very successfully at that. Luke was not in one of his expansive moods, and Jim also was *distrait* and absent.

So Katherine, directly the fish arrived, got on to the question of drinks. She felt that a little alcohol all round was what was needed. She had made, she explained, some claret cup, but there was also hock, and of course whisky and beer. Opinion unanimously rejected the hock and the beer, and was equally divided between her other two suggestions. William, Mant and Jim took whisky, Jim in quantity that made her open her eyes, and the other three had the cup.

During the fish course the going remained heavy, but when the fillet of beef had been served, things began to brighten up. Jim in particular seemed to be throwing off his depression. His laugh grew louder, and Katherine glanced with some misgiving at his glass, which he was just then replenishing with as large an amount of whisky as before.

Katherine, who was always allowing her imagination to run away with her, now began to sense a new danger. If Jim were to drink too much he would certainly quarrel with Mant. And clearly he was drinking too much. The spirit was beginning to take effect on him already. He was getting noisy and throwing himself about in his chair. Mant already was noticing it and glancing at him rather unpleasantly. Katherine felt that if Mant said anything, it would provoke an explosion.

She was not sorry when the last course, the trifle, had been cleared away, and she took advantage of Mant's having left the conduct of the proceedings in her hands to hurry on to the final act of the meal. Standing up, she said smilingly, "As presumably I am supposed to be still in the chair," she looked enquiringly at Mant, who nodded gravely, "let me announce that we have now come to the most important event of the evening. With the greatest pleasure and satisfaction I give you a toast – the toast of our Uncle William. May he have many happy returns of the day, and be speedily restored to his full health!"

They stood, raised their glasses to the older man, murmured "Uncle William," drank, bowed, and sat down. It was a simple ceremony, carried through in order not to break the custom of years, but passed over quickly to reduce to the minimum the strain on the invalid. Katherine wished he would not think it necessary to reply, but he did. He got up and with less hesitation than she had expected, thanked his nephews and nieces for their good wishes and the gifts by which they expressed their good will. They had had many such gatherings, but at this one they had a newcomer to the family circle. He took the opportunity of welcoming Mant, and considered that it was much better that a family should live together, rather than at opposite ends of the world. Jim had not been living at the other side of the world, and therefore did not need to be told that he was always welcome in that house: he knew it already. It was always the greatest pleasure to have Eva, and Luke also. About Katherine he couldn't say anything: he could never hope to repay all that she had done for him. He thanked them all again.

There was some clapping and then Katherine rose. "Come along, Eva," she said, "we've had enough of them for a while." Then to the four men: "Your coffee'll be here, but you're not to be long." Amid murmurs of, "We won't be long," the two women left the room.

Katherine had been feeling rather uncomfortable for some minutes, and as she walked across the hall, these feelings grew worse. She had some pain and was slightly sickish, and the movement made her a little faint. But as soon as she sat down she felt better, though not quite well. She wondered what could have upset her. She was not given to biliousness or digestive troubles: in fact she was unusually free from minor ailments of all kinds. How unfortunate, she thought, if she were going to be ill, that it should be on this night when she wanted to be at her best. However, if she didn't get worse, she thought she could manage without letting her feelings be known.

She and Eva chatted for some ten minutes. Eva spoke of Jim. She indicated that he and Mant were now getting on better than at first, and thought that Jim was finding his work at the office less irksome. "At all events," she said, "he hasn't complained to me lately, and I think all that row they had has been dropped."

The subject was interrupted by the arrival of Sarah with coffee, a small outfit for just the two of them. Katherine began to pour out.

She got up to carry Eva's cup across to her, and as she did so, a stab of burning pain and another qualm of sickness passed over her. Very uncomfortable, she felt ill. She sat down, panting slightly, and sipped her coffee. Presently the worst symptoms passed away and she began to talk to Eva about the literary luncheon of a couple of weeks earlier.

But she soon found that she could not continue the discussion. Another wave of sickness came over her, accompanied by a really horrible spasm of pain. What could it be? For an ordinary digestive upset, it was very severe. Then once again the worst of it passed, and she turned to Eva to renew the conversation.

But Eva herself was looking far from well. Her face was white and drawn and she was also panting. Then she spoke, in strained accents. "Do you know, Katherine, I'm not feeling very well. I think I must go upstairs and lie down."

"I'm not well either, Eva," Katherine answered. "I've got a pain and I feel sick and faint."

"So do I. What on earth can have happened?" They looked at each other in dismay, the same unspoken thought in both their minds. Something in the food! There had just been a case of that rare food poisoning known as botulism, and the papers had been full of the impossibility of finding out beforehand if food were so tainted. For the moment the public was nervous on the subject, and Katherine, again imaginative, immediately suspected that she and Eva had fallen victims to the complaint. Botulism, a horrible and dangerous disease! Katherine wondered should they not have the doctor.

Her mind was speedily made up for her. With a little groan Eva threw herself back in her chair. "Oh," she moaned, "I feel ill. I'm going to be ill! I must lie down! Help me, Katherine."

Katherine forced herself to her feet, but as she did so a paroxysm of pain and sickness came over her and she almost collapsed. "This will never do!" she thought. "I must get help." Setting her teeth, she struggled across the room to the fireplace and pressed the bell. Then, fearful that she would fall into the fire, she managed to reach a chair and dropped into it, all power of movement gone.

Presently the attack began to pass slightly away. She felt better, though still very far from well. She looked at Eva. Eva was lying as she had fallen into the chair, her face white and drawn and drops of perspiration on her forehead. Her eyes were closed and she was moaning. Something, Katherine felt, must be done at once. But no one came in answer to her ring. She must ring again.

But could she reach the bell? She really did not know. Then feeling a little better, and with the urge to get help strong within her, she decided she must go out into the hall and call the men.

With immense difficulty she pulled herself up out of her chair, and clutching on to the furniture staggered across the room to the door. There for a moment she could go no further, and stood clinging on to the handle, while desperately trying to beat down the waves of sickness. Then the paroxysm passed, and opening the door, she groped her way out.

The dining-room door was open and through it she could see into the room. It was empty.

As she gazed in mystification, Sarah and Mrs Fisher appeared coming from the back hall. Their faces were blanched with terror. They gazed speechlessly at Katherine.

"What is it?" Katherine gasped.

Sarah wrung her hands. "They're all ill, miss!" she cried. "They're all dying! Oh, what shall we do?"

"The doctor!" Katherine gasped. "Dr Jellicoe!" A wave of pain and sickness swept over her. She turned back into the sitting room and made for her chair, but her knees gave way and she collapsed on to the floor and lay moaning, conscious only of the pain.

– 5 –

THE APPLICATION OF RUNCIMAN

At much the same time as the birthday dinner was in progress at the Grey House Dr Runciman Jellicoe also was having his evening meal. He sat with a book propped on the table before him in the little room behind his surgery. It was not a pleasant room, nor for the matter of that was the house a pleasant house, and it was an ambition of the doctor's to move elsewhere. But the house had belonged to the man whose practice he had bought, and it occupied a good position in the Bromsley Upper High Street. Up to the present Jellicoe had found nothing that he liked better and which at the same time was equally convenient for his patients.

George Runciman Jellicoe was a man of forty or less, with a clean-shaven intellectual face and agreeable though rather grave manners. He was slightly below middle height and given a little to corpulence, both of which facts grieved him exceedingly. He had that dependable look and reassuring manner so invaluable to a doctor. The feeling of confidence he inspired, he himself would have been the first to admit, did as much or more for his patients as his various treatments. People who called him in added faith to medicine and grew better. Thus he achieved a reputation for cures and his practice grew.

Jellicoe indeed, when he looked back over his past career, was wont to grow a trifle complacent. He had done well. Not perhaps that a general practitioner in a place like Bromsley was anything very much to boast about. But there were special circumstances which made his present position peculiarly gratifying to him. He had started with almost every handicap that an adverse Fate could have devised, and in spite of them all he had forced his way forward. At an early age he had been left an orphan, and had been brought up in a perfunctory manner by a spinster aunt. This lady, who lived at Stockport, had neither the will nor the means to send him to a good school, and the choice held out to him was that of a junior clerkship in a chemist's or an office boy with a firm of architects. George took the clerkship and did quite well. But he did not intend always to remain a clerk. His ambition was to be a doctor. While therefore during the day he posted items in the chemist's ledger, in the evenings he worked at the books which by rigid self denial he had managed to buy. He got his reward. At the age of two and twenty he matriculated with a scholarship which enabled him to carry on his studies and take his final medical. Then he had some years in the hospitals. At last when he was thirty-six his aunt died. She left him her money. It was little, but it was just enough. He bought this practice from an elderly man who agreed to give him a start by taking him as a partner for a year. He got his start and never looked back. In three years he had nearly doubled his income. And recently he had been appointed police doctor for the district, a position which was giving him some useful, if specialised, experience.

His career so far had been an achievement, and he was proud of it. He was now earning well up to a thousand a year, and he believed that in a very short time this figure also would be doubled. Then he had proposed to sell the practice, and with the proceeds, added to what he had saved, he would buy a more important and lucrative one in Birmingham, or perhaps even London. Eventually perhaps he could retire from the practice and devote his time to the chemical research he loved, and which even now he tried to carry on. Certainly he had not a few months ago intended to remain a mere local practitioner all his days.

But recently a new factor had come into his life and had changed all his ideas and aspirations. He had met Katherine Shirley at a local tennis party and had straightway fallen in love with her. Up to now he had been too busy to think of women, and this was the first time that he had really lost his heart. As a result he lost it completely. The vision of a home life with Katherine as the presiding angel was so entrancing that all other desires receded into the background, and he felt that if he could win her, his earthly ambition would be complete.

But if Jellicoe was determined, he was also extremely cautious. He was desperately afraid of rushing Katherine. No matter what it cost him, he would wait till he felt the moment was propitious, before taking the plunge. He knew so little of women that he could not tell whether or not she liked him. But latterly he was becoming rather more hopeful on the point. Recently she had accepted his invitation to drive with him to Ludlow. They had had tea together there in an old timbered inn, and rather to his surprise, for he was not a vain man, she had seemed quite happy in his company. He was now indeed considering what circumstances might best pave the way to a proposal, with the object of trying to bring these about.

He slowly filled his pipe before moving to the little den at the back of the house which he used as a study and sitting room. Should he take advantage of what would look to Katherine – he called her Katherine to himself – as a chance opportunity, or would he be wiser to call deliberately at the Grey House to put his question? From his knowledge of her character he imagined she would prefer the latter. But he was by no means sure.

As he was pondering the matter the telephone rang. At first when he had had an evening call he had been delighted. It stood as a symbol of his increasing prosperity. But now he was busy enough to grudge work outside working hours, and he gave a half sigh as he passed into his consulting room and picked up the receiver.

As he listened his face changed. "What?" he said sharply; "six of you ill? What are the symptoms?" Again he listened. "Sick and faint, with abdominal pain? Right! I'll come immediately."

In a moment Dr Jellicoe's outlook upon life had been changed. Here was an urgent call upon his professional skill – six people ill with what sounded at first hearing like some kind of food poisoning. But it was not this – important though it might be – that set the doctor's heart beating with unusual and uncomfortable rapidity. It was the news which came with it. Of these six, Katherine Shirley was one.

Hurriedly Jellicoe seized his bag, which he knew was well stocked with the implements and drugs which he might want, and running downstairs, he jumped into his car and drove at considerably above the legal limit to the Grey House. Fortunately it was not far and he reached it within some four minutes of receiving the call.

The door was opened to him by Sarah Stedman, a Sarah with blanched face and frightened eyes. "Where are they?" he asked urgently as he pushed his way in. Cold as was the evening, he had not in his haste troubled with hat or coat.

"The ladies in the sitting room, the gentlemen in Mr Mant's study," Sarah answered, pointing towards the back hall.

Jellicoe ran down the hall to the study and glanced quickly in. On the floor, white and motionless, lay Mant and William. William, being his patient, he knew well, and Mant he had met. Another man whom he took to be Jim Musgrave was leaning over the table desk, his head in his hands. The fourth – Dugdale, he believed – was sitting up in an armchair, though looking white and drawn.

"That the doctor?" this fourth man said. "It's got us all, but I'm not as bad as the others."

For a moment Jellicoe glanced at the four faces. Then he swung back into the hall.

"Your telephone?" he asked Sarah, and at the same moment seeing it on a side table, he ran to it and began calling urgently to two of his colleagues to drop everything they might be doing and come immediately. "And get a couple of nurses as quickly as you can. Let them follow at once."

He swung round to Sarah. "And you, get blankets and eiderdowns and hot bottles. Quickly now!" She at all events seemed well. She hurried off while Jellicoe, seizing his bag, hastened into the sitting room.

On the floor Katherine and another woman in evening dress, he thought Mrs Dugdale, were lying, while kneeling beside them was a third woman, elderly and dressed like a maid. "Low pillows for their heads," he said to this third woman, "then help Sarah with blankets." He himself knelt down and spoke to Katherine.

"Tell me, if you can, how you feel and what you ate," he asked. Now that he was actually at grips with the case, the fact that Katherine was the patient receded and professional interest and responsibility calmed his mind.

At the moment she was feeling somewhat better and she was able to speak clearly enough. "We just had the ordinary dinner," she went on. "Soup and fish and joint and sweets: everything seemed all right. Then simply we all got ill," and she described her sensations.

Food poisoning of some kind, Jellicoe saw at once, though of what kind was not so obvious. The idea of botulism (he thought of it as botulismus) did occur to him – it was in everyone's mind at the time. But he did not think this was botulism. Its symptoms were usually referable to the central nervous system and included motor paralysis and other complications which did not seem to be present here. No, it looked more like ordinary infected food or some of the cruder poisons. That the attacks were serious was only too clear, and he realised that his patients' lives might well be in danger.

As these thoughts passed through his mind, he was working energetically, first with Katherine, then with Eva. Then he raced to the study to give first-aid to the men. All six would have to be got to bed, but in the meantime, he made them as comfortable as he could on the floor with pillows, rugs, blankets, and hot-water bottles. He knew that all his energies should be given to one patient and that he couldn't possibly cope with six, but he worked on as best he could till he heard the welcome sound of wheels, and two of his colleagues, Drs Mortimer and Gilchrist, appeared in the hall.

"Take the four in the study," he explained, running out of the sitting room. "I'll deal with the two in here. Apparently food poisoning: nausea, faintness, abdominal pain. What about the nurses?"

"They're following," Dr Mortimer answered as he and Gilchrist hurried down the hall in the direction Jellicoe had indicated.

Some ten minutes later the two nurses turned up, and then one by one the patients were carried upstairs to bed. Eva and Luke were put into the spare room and for Jim a second bed was put up in Mant's room, a large apartment and the only other one available.

All that night the doctors and nurses worked. The attack was severe in all cases, but Mant and William were obviously much worse than the others. Towards morning the three doctors held a consultation. In the case of the other four the balance of opinion was that they would pull through. In those of Mant and his uncle all reserved judgment.

But besides attending to their patients, the doctors had been active in taking all possible steps which might aid the investigation which would necessarily follow. Directly on arrival Jellicoe had ordered the maids to leave the entire remains of dinner untouched, the plates unwashed, the food where it was at the moment. As soon afterwards as he could, he had, with Dr Gilchrist's help, put all food and drinks into the larder, sealing the door. He also advised the maids, who had remained unaffected by the illness, to bring back to their minds every slightest incident connected with the dinner, so that they might be able to answer the questions which they would later be asked.

As the need for action grew less, everything possible having been done for the patients, another problem arose in Jellicoe's mind and grew more and more insistent with every moment that passed. Could he avoid reporting the circumstances to the police?

He feared it would be impossible. If either the Australian or the elder Carrington died there would be an inquest, and if he had not reported the illness at the time, he would be gravely censured. The thing, of course, was an accident: the mere fact that each member of the party was suffering proved that, but this would not be held a justification for silence. In all such cases the cause of the illness must be investigated and cleared up by responsible officials.

He was profoundly anxious to keep Katherine's name out of the affair, but he did not see how he could do so. It would be too grave a responsibility. And even if he were willing to take such a risk, his colleagues would refuse.

About five in the morning, when for the moment there was nothing to be done upstairs, he called them into the dining room, and over some whisky and bread and cheese he sounded them on the point.

Dr Mortimer seemed slightly uncertain as to what should be done, and Jellicoe thought that he could obtain his support for whatever course he himself advocated. But Gilchrist was adamant. The police must be told. It was madness to consider anything else. If Jellicoe didn't make a report to them, he would. "The fact of the matter is," he said, "it should have been done before now. You're a nice police doctor, I will say."

"I expect you're right," Jellicoe admitted. "I shall ring them up presently." He paused for a moment, then leaning forward across the table and instinctively lowering his voice, he went on: "Have either of you any views about this thing? I mean as to the cause?"

Gilchrist looked at him keenly. "With our present knowledge none of us can be sure," he declared, "as you're very well aware. But I know" – he shrugged – "the first test I should make if I wanted to find out."

Mortimer glanced up at him. "Reinsch?" he asked dryly.

Gilchrist nodded with decision. "Marsh-Berzelius for me," he answered. "But you've said it."

As his colleagues mentioned the two common tests for arsenic, Jellicoe experienced a feeling almost of consternation. Arsenic had, indeed, been what he himself had suspected. But he had hoped against hope that his friends might have fixed on something else. Arsenic in sufficient quantity to produce the effects they had found, must, of course, have got into the food by some quite definite accident. It was true that certain fish, notably Mediterranean shellfish, contained a considerable amount of arsenic, but no foods liable to such contamination had been served. Jellicoe wished he knew with certainty. He turned again to the others.

"Arsenic was in my mind also," he admitted, "but I should like to be sure. I suggest we slip round to my place and make a rough provisional test. It just chances that I have the apparatus set up. It wouldn't take long. In any case, the first question the police will ask is, what do we suspect? I should like to know more before I answered it."

"Do you mean, test the food?" asked Gilchrist.

"No," Jellicoe returned. "I don't think we should touch the food. It may all have to go to the public analyst. No, they've all been sick again and again: a small quantity of the ejection."

Gilchrist looked at Mortimer. "Yes, I think we might do what Jellicoe suggests. What do you say, Mortimer?"

"I agree. But I don't think we should all go. You and Jellicoe go, Gilchrist, and I'll stay and look after these people."

"I think you're right," Gilchrist approved. "Very well, if you don't mind staying, Jellicoe and I'll make the test. How do you happen to have the apparatus ready, Jellicoe?"

"I'm fond of chemistry and I do a little mild research between times."

"I didn't know that. I'm fond of it myself. If it's not a secret, what are you working on?"

The two doctors immediately became technical. Then they made their test, and in something under an hour were back again at the Grey House. Gilchrist was looking pleased and self-satisfied, Jellicoe more worried than ever.

He was indeed feeling extremely anxious. The test had shown arsenic present. Nothing could now prevent a detailed police enquiry. The affair would get into the papers and perhaps, if negligence could be proved, into the courts. The publicity would be horrible, and to this publicity Katherine would be exposed. And nothing that he could do would save her from it. She might, indeed, blame him for the whole thing.

He sighed. "Well, I'll go and ring up the police," he said despondently, turning towards the back hall.

"And not any too soon," Gilchrist added as he went upstairs to relieve Mortimer.

"I wish to speak to the officer on duty," Jellicoe called when he had got Bromsley police station. "It's Dr Jellicoe speaking from Mr Carrington's residence, the Grey House."

"Yes, sir; Station-Sergeant Browne speaking," came the reply.

"I'm sorry to tell you that Mr Carrington and five other persons who dined with him last night have all been taken ill, presumably by some kind of food poisoning: seriously ill. I think you people should know in case you wish to take any action."

"Yes, sir. Thank you. We shall probably have to make some enquiries. A man will go round in a few minutes. You will be there, I presume?"

"Certainly. Also Dr Mortimer and Dr Gilchrist. I sent for them at once, as six cases was more than I could handle with the necessary speed."

"Very good, sir. In about fifteen minutes."

Extremely worried at the turn affairs had taken, Jellicoe went upstairs to have another look at the patients before the police should come. Of all of them Eva Dugdale seemed the least seriously affected. For the moment she had dropped asleep, which the doctor thought an entirely good sign. Luke Dugdale also appeared to have got over the worst of the attack. These two, Jellicoe felt he might say, were definitely out of danger.

As to Katherine he was less happy, but here also her condition seemed promising. Standing looking down at her, his mind oscillated between professional satisfaction at her apparent improvement, and horror and tenderness because it was she who was suffering. Heavens, how he loved her! If before this disaster he had had any doubts as to the intensity of his affection, he had none now. How thankful he would be if only he could suffer this pain and misery for her! How he wished he could do more to ease her and make her comfortable! But he had done everything that his knowledge suggested. Arsenical poisoning is a painful thing: not as bad as that from strychnine and certain other poisons, but very distressing all the same. He lingered with Katherine, willing her with all his power to fight and triumph over the disease.

Jim Musgrave was not so well as Katherine, but even he appeared to be holding his own. So far as Jellicoe could see, only Mant and William were really dangerously ill. It would be touch and go with both, if indeed they pulled through.

A strange and baffling malady was poisoning: particularly arsenical poisoning! If you were to take any given number of persons and administer to each one grain of the stuff, you would almost certainly get an equal number of different results. Varying tolerances and constitutions produced varying effects. Here were six people. Probably they had all had about the same amount of the arsenic, and yet no two were affected precisely to the same extent. In the case of William, of course, the circumstances were not quite normal. He was older than the others and in a more delicate state of health, and it was not unreasonable to suppose that the irritant would affect him more than the others.

But Mant's attack was more severe even than William's, and in his case there was nothing like age or a delicate state of health to account for it. Dr Mortimer, who had attended Mant and Jim, was in the other room speaking to the nurse, and for the moment Jellicoe was alone with the two sufferers. He bent down and examined Mant more carefully.

Yes, the man was certainly very ill. There were all the symptoms of arsenical poisoning, indeed in a way it might be said that there were more. The poison had affected Mant strangely. There was a considerable flow of perspiration and saliva and the breathing was very laboured. The pulse when Jellicoe picked up the moist wrist was slow. All possible as a result of arsenic of course. The pupils were much contracted, and from a technical point of view this interested Jellicoe more than the other symptoms, as he could not remember having heard of it in connection with arsenic. He began indeed to visualise a possible paper on the subject at the next meeting of their local medical association.

His cogitations were interrupted by the front doorbell, followed by deep voices in the hall. He went down. Two police officers had just been admitted by Sarah. He recognised Inspector Kirby and Sergeant Scarlett, both of whom he knew to be pleasant and efficient men.

"Good morning, sir," said Kirby, saluting. "This is reversing the usual practice. It's generally we that have to call for you. You've had some trouble here? Will you tell me what has happened?"

"Certainly, inspector. Come into the dining room."

They sat round the table and the inspector and sergeant produced notebooks. "Yes, sir?" Kirby went on interrogatively. "Perhaps you'd just tell us the story from your own point of view: what was the first you heard of it, and then on till you rang us up?"

"The first I heard of it was a few minutes before nine last night, about five minutes to nine I should say. I had an urgent telephone call from Mr Luke Dugdale, who is a connection of Mr Carrington's, and one of the men who is ill," and Jellicoe went on to describe all he had seen and done during the night. The officers took copious notes, the sergeant an apparent verbatim report in shorthand, the inspector points or queries quickly jotted down.

Kirby was polite. He expressed thanks for Jellicoe's action about the food and plates, and judicious admiration at his quick test for arsenic, but allowed himself a discreet reprimand at the end. "Do you not think, sir, that it would have been better to have rung us up earlier?" he asked, with eyes keen and wide-awake for the doctor's reply.

"If you want to bother the patients with questions, I've rung you up too soon instead of too late," Jellicoe answered, determined to carry the war into the enemy's camp. "They mustn't be spoken to or disturbed in any way. I hope you understand that." Then relaxing, "Perhaps you are right, inspector. Perhaps we should have rung you up. But we were so busy trying to save our patients' lives that at first we had no time for anything else. Then, when the immediate business was over with them, I was anxious to make the test for arsenic before calling you. Directly it was made I did call."

Inspector Kirby nodded. "That's all right, sir; I just wanted to get your views. I think that'll be all in the meantime. Probably later we shall want to ask some questions and go into certain points more fully. Are you remaining here?"

"No, I want to get home as soon as I can. I expect to make some joint arrangement with the other two doctors about the care of the patients."

"Thank you, sir. I suppose for completeness sake we'd better take statements from the other doctors. Perhaps if you are going upstairs you'd kindly ask one of them if he'd come down?"

To the other doctors Jellicoe proposed a joint supervision of the case, but he found that neither of them wished for this arrangement. "They're your patients and it's your case and you can quite easily deal with it now yourself," Gilchrist declared. "We've our own to look after, so we'll just leave you to it. What do you say, Mortimer?"

Dr Mortimer was of the same opinion and Jellicoe agreed. "By the way," he went on, "the police would like a word with you before you go out. They're in the dining room."

He busied himself then in making arrangements for the day. He rang up for another couple of nurses to relieve the two who had been on duty during the night, and decided he would go home for a bath and breakfast and then come back to supervise the new nurses taking over. With further calls, say, before lunch and after tea, the medical provision should be adequate.

Before leaving he had one more look at the patients. Katherine was awake and conscious. Her lips moved. He bent down.

"What has happened?" she breathed.

"You've all eaten something which has disagreed with you," he answered easily, if somewhat unnecessarily. "You've had a very unpleasant time, but you're over the worst. You needn't worry. You'll be all right in a day or two."

"And the others?"

"The others, too," he declared with an assurance he did not feel.

"You've been so kind."

A rush of tenderness came over Jellicoe. He put out his hand and patted her shoulder. "My dear!" he said, and he could not keep the yearning out of his voice.

She closed her eyes and smiled, he almost thought, happily.

When he left the house, elderly man of almost forty as he was, his heart was singing.

But that night his complacency received a considerable shock.

He had finished dinner and paid a further late visit to the invalids when Dr Mortimer rang him up. He wanted a word with him and would come round if Jellicoe were not busy.

Twenty minutes later the two doctors were installed on either side of the fire in Jellicoe's sitting room, Mortimer with one of the cigars which his colleague kept for important callers, Jellicoe himself with his pipe, and both with glasses of whisky-and-soda at their elbows. For a moment they talked generalities and then Mortimer came to business.

"I've been thinking over this affair at old Carrington's," he began, "and I don't know that I'm entirely happy about it. I thought I should like to discuss it with you."

"I'm puzzled myself," Jellicoe admitted. "I'm delighted you came round."

"With me it's more than being puzzled. I'm definitely unhappy."

"I don't follow you there. Why so?"

Mortimer drew slowly at his cigar and absently watched the resultant smoke dispersing upwards. "I think I made a mistake this morning," he said at last and with obvious hesitation. "I wasn't altogether satisfied with Mant Carrington's condition. But one doesn't like to be fussy and in the end I said nothing. Since then I have been thinking the matter over, and I believe I should have asked you and Gilchrist to examine him."

Instantly Jellicoe recalled the curious symptoms he had observed.

"As a matter of fact I did have a look at him this morning when you were settling up with the nurse. I was curious about him, and I knew you wouldn't mind, as he was really my own patient."

"Oh," said Mortimer with apparent relief, "you did examine him, did you? I'm glad of that."

"I'm afraid 'examine' is not quite the word. I only looked at him and felt his pulse."

"That was enough. Tell me, were you satisfied with what you saw?"

Jellicoe hesitated in his turn. "I was a little surprised by some of his symptoms," he admitted. "But I didn't think them serious. Is that what you're upset about?"

Mortimer moved uneasily. "Well, it is," he agreed. "What rather puzzled me was the contraction of the pupils. I've never known that caused by arsenic."

"But we know it was arsenic. Gilchrist and I found it."

"I agree. All the same it was peculiar. And it was not only that. There was also difficulty in the breathing and an abnormally slow pulse. Ever hear of those coming from arsenic?"

"Never, but it didn't seem to me impossible that they should. The contraction of the pupils I found harder to explain."

"That was my view also, and since I got in from my round I've looked it up in all the books I have. And as far as I can see arsenic has never been known to give that reaction. I should look myself for an alkaloid."

"The contraction of the pupils certainly does suggest an alkaloid," Jellicoe agreed, "but I shouldn't like to say it proved its presence. Do you think we should do anything about it?"

"I thought we should ask the police to warn their analyst of what's in our mind."

"But if he finds an alkaloid, he'll say so in any case."

"No doubt. But if he finds arsenic he may stop his research in the belief that he has reached the cause of the trouble."

Jellicoe thought this over. "I expect you're right," he concluded. "It won't do any harm to warn the analyst, and it may produce something – unexpected. Will you move in it or shall I?"

"You," Mortimer decided. "It's your patient, and besides you're police doctor."

"Right. I'll do it now."

Jellicoe crossed the room to the telephone. "Is Inspector Kirby there?" he asked when he had got the police station. "Oh, speaking, are you? Well, look here, Kirby, I've got Dr Mortimer with me and we've been talking over this Carrington affair. Do you think you could look in for a moment? We should like to discuss a point with you...In ten minutes? Right! Splendid!"

Kirby was obviously impressed when Jellicoe had explained the point at issue. He at once agreed to ask the analyst to look for alkaloids or other poisons as well as for arsenic.

"But," he went on when this was settled, "let me be sure of this. It was only in the case of Mant Carrington that you found these symptoms? Not in any of the others?"

"That is so."

Kirby thought for a moment. "But are you sure, gentlemen, that they mightn't have been caused by the arsenic?"

Jellicoe shrugged and looked at Mortimer.

"I don't think either of us would say that," the elder doctor answered. "These poisons act, if I may use the word, freakishly. But neither of us have been able to find any record of such a thing having happened before. I think all we could say is that the circumstances are suspicious, and should be gone into further. Do you agree, Jellicoe?"

"I certainly do. You mustn't commit us, Kirby, to anything more than that."

"I'll get the tests made," the inspector declared as he stood up and thanked the others for their information.

"It's evident he doesn't believe in anything but the arsenic," said Mortimer when Kirby had gone.

"Clearly. However, thanks to you, we've done the right thing about it."

The two doctors sat for some time chatting and then Mortimer went home. But neither he nor Jellicoe put into words what lay deep in both their minds. If some alkaloid poison had been taken as well as the arsenic, the affair could no longer be explained as an accident. Intention would unquestionably be indicated.

But if there had been intention, only one thing could follow. Uneasily both men wondered could they be dealing with a case of attempted murder.

– 6 –

THE INVESTIGATION OF KIRBY

It happened that Detective Inspector Frederick Kirby was up and dressed when he received the summons from police headquarters to undertake the enquiry at the Grey House. He was, in fact, an enthusiastic gardener and he was building in his spare time a small greenhouse. This he wanted to be ready for the early sowing of seeds, and as he had been busy in the evenings recently, he had taken to getting up half an hour earlier in the morning to push on the good work. He was therefore able to leave immediately on receiving the message, and to have collected his stuff at headquarters by the time Sergeant Scarlett, his assistant for the job, arrived. Scarlett jumped into the waiting car and in another three minutes the two men had reached their destination.

Kirby was not much impressed by Dr Jellicoe's statement. Some mistake had been made, some carelessness had been shown. If the doctors were correct in their analysis, which apparently had been done so roughly as to be of doubtful value, arsenic had got into some article of food. Very regrettable, but not particularly interesting, at least to himself. The thing was obviously an accident, as no murderer would attempt to poison a family wholesale. Therefore no matter how efficiently he dealt with the case, there would be no kudos and probably no publicity. It might be a pleasant relief from routine, but on the other hand it would probably mean a lot of extra work. He wished someone else had been given the job.

But since it had been given him, he could not afford to do anything but his best. Kirby was a young officer, still ambitious and hoping for early promotion. A good deal might depend on how he handled the case.

It was obvious that the other doctors and the nurses would soon be going home, tired after their night's work. Equally clearly, before they did so statements should be taken from them. Kirby did not suppose that any of them would add much to what Jellicoe had already told him, and his anticipation proved correct. He therefore thanked them and turned his attention to the maids. One of these had gone to bed, and he asked the other to step into Mr William Carrington's sitting room, which had not figured in the story.

She was a tall gaunt elderly woman with a dependable face and a quiet, well-educated manner. She advanced towards the table with a questioning look on her features. Kirby was polite to her.

"Will you sit down, please?" he began. "We're trying to find out what has happened here, and we want your help. We'll not keep you long. Now will you begin by telling us your name?"

"Eliza Fisher."

"Yes? And you are?"

"Wife of John Fisher, who's gardener and chauffeur to Mr Carrington."

"Mr William Carrington?"

"Yes."

Mrs Fisher went on to say that before her marriage she had been a maid in several large houses, and knew how things should be done. For this reason when there was a party at the Grey House, Miss Shirley usually asked her in to help. There were not many such parties, but in the course of the seven years during which her husband had been with Mr Carrington, she had done it perhaps thirty times. On this occasion, she had come to the house about five to assist with the cooking. Miss Shirley, who was a good cook, had superintended the work, but she, Mrs Fisher, had dished the dinner and passed it to the regular maid, Miss Sarah Stedman, to take into the dining room. Everything had been done in a perfectly normal way and she could offer no explanation of the illness which had followed.

"That's very clear, Mrs Fisher. Now just tell me exactly what you did after the dinner had been served?"

"Well, you'll understand the first courses were coming out while the last were going in. As soon as the trifle went in, work in the dining room was over for the time being, and we had our soup, Sarah and I. We had a bit of fish next, and then Sarah went back into the dining room to clear the table. When she came out we had our joint. You understand we wanted to take it while it was hot, though even then it wasn't as hot as we should have liked. Then we had our trifle, and then I started to make the coffee, while Sarah put the plates that were to be washed over on the sink. The coffee was made on two trays, one with two cups for the ladies in the sitting room, and one with four for the gentlemen. Sarah took the trays and then came back and we started to wash up."

"Quite. Was the dining-table quite cleared at this time?"

"Yes, Sarah finished it at that time. She said she had had to take the coffee to Mr Mant's study, for the gentlemen had moved in there. Then when she was coming back she cleared the table. There was little on it but glasses at that time."

"Then you began to wash up. Did you complete the washing up?"

"No, we were only about half way through when we got to know about the trouble."

"How?"

For the first time Mrs Fisher's cool, businesslike manner became interrupted, and some feeling showed beneath it. "The sitting-room bell rang, and then as Sarah was drying her hands to go, we heard a fall," she said with a slight shudder.

"A fall?"

"Yes: someone fell in the study."

"And what did you do?"

"We went out into the passage to see what it was. We were a bit scared, if the truth be told. I mean, no one would fall if there was nothing wrong."

"Naturally," Kirby admitted. "And what did you see?"

"Mr Dugdale came out of the study as we got to the passage. He was looking queer, sort of wild and his face was white. He saw us and he said, 'Are you two all right?' just like that. We said, 'Yes.' Then he said, 'Well, they're ill in there,' and he went on to the telephone, sort of staggering."

"Did you hear what he said?"

"Yes, it was to Dr Jellicoe, and he said they had been taken ill and to come at once. Then he looked at us again and said, 'See to the ladies,' and went back into the study."

"And what did you do?" Kirby repeated.

"We looked into the study through the door: Mr Dugdale had left it open. Mr Mant was lying on the floor. It had been his fall that we had heard." Again Mrs Fisher shivered, but with an obvious effort she went on. "As we looked, Mr William – just sort of rolled out of his chair – on to the ground. Sarah let a scream."

"I don't wonder," Kirby said sympathetically. "Did you see the other two gentlemen?"

Mrs Fisher nodded. "Mr Jim had his head down on the desk like as if he was ill too. Mr Dugdale had sat down. He didn't look too well, either."

"And what then?"

"We stood for a minute: we just couldn't do anything what with the shock and that. Then Sarah said, 'We'd better see about the ladies,' and we both went on to the sitting room. Miss Katherine was standing swaying about at the door. She looked like death. She asked what was wrong, and Sarah told her. Then she sort of whispered to call Dr Jellicoe and turned back into the sitting room and fell on the floor."

"You followed her in?"

For a moment the witness appeared to have difficulty in proceeding. "Yes. She was lying on the floor," she said at last, "just inside the door. She was – on her face – all bunched up. I thought she – was dead. We turned her over on her back and got a pillow under her head. I think she fainted. Anyhow she shut her eyes and didn't speak. Mrs Dugdale was ill, too: she had slipped down on the floor from her chair."

"And did you attempt any kind of first-aid?"

"We didn't know just what to do. But they both felt cold to the touch, and we were going to get some blankets when we heard the doctor's ring. Sarah let him in and he told us to get blankets and hot bottles."

"So that your own idea was correct," Kirby encouraged her. "Now tell me, did you do any more washing up?"

"No. We were too busy to think of that at first. Then Dr Jellicoe came out and told us on no account to touch anything. Then later he and the other doctors put the food that was left over away in the larder and sealed the door. Which they needn't have done for no one was going to interfere with it."

"You needn't mind that," Kirby explained. "They were only doing what the law requires. Now once again about what you and Sarah had to eat. You can see why I want to know about this. You and Sarah are not ill, so nothing that you had could have been infected."

"I see that right enough, and I've been thinking about it myself, and I don't understand it. So far as I know, we had everything that they had in the dining room."

"Oh?" said Kirby, glancing at her shrewdly. "You said you had soup, fish, meat and sweets. Were these just the same as they had in the dining room?"

"Just the very same in every particular."

"I see. Now what about drinks: at dinner or before or after?"

"Well, there was claret cup that Miss Katherine had made, and there was hock and there was whisky and soda. But they didn't take any hock, so that needn't be counted. Three of them had the cup and three whisky-and-soda, so Sarah told me when we were talking about it. There were no cocktails."

"Quite. Now did you or Sarah or both of you have any of those drinks?"

"Sarah had some of the claret cup. But I don't care for those sort of things and I didn't have any. I just took a little milk."

"I see. Then you all had coffee?"

Mrs Fisher made a sudden gesture. "I did forget about the coffee. No, we didn't have any coffee, Sarah nor I. But," she grew thoughtful, "there couldn't have been anything in the coffee. I made it myself and I *know* it was all right." She looked at Kirby with a puzzled expression.

"I'm not doubting that, Mrs Fisher," the inspector returned diplomatically, "but we've got to get a record of the facts. Now we've got one thing the family had that you and Sarah didn't. Coffee. Any liqueurs with it?"

"No, none."

"Just so." Kirby studied his notes. "I think that's about finished with the food. Is there anything else you can tell me that might be helpful to me?"

Mrs Fisher thought not, skilfully conveying the impression that she considered she had done extraordinarily well for him up to the present and that to ask for more information was in the nature of an impertinence.

"Very good. Then I'd like a look at the rooms."

They inspected the dining room, Mant's study and the sitting room, but Kirby could see nothing which threw the slightest light on the affair. Then they went on to the kitchen premises.

The accommodation was very different from that obtaining in a modern house, and consisted of no less than five rooms: a kitchen, a scullery, a service hall between the kitchen and the dining room, and off the scullery, a larder and a pantry. Kirby took the rooms in turn.

In the kitchen, service hall and pantry there seemed to be nothing to be learnt. In the scullery were the partially washed up utensils. The plates which had been used Mrs Fisher pointed out in their drying-rack. They had all been washed and were therefore useless. On the draining board were sundry etceteras of the meal, including six upturned goblet-shaped tumblers of Czecho-Slovakian glass which shone with a faint blue iridescent sheen. These also had been washed, though not polished. In a basin of water in the sink were the spoons and forks.

"Now for the larder," said Kirby, moving across to the door and breaking the seals which the doctor had affixed.

Here Mrs Fisher pointed out the various viands.

Besides the soup, fish, meat, vegetables, and trifle Kirby was delighted to see two trays with coffee-pots, milk, and sugar. On one were two cups and on the other four, all with grounds sufficient for analysis. There was also the jug of claret cup.

"Now tell me," Kirby went on. "Was there any other person in the house yesterday evening besides the dinner party of six and yourself and Sarah?"

There had been no one. So Mrs Fisher assured him, and he did not see how anyone could have entered without her knowledge.

Kirby's activities now followed the usual routine. Leaving Sergeant Scarlett to guard the "exhibits", he rang up the police station for a van, in which these could be removed. Then he insisted on seeing Sarah Stedman, much to that lady's indignation. She, however, had nothing fresh to tell. He importuned the nurse to be allowed to question the victims, which request she turned down with scorn.

Presently the van arrived and Kirby superintended the removal of the food to it, together with the whisky, and soda siphon which had been used. Dr Jellicoe had returned by this time, and he handed over sealed bottles containing the ejections from the stomachs of the patients. Kirby went back to headquarters with the van, and arranged for these latter exhibits to be sent to the police analyst for report. Then he settled down in his office to get his notes in order.

He was a good deal puzzled by what he had learnt. The case did not seem so simple as he had imagined at first sight. It was confoundedly difficult to see, firstly, what particular article of food or drink had contained the poison; and secondly, how or by whom the poison had been introduced into it.

In the first place there was the outstanding fact that all the food which the sick persons had eaten had also been taken by the maids. The maids were not affected: therefore it surely followed that the poison was not in the food, but in one of the drinks.

If he were right so far, there could be little doubt which the drink in question was. The claret cup was out of it for the two excellent reasons, first, that it had also been drunk by Sarah, and second, that three of the six victims had not had any. Similarly it was obvious that the dope was not in the whisky-and-soda, as the other three had not taken it.

Obviously the coffee was the only liquid which met all the requirements. But it did meet them all. It had been taken by all six victims, and by neither of the maids. Moreover it was the only thing of which this could be said.

If so, the poison would be found in the grounds. Kirby had, of course, considered the possibility of the original coffee and grounds having been emptied out and fresh substituted. But he soon came to the conclusion that this would have been out of the question. The separate trays appeared to have remained in the study and sitting room respectively until the arrival of the doctor. Before that they could not have been tampered with, unseen at least by Luke Dugdale, who had remained in full possession of his senses, and after Jellicoe's arrival no one would have dared to attempt it. Besides only the maids could have done such a thing, and on general grounds their guilt was so unlikely as to be out of the question.

All the same, by some quite amazing accident arsenic had got into the coffee. How, he could not imagine, but he supposed he would be expected to find out.

Having thus cleared up the affair in his mind, Kirby went in to Superintendent Wakefield's office and made his report. Wakefield was a big bovine man with sleepy eyes and a drawling manner of speech. But if anyone assumed that he was either sleepy or slow, and acted on his assumption, he usually received a rather unpleasant surprise. For all his easy-going manners, there were few more wide-awake and efficient men in the force.

He listened now to Kirby's statement without moving a muscle or asking a question till the inspector had finished. Then lazily he asked: "And what do you propose?"

"Analysis, sir," Kirby answered. "It seemed to me we should get the stomach ejections of all six patients analysed to make sure it was arsenic, and I have arranged for this to be done. Then I thought the coffee-grounds in all six cups should be done also. I expect we shall get the same result from both," and he explained his reasons. "It seems to me that it would be waste of money to get all the rest of the food and drink analysed, but that's whatever you say."

Wakefield considered. "I agree," he said presently, "with the proviso that you keep all the rest of the food till the result of the coffee analysis is known."

"Certainly, sir. I brought it here with that intention."

It was just as this interview terminated that Kirby was called up by Dr Jellicoe. He was not greatly impressed by the doctor's fresh statement, believing that the arsenic was the cause of the trouble. He had the policeman's scepticism of the conclusions of expert witnesses, and the plain man's desire to accept the obvious explanation. Here were sick persons, and here was arsenic, and what more could anyone want? However he was careful to instruct the analyst not to content himself with establishing the presence of arsenic, but to look for other poisons as well, particularly alkaloids.

In due course he learnt that it would be two or three days before the analyses would be available. During these days he was much at the Grey House. But none of the patients were well enough to be questioned, and he had to possess his soul in patience.

Then at last came the analyst's report. As Kirby read its three main conclusions, his surprise and mystification grew steadily deeper.

The first was that in the ejections from the stomachs of all six victims there was arsenic: a comparatively small quantity in each case, enough to cause an unpleasant illness, but not enough to cause death.

The second was that in Mant's stomach, and in Mant's only, there had been a second poison, eserine or physostigmine, in sufficient quantity normally to cause death.

The third was to Kirby the most astonishing of all. In the coffee there was no trace of either of these poisons: neither in the dregs in the cups, nor in the coffee-pots, nor in the milk.

Kirby swore luridly as he went in to discuss this new development with Superintendent Wakefield.

– 7 –

THE INTERROGATION OF KATHERINE

The two or three days following that of the dinner party were for Katherine a nightmare period of pain, sickness, and misery. For the first twenty-four hours, indeed, she was in a state almost of coma, when she lay vacant minded, or dreamily wondering in a detached way whether or not she was going to die. During this period she was vaguely conscious of the occasional shadowy presence of unrecognisable figures, which vanished disconcertingly as soon as she tried to discover their identity. Then later she realised that her most frequent visitor was a nurse, while another who came seldom – far too seldom – was Dr Jellicoe.

"I've been ill?" she whispered faintly when first she realised he was beside her.

"Yes, but you're getting better," he answered in such a convincing way that she knew at once that it must be true and that she was not going to die.

"Keep quiet and don't try to talk," he went on, and immediately she felt that here was the solution that she had been dimly seeking, the thing of all others that she wished to do.

But this sojourn in the land of shadows passed slowly away, and presently Katherine was her old self, very languid and weak, able to do little more than turn in bed, but still well again, in the sense of being free from the terribly distressing pain and sickness. Not able to talk very much when Jellicoe came to see her, but able to enjoy his presence with every fibre of her being.

Practically her first question was an enquiry for the others.

"Doing well," Jellicoe answered, seating himself beside her. "A sharp attack in each case, but all getting better. Mr Mant was the worst; in fact I don't mind confessing that for a time it was touch and go with him. But I think I may say he's out of danger now."

"Was it really as bad as that?"

"In his case, yes. But don't think about it. It's past and over. All that you have got to do now is to stay quiet for a while, and you'll all be as right as rain."

Katherine lay for a time without speaking, basking in his mere presence. Then she asked another question. "What was it? I mean, what made us ill?"

Jellicoe became slightly evasive. "Well, that's just the question. Something you ate, of course. But the food and drink you had at dinner has been examined, and it was all found to be good."

Katherine stared at him. "I wondered about botulism," she said faintly. "I've heard that you can't trace it in the food."

"It wasn't botulism. That was the first thing I thought of, but you hadn't the symptoms. No, it was poisoning of some kind, and what we shall want to know, when you're all well enough to answer questions, is where you got it."

"We had nothing but what we took at dinner. Or perhaps," she checked herself, "I should say, I had nothing. I can't, of course, speak for the others."

Jellicoe got up. "Well, don't worry about it now. Later on we'll have a chat."

She wanted to continue to discuss the affair, but he was firm that she must rest. She wished he would say something more personal, and yet she was blissfully happy. She was sure from the look in his eyes, from the tone of his voice, that he loved her, and she felt the declaration would come in due time. At present she knew that considerations of professional honour would prevent him from speaking. And, of course, he was right. She thought the more of him for it.

But next day, after satisfying himself that her improvement continued satisfactorily, he began to speak with signs of some embarrassment. For a moment her heart beat faster. But it was only the poisoning affair of which he wished to talk.

"I'm afraid I have something to tell you that will upset you," he began. "I would have done anything, *anything*, to have saved you the annoyance, but it's out of my power. And I have come to the conclusion that it may be easier for you to hear it from me, when we can talk about it here, as it were, privately. It's nothing to be the least alarmed about, but I'm afraid it will distress you."

She looked at him without misgiving. If he loved her, and his words confirmed her belief of the previous day, what else mattered? In spite of his bad news, her heart sang within her.

But what he had to tell her speedily brought her back to the present. "There are two things," he said, "both unpleasant. The first is that what upset you all was arsenic."

She stared, her attention at last fully on the matter. "Arsenic?" she repeated. "But how could arsenic have got into the food?"

"That's just what we don't know," he answered, "and what we have got to find out. So far we haven't been able, and that's where we want your help."

"But I can't help you. I haven't the least idea where it came from."

"So I should imagine. But you'll be asked for all that. Well, that's one of my bad pieces of news and the second is this: You will understand that in such a serious case, it was impossible to keep the matter from the police."

At last she was dismayed. "Oh," she said in long-drawn-out tones. "Was that really necessary?"

"I'm afraid absolutely," he answered regretfully. "Even if we doctors had been willing to keep it secret, we couldn't have done so; the police would have come of their own accord to make enquiries. No, believe me, if it could have been avoided, it would have."

"I'm sure of it, of course," she answered with a rather wan smile. "I know you would do what you could. And you wanted to warn me that they would come making enquiries. That was kind of you, and I'm grateful."

"You're very good," he said with evident emotion. "I did wish to warn you, as you say. But I'm most dreadfully sorry to tell you that that isn't the whole of it. Indeed, I have still to tell you the worst. I don't, indeed, know how to do it."

Her heart sank. "Tell me," she said in a lower voice.

"They think, the police think – that there was something wrong about the affair – I mean, they think it was not an accident."

She stared uncomprehendingly. "Not an accident? What on earth do they mean?"

He bent down and spoke very gravely. "They think the arsenic was put into the food – deliberately."

"But that" – still she stared as if unable to take in his meaning – "that would be – "

He nodded. "They think it was attempted murder." For a time she could scarcely realise the full import of the suggestion, then its obvious absurdity appealed to her.

"But what nonsense," she declared. "Who would want to murder a whole family? Besides, what had we done?"

Jellicoe shook his head. "My dear" – the term slipped out in spite of himself, and in spite of his news she noted it with a faint flush of warm feeling – "I can't tell you. I only wanted to prepare you for their visit. They'll ask searching questions, you know."

"But you don't think they're right?"

He shrugged. "Unfortunately it doesn't matter what I think. It's what they think that will decide their actions. But I have to tell you also that I have broken a pledge to give you this news. As a police doctor I'm not supposed to repeat what they said. And you mustn't tell anyone else."

"Of course not," Katherine said unhappily. She paused. "The more I think over it," she went on, "the more utterly incomprehensible it seems. Can you understand it?"

"No, not the least little bit." This time he could answer readily. "I confess it's a complete mystery to me."

"Tell me more about the action of arsenic."

He told her a little, as little as she would let him off with. Again she remained silent, lost in thought. "But surely the police idea is nonsense," she went on presently. "No one could have got at the food except ourselves and the servants. I don't suppose even the police imagine we tried to poison ourselves, and to suppose either of the maids did it is just as absurd. Do they think someone broke into the house and tampered with the food?"

Jellicoe shook his head. "I can't imagine."

"It all seems mad. I can't make head or tail of it."

For the first time Jellicoe smiled. "That's the correct view at last," he declared. "You can't understand it, and I can't understand it, and the police can't understand it. They're completely puzzled, and you know what the police do when they're puzzled: they suspect everyone. So you mustn't allow their questions to worry you. And now I've stayed far too long and tired you out, and I'm already late for several other appointments. I really must run."

He didn't run, but after some minutes of further discussion he took a dignified departure.

The news he had given her did not distress Katherine so much as he had seemed to think it should. The theory of the police was surely mere midsummer madness. And yet they were anything but fools. If they seriously held an opinion, there must be something pretty convincing to support it.

Katherine was feeling better this afternoon, and now she lay back and closed her eyes as she went over in her mind all that she remembered of that dreadful evening in the light of what Runciman Jellicoe had told her.

In the first place it was obvious that the arsenic had been taken at dinner. Her previous meal was tea, which she had had about half past four. But if she had taken the arsenic at half past four, she would have been ill by five or, at latest, six. Besides, neither Mant, Eva, Jim nor Luke had had tea with her. And she had had nothing else after tea but dinner: no sweets nor drinks, nothing. Therefore, beyond any doubt whatever, they must all have had the poison from some common source at dinner.

But what source? She went over each item they had had in her mind. Not from the soup, the fish, the joint, the sweets, the claret cup, the whisky, the soda, or the coffee, because there was some of each of these left over and there was no arsenic in any of them. And they had had nothing besides these things. At last she appreciated the difficulty of the problem. No wonder Dr Jellicoe said that both he and the police were puzzled.

How could the stuff have been taken? Katherine worried over the problem till the nurse threatened her with sleeping-draughts and other dire penalties unless she gave it up.

But though she could reach no conclusion as to what actually had occurred, Katherine felt there was something dreadful behind the whole affair. If it were impossible to suspect anyone of attempting to murder them all, it was equally difficult to understand how the presence of the arsenic could be accidental. The very fact that no trace of it had been found in the food surely showed that it had been administered in some extraordinarily skilful way, deliberately designed to cover up the traces of what had been done? If it had got into the food accidentally, it would be in what was left over as well as in what had been eaten.

Besides, there was no arsenic in the house. It must have been brought in, and this bringing of it in had been done secretly. Further, as it was required for no legitimate purpose in the house, it could surely only have been obtained for something criminal.

Altogether the whole thing looked very badly and was very distressing. Katherine grew more and more unhappy. There really was after all a considerable justification for the police opinion that murder had been attempted.

How horrible! How unutterably ghastly!

And how overwhelmingly mysterious!

Katherine was beginning in imagination to live through the whole circumstances again in the hope of seeing some helpful point which up to then she had missed, when the nurse bore down on her. "You're very bad," she said severely. "I told you to give up worrying and to go to sleep. Now you must take a draught."

Katherine submitted meekly, and soon fell into a heavy sleep, filled with confused dreams, in which she struggled ineffectively to escape from vague but imminent dangers not unconnected with the police.

But in spite of the nightmares the sleep rested her and next day she felt physically a good deal better. There was a corresponding improvement in her mental outlook. Her fears had receded and she could almost laugh at her earlier forebodings.

All the same it was with some uneasiness that she heard that Inspector Kirby and Sergeant Scarlett were waiting to speak to her. Jellicoe had just been to see her and had said he was afraid he could no longer say she was too ill to be questioned.

Kirby was polite when he and his companion were at last shown in. He apologised for having to trouble her when she was still not quite recovered from her distressing experience, but pointed out that so serious an accident must be investigated while the details were still fresh in the minds of everyone concerned.

Katherine said she quite understood and was only too willing to do anything possible to help.

A satisfactory understanding having thus been reached, Kirby got to work. "You will forgive me if I ask you a lot about your family," he went on, "because in a case like this we must start with a knowledge of who everyone is." He paused and looked at her interrogatively.

"Of course," Katherine agreed.

At first the questions were inoffensive. He began by asking about her own life, then about her uncle's, Jim's, Mant's, Eva's, Luke's, the maid's, and Mrs Fisher's. The histories of all of them, so far as Katherine knew them, were brought out and taken down by the sergeant, who wrote shorthand. Then Kirby, speaking in a very matter-of-fact voice, went on to ask about the relations of each to the others. Particularly he wanted to know of any disputes which might exist or have existed. Katherine, hoping her manner was normal, knew of none. The inspector was courteously sceptical. It was a strange household in which there were no differences of opinion: she surely didn't mean what she said quite literally. Katherine pointed out that she had answered what she took to be the spirit of his question: she knew of no differences of opinion which could be called disputes. He looked at her shrewdly, seemed to meditate a further attack, then thinking better of it, turned to another subject. Would she now give him a complete account of the dinner party, detailing in particular all she herself did on that evening, say from five o'clock on?

Here she felt on absolutely firm ground, and she answered all his questions without hesitation, until he asked one which seemed to give some hint – a horrible hint – of his ideas.

"Now you have told me that you accompanied Mrs Dugdale upstairs on her arrival, when she was taking off her things, and that you then went to the kitchen to see that everything was right before returning to the sitting room. Where did you part from Mrs Dugdale?"

"Upstairs in my bedroom," Katherine answered promptly.

"Quite. And about how long – I realise that you can't say to a second – but about how long was it between the time you parted from Mrs Dugdale upstairs and your return to the sitting room?"

"Oh," Katherine thought, "perhaps three or four minutes."

"Had Mrs Dugdale returned to the sitting room when you reached it?"

"No, she came in three or four minutes later."

"So that she was alone upstairs from six to eight minutes – approximately of course?"

"Yes, she was changing her shoes and so on."

"And was anyone in the dining room during that six or eight minutes?"

It was this question which caused Katherine to hesitate. What did it mean? Did it contain a suggestion: a hideous suggestion? Was he hinting that Eva might have been dealing with arsenic in the dining room during those minutes? But no, it couldn't be anything so foolish.

"No, not that I know of," she answered.

The inspector was watching her curiously. "My question has suggested some train of thought, Miss Shirley," he said, keeping his eyes fixed on hers. "What was it?"

Katherine was slightly taken aback. "Oh no," she declared, "I was just trying to remember. All these small details are not easy to recall."

"But," Kirby insisted, "it was quite unmistakable. Your expression changed. Something unquestionably occurred to you. I'm afraid I shall have to ask you to tell me what it was."

Once again Katherine hesitated. She did not know what to say. She had always heard that these police enquiries were terrible. Up to the present it had been easy, but this looked like the beginning of trouble. She must answer at once. But how?

Then just as the pause was lengthening significantly, she saw her way.

"You might guess, I think," she said slowly. "Your question was suggestive: almost as if you imagined that Mrs Dugdale had tampered with some of the food." She paused again, then decided to carry the war into the enemy's camp. "I don't suppose you did think anything so silly, but the suggestion was offensive."

She saw slight surprise in his face, but he still kept his shrewd eyes on hers. "It might have been offensive if I had made it," he returned quietly, "but I did not do so. I asked if you were in the dining room at that time, but I don't suppose you imagined that I was going to accuse you of doing anything wrong. However, to show there's no discrimination or ill will, let me put the same question about each of the other guests. Could Mr Jim Musgrave, for instance, have visited the dining room unknown to anyone else?"

The honours, Katherine realised sickly, were with Inspector Kirby, and yet she did not think she had given herself away. But she was genuinely astonished to find, as he probed her with searching questions, that not only she herself, but each other member of the party could have had at least a minute alone in the dining room. Her Uncle William she had met there when he was looking for the cigars. Mant could easily have slipped in during the time he was supposed to be dressing. Luke, she now remembered, had been in the cloak room when she had gone back into the sitting room. The cloak room adjoined the dining room, and Luke had not followed her to the sitting room for at least a couple of minutes. And Jim! Suddenly she remembered about Jim. Jim had been in the sitting room when she entered; he had been there until the whole party had assembled. Then he had gone out of the room for a couple of minutes! He had said that he had left his present in his coat pocket, and had gone for it. In spite of herself the word "ostensibly" forced itself into her mind. How had Jim come to forget his parcel? Was it likely that such a thing on such a night would be overlooked? Once again Katherine felt a little sick, and once again she strove with all her will-power not to betray her feelings to this terribly keen-sighted policeman.

But she found she could not put his enquiries off. Relentlessly he pursued his way until the whole events of that ghastly evening were as clear in his mind as they were in her own. He did not say he had learnt that each member of the party had had an opportunity of secret access to the dining room, but she was quite satisfied that he realised it perfectly.

However, he made no comment on the evidence, but apologised for keeping her so long and said there were just a couple of other points.

"You are a gardener, Miss Shirley?" he went on.

Katherine, wondering where this new attack would develop, agreed that she was fond of gardening.

"Quite. And no doubt you have weed-killer among your stores?"

Fool! She should have thought of this. "Yes," she answered, "there's a tin in the shed in the garden. I've had it for quite a while."

"Open to everyone, I suppose? I mean, the shed's not kept locked, is it?"

"No."

"Can you remember how long it is since the weed-killer has been used?"

"I'm afraid not; not for quite a long time at all events."

"Do you think you would know if it had been tampered with?"

Katherine shook her head. "I'm afraid not," she repeated, "though of course I might if I saw it."

Kirby took a card out of his case and passed it over. "There's a photograph of the shed showing the tin. Can you say if it has been moved?"

Katherine's brain whirled. So when he asked her if she had the stuff, he had already found it and taken a photograph!

"I don't think so," she said. "That's where I kept it, though of course Fisher might have moved it."

"Another question – a general one," he smiled, "so that it may convey no suggestion. All of the dining party and the maids had access to the shed, or have had access at some time in the past?"

Katherine, again a little sick, had to admit that they had.

"There was another point," Kirby went on in a reminiscent tone, turning the leaves of his notebook backwards and forwards. "Oh yes, here it is. Tell me, Miss Shirley, have any of your family suffered from eye trouble lately?"

Eye trouble! What was he on to now? Katherine felt instinctively that it must be something important. That forgetfulness had been well done, but not just well enough. However, she couldn't prevaricate. Anyone in the house could tell him the answer, and probably had.

"Yes," she said, "last year I had some trouble myself."

Kirby took a small bottle from his pocket. "I saw this in the medicine cupboard in the bathroom," he explained. "Is it yours?"

It was a little bottle half full of tiny pellets.

"Yes," she agreed, "those little tablets are called lamellae and they contain eserine. It was part of the treatment to put them inside the lid of my eye, where they dissolved."

"Quite. I thought they were used in that way. Well, Miss Shirley, I'm greatly obliged to you for your help," and with further apologies for the length of his stay, Kirby took his departure, followed by his attendant sergeant.

– 8 –

THE DETERMINATION OF RUNCIMAN

It was a special pleasure to Katherine when next morning Dr Jellicoe came in to pay his daily visit. She wanted to tell him of her interview with the police, and to find out if he could throw any light on what was going on. She wanted to talk to him, not only as an end in itself, but because she felt she must get some relief from the rather terrible thoughts which persisted in her mind.

So, when he had taken her temperature, felt her pulse, and otherwise satisfied himself as to her continued progress, and had sat down for the little chat which he allowed himself she plunged at once into her subject.

"Well, I had Inspector Kirby and Sergeant Scarlett here for a couple of hours yesterday."

"I was thinking of you," he said. "I needn't ask how you got on, but I do hope it wasn't as bad as you feared?"

"In one sense it wasn't bad at all. The inspector was extremely polite. But in another it was dreadful. Tell me, Dr Jellicoe, exactly what it is they suspect?"

He looked more gravely at her. "What did they say?" he asked.

"They said nothing, in the sense of making statements. But their questions were terribly suggestive."

"Tell me."

"I expect I misunderstood, because what they appeared to suggest was too utterly absurd. They seemed to think that someone in the house had poisoned the rest deliberately."

Jellicoe nodded slowly. "I'm dreadfully sorry," he declared, "but I'm afraid that's what they do think. You remember, I gave you a hint of it yesterday."

"Yes, but it's so ridiculous."

"I gathered that it doesn't seem so to them. What exactly did they ask you?"

"They found out, first, that every single creature in the house could have gone into the dining room for a minute or so before dinner, alone and unknown to any of the others. Then they found out that there was a tin of arsenical weed-killer in the tool shed in the garden, and that everyone of us could have known it was there, and at some time or another could have gone to the shed and taken some. Dreadful, isn't it? And they also asked if there had been any disputes or ill feeling between the members of the family."

"And had there been?"

"No, of course not."

To say so was Katherine's normal and immediate reaction. But as she spoke, the dreadful thought which had been so long lurking in the recesses of her mind, recurred to her more vividly than ever.

She was wrong! That look she had surprised on Jim's face!

For a moment she felt quite overwhelmed, then her reason reasserted itself. If Jim had any such feeling it was against Mant, and Mant alone. Jim was extremely fond of his sister, Eva, and to Luke Dugdale and to herself, Katherine, he wished only well. And to William too, she believed.

She had been silent as these thoughts passed through her mind, and now she saw that Jellicoe was looking at her with a mixture of love and intense longing. In spite of herself she flushed slightly. He withdrew his eyes and moved deprecatingly.

"My dear," he said, "you are worried about something. Is there anything I can do to help?"

The impulse to tell him everything was overwhelming. This dreadful nightmare idea would be dispelled if only it could be put into words. If she could share her trouble, she would be comforted.

But there was one thing that she *must* understand first: if he could explain it. Impulsively she asked her question.

"Tell me," she said, "what the police really suspect? Surely they *cannot* imagine that one of us actually tried to kill all the rest, including him or herself? It seems to me too absurd. Can you explain it?"

"Well," he answered, "I'd much rather not talk of it, but if you must know, I'll tell you. But again it's confidential."

"Never mind. Tell me. I won't repeat it."

"Very well. They don't suppose that one of the party tried to kill all the rest. What they think is that one of the party tried to kill Mr Mant."

The blood surged from Katherine's face, leaving it blanched and drawn. "Mant?" she gasped. "Oh, how?"

He paused as if to choose his words. "Well, you see," he went on, apparently speaking with regret, "there is one fact which I must admit is suspicious. And that is this: Mr Mant has been very much more seriously ill than any of the other members of the party: *very* much more. While you other five had a sharp attack, extremely unpleasant and all that, none of you were really dangerously ill. But Mr Mant nearly died: it was touch and go with him."

Katherine shook her head. "I don't see what that has to do with it," she explained. "Surely that depends on what I think is called a person's tolerance to the poison, and that could scarcely be foreseen?"

"No, I'm afraid it means more than that. I'm dreadfully sorry, but you'll have to know it sooner or later. While all of you received a small dose of arsenic, Mr Mant also had a second poison – a fatal dose of eserine."

Katherine stared with horror-stricken face. "Eserine! That explains the inspector's question!"

"Oh," said Jellicoe. "What did he ask?"

"Oh, dear, isn't it *awful!* He had found the bottle of lamellae I had for my iritis some months ago, and he asked whose it was."

"Did he ask who had access to it?"

Katherine groaned. "No, but it was in the bathroom cupboard. He must have known we all had."

Katherine would not allow herself to think. The dreadful idea was hammering at her consciousness: Jim could have got it! Jim could have got it! Resolutely she tried to force it out of her mind.

"But," she said tremulously, "I don't understand. You say Mant had a fatal dose. Why then – did he not – die?"

"It seems an absurd thing to say," Jellicoe returned gravely, "but it was because of the arsenic. The arsenic really saved him. I'll tell you. This poison, eserine, is obtained from the calabar bean, and it's the poison the African witch doctors use in their ordeals. I expect you've read about it. Someone is suspected of crime and they give him a dose of calabar beans. If he lives they say he's innocent, and if he dies they say he's guilty. Now the witch doctors can arrange beforehand which is to happen, and without suspicion falling on them. For the strange thing about this poison is that a moderate dose kills, while a large one is safe. The reason is that a large dose makes the patient sick and he gets rid of the poison. A small dose on the other hand does not, and he retains it and it kills him. Now in Mr Mant's case the arsenic made him sick and he got rid of a lot of the eserine. So we may say the arsenic saved him."

"*Oh!*" Katherine breathed. "But still I don't understand. Suppose he had two poisons. Why should the rest of us have had any poison at all? And how could the doses have been given?"

"Unfortunately the police have put up theories to answer both your questions. They can't prove them of course. But here they are for what they're worth. They think that the murderer decided to dose all round so that accidental illness should be assumed and murder not suspected. You see, assuming they're right, it would have looked – and did look – and does look – very much like it. Only for what I may call the murderer's extraordinarily bad luck, it would have been accepted without question. You can see that for yourself. It never occurred to you to suspect anything but accident – simply because the whole party got ill. You see, it was really a very clever move on the murderer's part."

The further Jellicoe went on, the lower sank Katherine's heart. "What was the bad luck?" she asked tonelessly.

"Simply that some of everything that was eaten was left over. If one item of the meal – suppose for argument's sake the soup – had been finished, the conclusion that the soup had contained the poison would have been irresistible. If the claret cup had been finished, the same would have been argued about it. Because the murderer evidently assumed – and correctly – that the plates and glasses would have been washed up before the symptoms appeared. If, as I say, one single dish had been finished and washed – as he had every right to expect would be the case – the murderer would have been safe."

"You speak as if you believed there was a murderer."

The doctor shook his head. "On the contrary: I'm trying to leave my views out of it altogether and to tell you only what the police think. I know what they think because they consulted me as to its possibility from a medical point of view."

Katherine felt almost sick with dismay. Simply she couldn't bear to think of what his words might involve. Involuntarily she gave a little moan, then pulled herself together and repeated her question as to how the doses could have been given.

"Katherine dear," Jellicoe said; "you must let me call you Katherine in this trouble. I would do anything to spare you this worry, but you have asked me, and indeed I think it better that you should know what is being considered. The police have a theory as to how doses of any kind could have been given to all those at the dinner. Here again they haven't proved their theory and I don't see how they ever could."

"Tell me," she said again.

He nodded. "I'm going to. They had evolved the idea, as you guessed from their questions, that someone slipped into the dining room just before dinner and dispensed the poison. They reached that opinion by elimination – they thought there was no other time at which it could have been done. Then they tried an experiment. They had the dining room prepared exactly as it was on that night. The table was laid in the same way, the chairs arranged as before, the fire and lights just as they were. No food was prepared because their idea was that the poison had been arranged for before the food came in. Here they tried again by elimination.

They removed from the room everything that couldn't possibly have been used. And they finished – with a definite theory."

Katherine didn't speak, but looked her question.

"They found that it was possible to drop as much as four drops into those goblets without the liquid being seen. Remember the shape of the goblets, deep and narrow at the bottom, and with thicker glass at this place, and particularly the bluish tinge of the glass. Then the light was dim, only four small electric candles. The police suggested that three or four drops of arsenic had been put into all the glasses, and a number of eserine lamellae into Mr Mant's in addition."

Katherine was stunned. It sounded not only possible, but hideously possible. And Jim – had forgotten his parcel.

But Jim *couldn't* have done such a thing! He hadn't it in him. Eagerly she clung to her knowledge of his character, known all through his life. No, if anyone was guilty of this ghastly crime, it was not Jim.

Then again the devil of doubt whispered, Would she have believed that Jim could look as he had? And she knew that if she had not seen it herself she would not.

Presently she realised that Jellicoe was speaking. "I can see," he was saying, "that this has worried you greatly. I don't know if I can help you in anything, but if I can, I do beg of you to let me try."

She glanced at him gratefully. What a relief it would be to take him at his word and tell him all that was in her mind! But she dare not. Not even to him. If it had been she who was open to suspicion, how quickly she would have done so. But a doubt of Jim must not be breathed to anyone on earth. There might be danger in the slightest whisper.

In any case, she reminded herself, there was nothing to tell and nothing to hide. It couldn't have been Jim.

And yet...

But this morning, though it brought this terrible fear to Katherine, brought her also a thrill of unbelievable happiness. Jellicoe when leaving had taken both her hands and pressed them while he said – and she could feel how strong and how repressed was his emotion – "Dear Katherine, do believe that there's nothing in the world I wouldn't do to save you this worry, if only I could." And then he had paused and gone on hastily: "When you're well I want to put something before you. *Please* don't come to any conclusion about the future till you have heard me." With that he stooped, kissed her hands quickly and vanished.

She knew she loved him and she knew that when he asked her to marry him she would do so. She wished only that he had asked her then and there, but she understood that his ideas of professional honour would not allow him to do so while she was still his patient. But there could be no doubt of what he meant.

Katherine lay swayed in her anticipation from ecstasy to something approaching despair. On the one hand, what unmixed joy was promised: on the other, what a ghastly fate might be hanging over them all! And if this dreadful horror really materialised, it would be the end of her happiness. Even if the doctor would marry her – and she believed he would even under such terrible circumstances – she could never marry him.

Again and again she told herself there was no use in worrying about it, as nothing she could do would affect the result. But this recommendation suffered the usual fate of good advice.

The next day marked a stage in the party's convalescence. On it Katherine was allowed up, and on it Eva, Luke, and Jim were able to return home. William was much better, though not yet up, and even Mant was beginning slowly to improve.

When she saw the others Katherine found that they had been visited in turn by the police, who had obtained from each a similar statement to that she had herself given them. Once again she saw the hopelessness of trying to prevaricate to the police. With all these separate statements to compare, the slightest individual inaccuracy would instantly stand out, shrieking for attention. Thank heaven, everything she had said had been the literal truth!

Now came for Katherine a succession of dull and monotonous days, during which she slowly regained health and strength. She must, she felt, have been more seriously ill than she had imagined, her recovery was so gradual. And the same applied to the others also. In the cases of Eva, Jim, and Luke improvement was steady, though as slow as in her own. But Mant and William, though better, still remained prostrated. Mant, she now understood, had survived almost by a miracle, the result of his splendid constitution; and William's age and low state of health at the time told heavily against him.

As she talked with the others she quickly came to the conclusion that all five were completely puzzled as to what could have happened. None, she felt sure, had guessed the theory of the police or evolved any theory of their own to account for the facts.

Nor had the police, during these days, made any further move. What they were doing, if anything, Katherine could not imagine. No information had been given the family or published in the papers as to the result of their enquiries.

Katherine had one day met Inspector Kirby and had asked him how his investigation was progressing, but he had been politely non-committal in reply.

On one point she was profoundly thankful. Her terrible fears about Jim had died away. When she had met him and talked to him about the affair, he had spoken in such a way that she felt immediately satisfied as to his innocence. Jim was no actor and he could never, she felt sure, have displayed the feeling he did, had he had a guilty conscience.

Then one afternoon there came for Katherine what she believed was the most important day in her life. Runciman Jellicoe called and asked her to be his wife.

His manner was just a little cold and formal, and for a dreadful moment the suspicion leapt into her mind that he believed he had committed himself during her illness and was now only proposing from a sense of duty. But she soon saw that beneath that manner there was intense repressed feeling, and she realised that he spoke as he did in order not to embarrass her should she decide to refuse him. For this she loved him only the better, and she longed for nothing so much as to throw herself into his arms and feel them about her. Almost overwhelmingly she was tempted to accept him instantly and without condition.

But she did not do so. There was, she told him, this shadow hanging over the family, and until it was removed she could not even consider such a question.

"That," he said in his slightly precise way, "is not the question that I am immediately interested in. What I want to know, and what I do most earnestly beg you to tell me, is whether you think you could put up with me? I do love you so completely; it means more than anything else in the world to me. Could you, Katherine, love me a little in return?"

"Yes," she said then: she could hold herself back no longer. "I do love you, but I won't marry you or allow any engagement while there is the chance of something dreadful happening."

He looked overwhelmed, as if the shock of almost unbelievable happiness was too much for him. Then suddenly his manner changed. He dropped his cool precise manner, and, trembling with repressed excitement, he moved over to her and picked her up in his arms and kissed her as if she had been a child.

"My dear," he murmured with a kind of triumph in his voice, "when you've admitted that, you can't refuse to marry me. I couldn't urge you before; now I can. You love me! Nothing else matters. When you love me and I love you nothing can keep us apart. You will marry me, Katherine? You will?"

She clung to him. "I love you, Runciman," she answered, "but until this terrible shadow has cleared away I cannot marry you."

He kissed her again. "What is it you fear, my darling?" he asked. "What can anything outside our two selves matter to us? If trouble is coming, it is at your side that I should be, and will be," he added, a note of determination coming into his voice. "Katherine dear, we must be married before trouble can arise. Then I will have the right to face anything with you publicly." Still again he kissed her, then went on. "But don't let us be gloomy. It's very unlikely that the trouble you fear will arise at all. If the police had been going to move, they would have done so before now. No, give me this happiness, I implore you. Consent to an engagement. This is not really committing you" – he smiled whimsically – "you can always break it off later if you want to. But it would give me the right to stand at your side."

For an hour they discussed the matter, he putting up argument after argument and protesting that his entire happiness was dependent on her consent, she fighting against her almost overwhelming desire to agree.

"But don't you see," she repeated again and again, "if there is an arrest and a trial for attempted murder, quite apart from how that trial turns out, we'll all be ruined. If you're engaged to me, you'd be ruined, too. Who would consult a doctor whose wife was mixed up so closely in such a thing? You know it would be the end of your career."

In the end they compromised. Katherine agreed that while at the present she would not allow any engagement, she would reconsider the position at the end of a month, if by that time the police had made no move. With this, sorely against his will, he had to be content.

But Katherine could not keep her secret, though no word of it was spoken. Her heart sang within her and her face reflected her joy. Dr Jellicoe's long calls had already been noted, and these facts each counting as two, were put together, and the answer was found to be four.

Day after day passed and at last the month came to an end. The police had made no sign, and the affair of the poisoning was being forgotten. In his position as police doctor Jellicoe had tried to pump Inspector Kirby as to whether the case had been dropped, though with indifferent success.

However, the fact that the matter seemed to be dead had its effect on Katherine. When at the end of the month, to the very minute, Jellicoe called to press his claim, she consented to an engagement. But she insisted that there was to be no marriage till at least six months had passed, by which time practically all fear of the case being reopened would have vanished.

By this time all six invalids had recovered enough to take up again their usual avocations. But none of them was really well. Mant still remained so weak that he could only go to the office for an hour or two in the morning, and William was also far from being his old self. The other four were more normal, but even they felt languid and washed out and not able to do a day's work.

"You must go away," Jellicoe said for perhaps the twentieth time. "The whole lot of you must go away for a complete change. Take a voyage somewhere. What about Para and Manaos? There you cross the calmest part of the ocean and you get sun and there'd be nothing for you to do, so you'd have to lie up and rest. I don't care where you go, but if you want to get well in any reasonable time you must all go somewhere."

It was at this precise moment that something happened, in itself the most trivial of events, but which had a profound effect on the fortunes of the family. William, as a former client, received an advertisement of that season's Olympic cruises. Jellicoe happened to see it in his hand and said, "There you are! All of you go on one of those. I prescribe it as a cure."

For the first time William did not instantly turn the proposal down.

– 9 –

THE INVITATION OF WILLIAM

That night Runciman Jellicoe's suggestion was seriously discussed by William, Katherine, and Mant. Rather surprisingly, the idea appealed to all of them. William admitted that he had enjoyed his experience of the previous year, and had regretted having had to leave the ship at Marseilles. Evidently the idea of repeating what he had done and prolonging the cruise to the Eastern Mediterranean appealed to him. Mant expressed no enthusiasm about the cruise, but agreed that he couldn't get on with his work and must have a rest and change of some kind. As far as he was concerned, this Mediterranean excursion would do as well as anything else. As for Katherine, she declared that she was fed up with the common round of everyday life, and would give anything to get away for a time.

What Katherine really was considering was whether Runciman Jellicoe could go with them, but even if he could not, she felt she would not turn the idea down if William and Mant wanted to go.

"What exactly is the proposal?" she asked when this agreement in principle had been reached. "What places should we go to and when should we start?"

William picked up the attractively printed advertisement. "Here you are," he answered, "you'll find all particulars here." He turned the pages and began to read. "If we went at all, I think we should do two cruises, the first from Glasgow to Marseilles, the second straight on from Marseilles to the Greek Islands, Palestine, Egypt and so on and back to Marseilles, and so home overland. We should call at places which none of us have ever visited and at many of which there are excursions. What I saw of the arrangements last year was good and I shouldn't mind going again."

"That sounds splendid," Katherine approved. "You didn't say when it would be?"

"Pretty soon: in about a fortnight. We should have to leave Glasgow on Saturday, 20th of February, and we should be back in London on Saturday, 3rd of April. That's exactly seven weeks."

"Too long," said Mant.

"I don't know," William returned. Jellicoe keeps harping on two or three months. If we go at all we might as well do the thing properly. I haven't taken a real holiday for years, and I mind confessing I'd enjoy it."

"May I see?" Katherine asked, taking the programme. "Oh," she went on, "this looks delightful. From Glasgow to Cadiz, Gibraltar, Ceuta, Malaga, Marseilles, and then Ajaccio, Athens, and a lot of Greek places, Istanbul, Palestine, Egypt, and Majorca. Of all those places, I've only been at Marseilles. Yes, I think this is quite an idea."

She tried to seem enthusiastic because she thought the cruise would be so good for William. But really she was not wholly pleased. If she went, she would not see Runciman Jellicoe for seven whole weeks. She supposed there was not the slightest chance of his joining the party. Oh, if that were only possible! How splendid the adventure would then become!

There was also the question of Eva and Luke and Jim. Katherine felt she would not be quite happy going off on such a delightful trip, if her cousins were unable to enjoy it also. And she rather doubted if any of them could afford it.

"What about the others?" she asked. "Eva and Luke and Jim? I don't know if they could rise to it, and somehow I don't know that I'd care to go without them."

"I've thought about that," William said unexpectedly. "If we go, I invite the whole party as my guests except Mant," he looked at Mant with a smile. "Mant is now the millionaire in the family and can well pay for himself. But the rest of you, including Luke, I invite. And what's more," he looked shrewdly at Katherine, "I'm not going to trust myself to any steamer sawbones. I shall ask Jellicoe to come with us on the same terms."

Katherine could scarcely believe her ears. Here was a vision of happiness such as she could never have imagined. A cruise in such conditions would be like a peep into heaven. Impulsively she stepped forward and kissed William on the forehead.

"How splendid of you, uncle," she exclaimed warmly. "That would make everything just right."

The old man seemed pleased. "It's not altogether altruism," he declared with a twisted smile. "For my own sake I want you all to be happy and contented on board." Then more seriously: "As a matter of fact I feel some responsibility about the poisoning affair. It took place in my house, to my guests, and I think I should do what I can to help them over it. The doctor's different. He's going to have to work professionally for his tickets."

Though it made her feel rather a beast, Katherine could not help being surprised at both action and explanation. It was much more thoughtful and unselfish than she would have expected from William. He had always been just, but seldom generous. And this action was generous to a fault.

"And what about the others?" she asked presently. "Have you mentioned it to them yet?"

William, it appeared, had only just conceived the idea, and so had mentioned it to no one else.

"I tell you what," Katherine went on, "let's ring them up and ask them to come round. What about it?"

"Jim and Eva and Luke by all means," William answered. "But I'm not so sure about Jellicoe. After all between him and me it's a matter of business. You say what you like to him, but I think I'll make the suggestion when he calls professionally, as he will tomorrow."

Katherine could not but agree as she went to the telephone. William was right. He had been extraordinarily nice about the whole thing.

"Oh, Eva," she said when she had got through, "will you and Luke come round here now? The most wonderful prospect has opened out and we want to discuss it with you. It's something quite splendid. I can't tell you over the phone, but do come at once."

Eva, mystified, said they would start immediately, as did Jim in his turn, and a few minutes later all six were seated round the fire in the Grey House sitting room.

"It's this blessed doctor, whom we mustn't call Jellicoe any more, but Runciman," William began when Katherine had explained that he was going to make the great announcement. "He has, as you know, been urging us all to go away for a change, and at last I can stand him no longer and I've decided to go. But I don't want to go alone, so I've decided to invite all of you to come with me. Mant and Katherine are coming, and I hope you three will too. What we propose is – " And he went on to describe the Olympic tour.

Eva was enchanted with the proposal. She also sprang up and kissed William. She thought it would be perfectly heavenly and just what they all wanted to put them right after their illness. Uncle William was a dear to think of it. She would go and so would Luke, and many thanks.

Luke was accustomed to being spoken for in this way and didn't seem to mind. He said immediately that there was nothing he would like more, and expressed his thanks for the invitation. Jim, on his part, seemed a little overwhelmed. He said it was extraordinarily good of his Uncle William to include him and that he would be only too delighted to join in.

"One thing occurs to me," Luke put in. "Is it all right for every member of the family to leave the works together?"

"I think so," said Mant, who up to now had taken little part in the conversation. "All of us left it when we were ill, and we didn't seem to be missed. Beecher carried on quite well without any instructions, and he can do it again."

"Then," said William, "we have only to find out about Jellicoe, and I'll do that tomorrow when he calls."

"Runciman," corrected Jim. "He'll be all right. Trust Katherine to see to that."

"Your responsibilities beginning already, Katherine?" enquired Luke with heavy jocularity.

"Nice to hear them all admitting they have to do what they're told," Eva pointed out.

"The conversation is becoming embarrassing," Katherine smiled. "I move we take the next business. What is it, Uncle William?"

The old man was obviously impatient. "The next business is tickets and cabins. Now you and I, Katherine, are going up to Town on Tuesday. We'll fix them up then, what do you say?"

The visit was to enable William to attend the annual lunch of a society of manufacturers of electrical apparatus. He usually went up by himself, but this time Jellicoe had refused his consent to the journey unless Katherine travelled with him. Indeed only that the old man had set his heart on going, the doctor would have prohibited the expedition altogether. Katherine, however, was glad of the two or three days in London, now specially that she would require some new clothes for the cruise.

Next morning she waylaid Jellicoe when he was leaving William's room to learn his decision.

"Need you ask?" he put it to her as they turned into the sitting room. "I feel badly about it, because I cannot but believe that his wanting my opinion is only an excuse for inviting me. But since you are to be there, I simply hadn't the strength to refuse. Of course I needn't say how I shall enjoy it and how grateful I am to Mr Carrington for making it possible."

"Uncle William," Katherine said correctingly.

"I don't know. He mightn't like that," Jellicoe protested.

"Uncle William," Katherine repeated inexorably.

He smiled. "All right: Uncle William. I'll tell him you're responsible."

Two days later Katherine went up to London with William and he duly attended his luncheon. After it she left him installed in a sitting room in their hotel while she went out to do some shopping. He seemed a good deal better from the change and she felt disposed to take a rather high tone with him.

"Now remember you're to rest," she declared, warningly. "You're not to go out. You've had quite enough excitement for one day."

"I'm not going out," he protested. "I should like to go and see old Hamilton later, but I'll wait till you come back."

"Well, we'll see how you are then," she agreed, and left him on the sofa with books and papers and cigars within easy reach.

She spent more time in the shops than she had intended, and when she returned to the hotel it was nearly six. Too late for a visit to old Mr Hamilton, she thought. Her uncle would just have to wait till the next day.

But when she reached the sitting room William made no reference to the proposed visit. He was full of another subject. His interest in it indeed made him much more like his old self than he had been since his illness began.

"I've been having quite a pleasant time," he declared. "I got bored when you went out and I thought I'd go to Cunn's and fix up about the cruise. Then I thought that if I did you'd kick up such a shindy that it wouldn't be worthwhile, so I rang them up and told them to send a clerk here with all particulars. He was here for an hour and more: he's just gone indeed. But I fixed up everything. All the tickets are taken and the berths engaged."

"Oh, Uncle William, how splendid!"

"Ah, yes," he said, "but there's a snag. Several snags indeed, and some of them rather serious. We can't get the accommodation we should like and that I asked for. The ship's booked up almost completely. And I'm going to be selfish and take the best cabin for myself."

Katherine laughed. "I don't know who has a better right to it," she said. "Tell me."

"I've taken one single and two two-berth outside cabins on B Deck, adjoining each other. It was the merest chance that I got them. They had been reserved weeks ago by a party of five, and just this morning they had written that they couldn't go. So that was a piece of luck and I plumped for them."

"I should just think so."

"But that was as far as the luck went. I thought of those three I should be selfish and take the single one. Then another would do for Luke and Eva. The next one would have to be for Mant and Jim. But I wasn't sure how that would work."

Katherine did not feel so sure either. It was not a combination that she herself would have chosen.

"Then," went on William, "I'm extremely sorry to say that there were no single-berth cabins left for you and Jellicoe. You will both, I'm afraid, have to share with other people. I've secured one berth in a two-berth cabin on A Deck for you: an outside cabin, and one in a two-berth inside cabin on A Deck for Jellicoe. I'm so sorry, Katherine, but there were simply no others to be had."

"Oh, but that'll do splendidly!" Katherine declared. "I shall be perfectly all right."

"I don't see that we can better it," William went on.

It took me most of an hour to get even that arranged. You think you can manage?"

"Of course I can manage," Katherine assured him warmly. "I think it's just perfect."

And it was, she really did think. Seven glorious weeks of change and travel, with Runciman! What more heavenly prospect could be imagined? What did she care where her cabin was, or where the ship went to or who else might or might not be on board? These things were trifles – so infinitesimally small as to be practically non-existent. Change, travel, sun, scenery, comfort, interest: all these were good, excellent indeed in their way, but not one of them counted for anything compared to the great overwhelming fact that during these seven weeks she would be with Runciman.

The one unsatisfactory feature of the arrangement was that Mant and Jim must share a cabin. But this she did not think so serious as she would some weeks earlier. Since the illness Jim seemed to be getting on much better with Mant. Apparently there had been no further friction, and she had more than once heard them talking quite amicably. Perhaps indeed this sharing of the cabin would teach them each other's good points and turn them into real friends.

When they returned to Bromsley William called a meeting of the party to report progress. All concerned expressed themselves as delighted with the arrangements.

Time, which for all of them had dragged leadenly since their illness, now began to hasten by with incredible and inexorable speed. The nearer the great day approached, the more Katherine found she wanted to do before the start. It was astonishing how many clothes seemed to be necessary. She asked the people in Cunn's office whether they might expect warm weather or cool, but could get no satisfactory answer. Probably, it appeared, there would be both. All were agreed that it would be cold going down to Gibraltar, but no one seemed able to forecast the temperature in Egypt or Palestine. Nor could she find out whether fancy dress would be wanted for dances. In the end it looked as if she would have to take her whole wardrobe, and it was only then that she began to discover how depleted that wardrobe was. This meant more shopping, and as usual, the things that she particularly wanted were out of stock. So she had to change her plans, which gave her still more to think about.

Whether it was this need for preparation, or the mere anticipation of approaching pleasure, she began to feel much better and more like her old self. And she noticed the same phenomenon in each of the other members of the family. William in particular began really to improve. Not only did his physical health seem better, but mentally he was less depressed and appeared to have regained some of his former grip and energy.

"It's what he has wanted for a long time," Jellicoe told Katherine during one of his evening calls. "His mind was occupied with the works, then when he got this illness and had to retire he really had nothing to think about. All this looking forward to the cruise has been new life to him."

At last the great day dawned. The ship was sailing from Glasgow and all passengers had to be aboard by seven o'clock that evening. A convenient train left Birmingham about midday and reached Glasgow at 6.25. This would just do.

Allowing for their various ages and temperaments, the travellers made an excited little party as they took their seats in the train. In spite of the fortnight's preparation Katherine had found a number of things to do at the last minute, and it was with some slight feeling of relief that she settled herself into her place. If something vital had been forgotten, well, hang it all, it was too late now to worry any more. She rather gathered from disjointed remarks from Eva that her experience had been much the same. The men took things more calmly, being apparently chiefly concerned with the purchase of magazines and the securing of seats for lunch. William had handed over the whole matter of tickets, passports, and such managerial details to

Jim, as his contribution to the expedition, while Luke had taken charge of the luggage. On the strength of their seven tickets a first-class compartment had been reserved, but Katherine and Jellicoe found that you could not conveniently put seven people into six seats, and had sought sanctuary elsewhere.

The day had started promisingly with a thin though watery sunshine, but as they climbed through the Westmorland hills cloud had rolled up and at Carlisle it was dropping rain. The evening closed in early with a sodden downpour, and gradually the carriage windows grew black and streaked with horizontal lines of drops. The wind also had risen, and at Glasgow it was blowing gustily, sweeping little deluges of rain in eddies round the buildings and along the streets. It had been a source of disappointment that they were going down the Clyde during the night, but this was no longer felt to matter, as in this weather they would have had no view of the Firth.

Had Katherine been superstitious, the drive from the Central Station to the Princes Dock would have struck her as a bad omen for the cruise. The howling of the wind, the cold raw air, the splashing rain, the streaked reflections of the street lamps on the streaming footpaths, the hurrying figures, bent miserably forward for shelter, all seemed as uninviting and unpropitious as she could well imagine. And outside, away down the coast, where they would be before morning, she could picture a sea running, with great white-capped waves, a rolling, plunging ship, and herself...

"Ough! Jolly to be clearing out and leaving all this behind us," Eva's voice broke in on her thoughts.

Katherine felt that this, and not hers, was the way to look at the matter and she became more cheerful. And she was better pleased still when after a few unpleasant moments in the rain they struggled up a steeply sloping gangway and disappeared through a door into *Patricia*'s towering black side. It led into a small room in which officers sat at a desk and checked the tickets and passports of those coming aboard. A short delay and they were satisfied by Jim that his party was all it should be, and a move further was made.

The little room connected with a long narrow corridor, stretching endlessly in both directions. The miracle of this corridor seized Katherine's imagination, and during the whole time of her stay on the ship she never lost her feeling of wonder at its length. It was straight horizontally, but sagged slightly in the vertical dimension, following the curve of the decks. She afterwards found that it was one of several which stretched nearly, though not quite, the whole length of the ship.

Now the party separated and were ushered by their respective stewards to their respective cabins. Hers was A 60, a two-berthed cabin on A Deck amidships on the port side. Her stewardess appeared immediately and proved to be a slight middle-aged woman with a kindly face, a capable manner, and an accent which could only have come from "Glesca".

"Good evening, madam," she greeted Katherine. "You'll be Miss Shirley, I'm thinking?"

Katherine was thinking so too.

"Then this'll be your berth." The woman pointed to that beneath the closed and curtained porthole. "Mrs Ingram, that's her that has the one opposite, has just got her things put away. A nice lady from the north of Ireland."

Katherine could see some rather costly looking wraps hanging from the wall brackets beside her neighbour's wardrobe, and the corner of a suitcase and a number of pairs of shoes beneath the opposite berth. For a moment her heart failed her when she thought how extremely intimate her relations with this stranger would be during the next few weeks. However, Mrs Buchanan, as Katherine found the stewardess was called, had given the woman a good character, and the fact that her berth was not littered over with clothes suggested that at least she was tidy.

Katherine would have liked a bath after the long train journey, but it appeared that no baths were possible in port. There was, however, a good supply of hot water to the basin in the cabin and she quickly put away her things and got ready for dinner. On this first night, so she was assured, no one changed, and indeed there would have been scarcely time for this when the dinner bugle sounded.

Just as it did so her room mate knocked and entered. She was a tall middle-aged woman with intelligent eyes and greying hair. Her expression was grave, but when she smiled, as she did at Katherine, her face lit up as if illuminated by a lamp, and became wholly attractive. A feeling of relief passed through Katherine's mind. This surely was a woman with whom it would be a pleasure to travel.

"Miss Shirley, isn't it?" the newcomer said in a low musical voice with a slight accent which Katherine supposed must be north of Ireland. "I'm Mrs Ingram and we're to share the cabin. What a dreadful evening."

Katherine agreed and repeated Eva's remark about how splendid it was to be going south away from British weather.

"Yes, it's not England's star month, is it? Are you alone or a member of a party?"

"A party," Katherine answered. "As a matter of fact we are seven."

"Oh, you're lucky. I'm quite alone. However, I've already made a friend: a nice Canadian woman I've just been talking to. We're to sit together at meals. Do you know your table?"

"No: I leave that to the men. I've been staying put so far on the trip, and I suppose I shall go on doing so till the end. It saves a lot of trouble."

Mrs Ingram laughingly agreed, and they left the cabin. Jellicoe was hovering in the alleyway and came forward.

"Hullo, Katherine. Let me show you the way to the dining saloon. It appears that we can sit anywhere we like tonight. Tomorrow our permanent places will be given us."

"Let me introduce Dr Jellicoe," Katherine said. "My cabin mate, Mrs Ingram."

Chatting, Jellicoe led them along the alleyway to the main staircase, which led at C Deck level into the dining saloon. They went down and seized a four-seat table close to the door.

"Won't you and your new friend join us for tonight?" Katherine asked Mrs Ingram.

Mrs Ingram said she would be delighted, and presently captured the Canadian. Jellicoe was polite, but looked a little wistfully at a small two-seat table in the corner of the room. Katherine had already seen that there were four such tables and decided that if it were humanly possible, they would have one.

Though there was a good deal of unrest during dinner, people coming and going and moving about the saloon to talk to their friends at other tables, the meal was excellent and admirably served. Mrs Ingram seemed a really nice woman, and Katherine thought she was lucky to have her in her cabin. The Canadian was lively and pleasant, and altogether Katherine felt that at last the omens for the coming trip were of the best.

Certain muffled ringings of bells and other faint sounds presently indicated that they were moving out of the dock. In A Deck lounge, where the Carrington party was sitting, they felt nothing except once, when a slight vibration passed through the ship for a few seconds: the engines being put full speed astern, explained the ship's doctor, who at the moment happened to be chatting to them. Otherwise the only way in which they could tell whether or not they were moving was by looking out and seeing the slow passage of the shore lights.

For some hours after she went to bed Katherine could not sleep. How she hoped that this trip would not only restore all of them to complete health, but would heal the unhappy rift between Jim and Mant which might so easily destroy the happiness of all of them! How she wished to see her Uncle William well again, as he was during those uneventful though not unhappy years during which she had kept house for him! Above all, how she looked forward to being with Runciman, and how she trusted that nothing would occur to disturb the almost rapturous joy that now filled her mind!

Presently she grew drowsy, and then almost immediately she was wakened by the stewardess with her morning tea.

Instantly she realised that they were out in the open. *Patricia* was pitching, slowly and easily, but very perceptibly.

"Where are we?" she asked as she sat up and took the tea.

"Off the coast of Ireland, madam: County Down. We've left bonny Scotland behind."

"I hope we've left bonny Scotch weather, too," said Mrs Ingram with a smile.

The stewardess eyed her shrewdly and appeared satisfied. "Yes, madam," she replied meekly. "We've got to Irish weather here. Rain blowing on to us off the land."

Mrs Ingram laughed good-humouredly. "Ah, well," she concluded, "the less either of us say about it the better. Is there much of a sea on?"

"Just a wee jollop, madam. Nothing to signify."

"The nautical attitude, I'm afraid. I wonder shall I risk getting up?"

Katherine, who didn't mind the motion, got up and went on deck. It was an utterly depressing morning, and yet in a way she liked it. The wind was high, whistling and howling through the ship's upper fittings, and dashing the rain almost horizontally against the windows of the deck-houses. The atmosphere was grey and murky and visibility, as she thought she should now say, was poor. A dull lead-coloured sea heaved and churned, the wave crests seething with dirty white. Standing in the shelter of a boat, she watched the bow climbing slowly up into the sky, up and up and up, hanging there for a moment, and then falling, falling, falling, as if the ship was heading for the bottom. Then there would be a burst of spray over the bows, and the slow climb would begin again.

They were unlucky that day in that the weather remained too thick to see land. By dark they had left Ireland astern and when Mrs Buchanan brought Katherine her tea on the following morning, they were well round Land's End.

As, after the call at Plymouth, they crossed the end of the English Channel and reached the edge of the far-famed Bay of Biscay, the weather improved. The wind died down and the rather heavy swell which had been running began to flatten out. The sun burst through the heavy pall of clouds and patches of blue sky appeared. By the time they passed Finisterre they were in a different climate.

By then also the passengers had settled down to life at sea. They had fallen in with the routine of the ship, formed a new set of habits, made fresh contacts, and adapted their various characters and idiosyncrasies to their changed conditions.

Katherine had not, after all, been entirely happy while the weather had continued bad. She was not actually sick, but neither did she feel quite comfortable. She developed a passion for the deck, and enlisted stewards to carry the lighter kinds of food to where she sat, enveloped in rugs, in the shelter of the A Deck lounge.

But since the sun had come out and the sea had fallen she had begun to enjoy herself without any physical or mental reservation whatever. She had a comfortable cabin, a pleasant cabin mate, a shipload of people who all seemed out to be friendly, and more than all of these put together, she had Runciman Jellicoe. Already the nightmare of her fears about the poisoning was receding and she was feeling better in herself.

She had taken also very warmly to the ship's routine. She had always been an early riser, and she found that before breakfast was the best time for a walk. Later chairs covered a good deal of the deck, but at that hour comparatively few people were about. Then came breakfast and after it she generally looked over the wireless news posted on the stairs and in A Deck lounge, read for a while, and chatted or played games till lunch. After lunch was the hour sacred to deckchairs, sometimes spent in chatting, sometimes reading, sometimes lying lost in a dreamy muse, and sometimes wholly oblivious to what was going on. But tea was the time for rousing up, and then there were more games till it got dark, when bridge became a never-failing stand-by. Too soon it was necessary to change for dinner, and after dinner there was more bridge or talk, or a lecture or dancing, singly or combined to taste.

And then came the first real excitement of the trip. On the Thursday morning Katherine came on deck to find they were lying in the estuary behind Cadiz.

With a thrill she looked forward to stepping for the first time on Spanish soil, when they should take their first excursion: a morning drive through the fine old city. Her first foreign excursion – with Runciman! Truly this cruise promised to be the most tremendous success.

– 10 –

INTERLUDE – INTRODUCING TSS *PATRICIA*

Evening at Cadiz! While Katherine was yawning over her book on the after-deck and trying to assure herself that it was not yet time to go and dress for dinner, innumerable activities were in progress all over the ship.

For the cabin and bath stewards it was one of the rush hours of the day. The former were brushing and laying out evening clothes and carrying jugs of hot water to those cabins in which only cold was laid on, the latter coping with their perennial problem of how to supply more baths simultaneously than there were bathrooms. Above, the deck stewards were beginning to fold up chairs and collect rugs and the library steward was opening up his bookcases. Already the smoke-room staff were getting cocktails ready, and in the dining room the last touches were being given to the tables. Below in the kitchens the cooks sweated over their pots and pans and the wine steward anxiously counted his bottles. Everywhere preparations for dinner were under way.

Tonight in Cadiz, however, was one of the easiest of the cruise for the non-technical staff. Nearly half the passengers had taken the overland tour to Seville, Cordoba, and Granada, and would rejoin the ship three days later at Malaga. Numbers were therefore small and work correspondingly light.

But some of the passengers remaining had contrived to give those in command some anxiety. A party who had not taken the official excursion to Jerez had gone ashore after lunch to explore for themselves thc delights of Cadiz. Some of these had not turned up on the landing stage at the prescribed hour, and a boat, manned by exasperated officials, was awaiting them. The mere lateness in itself would not matter much, but what was annoying Captain Goode was that the tide was ebbing, and that if it fell much lower some risk of grounding might attend their passage to the sea.

In the landing room on B deck, with which the side ladder communicated, the officers on duty at the embarkation were congregated. The second officer was in charge of the operation and he sat chatting with his *confrère* from the purser's office who was responsible for recording the entry or exit of all passengers into or out of the ship. On *Patricia* a system obtained by means of which it was known at any given moment which passengers were aboard and which were not. Each was given a numbered card which had to be shown on leaving or returning to the ship, and these numbers were checked off on a sheet as the card holder passed the recording officer.

Below, on the landing platform itself, two seamen exchanged bilingual chaff with the crew of the launch belonging to the Spanish passport and harbour authorities. The launch was tied up to the platform awaiting the return of the emissaries who were still "up above", presumably drinking a glass of wine with the captain. Whatever these Olympians thought of each other in their secret minds, there was no doubt of the friendliness between the sailors.

The Spanish motorman had worked in Cardiff, and most of what he said was intelligible to the Englishmen.

Far below the water-line, in the engine room and stokehold, preparations for the start were in full swing. Here the outstanding question was steam. "They" up there on the bridge had a nasty habit of suddenly wanting full speed from one or both turbines, with the result that forecasts as to the amount of firing to be done in preparation were apt to be somewhat upset. The great thing was to have all the steam that could at any time be required, without wasting any of it by blowing off at the safety valves. A nice judgment was necessary for these requirements and Mr Mackintosh, the Chief, prided himself that they were practically always achieved.

In the seat of government, high up on the navigating bridge, indications that something was about to happen were also apparent.

Mr Claverton, the first officer, who was in charge of the ship, stood in the starboard cab, glancing from the last ship's boat, now rapidly approaching from the shore, to that of the Spanish authorities at the foot of the ladder below. The first officer was frowning slightly. This taking of the ship out was always just a trifle ticklish. With the falling tide there was very little margin between the depth of the water in the channel and *Patricia*'s draught. A little deviation from the fairway and the results for all concerned might be unpleasant. Of course they would have the pilot in charge and the old man himself would be on the bridge, but to ground the ship would be no better for the officer of the watch than for anyone else aboard. Not that Claverton was in the least nervous – he had taken ships out of port too often for that – but he did look graver than if they were out in the open. Mentally he cursed the errant passengers. If he had had his own way they would have been left behind.

He turned and glanced forward. All appeared to be in readiness on the fo'c'sle. The officer was in charge, and the men required for the raising of the anchor were at their posts. A faint waft from a leaking valve showed that steam was on the windlass.

At that moment the quartermaster who was to take the first trick at the helm came up the bridge ladder and entered the wheelhouse. Claverton followed him in and let his eyes run over the room and its contents.

The bridge, about five feet wide, ran across the ship for its full width. Indeed, it was rather longer than the width of the ship, for the two "cabs", or small, covered, and glass-panelled shelters at its ends, projected slightly out over the water. In the centre it was covered by the wheelhouse, a structure some twenty feet wide by ten deep. Along the front of the wheelhouse were spaced five Chadburn telegraph standards. Those at the ends next the bridge doorways duplicated each other and worked in unison. These led to the engine room, and each bore two handles and dials, referring to the port and starboard propellers respectively. Two other telegraphs communicated, one with the bow and the other with the stern, and covered every conceivable operation connected with mooring, warping, and casting off, as well as raising and letting fall the anchor. The fifth telegraph was for use if the steam steering engine broke down and recourse had to be made to the hand-steering apparatus, and indicated to the helmsmen astern how their wheel was to be moved. It contained a telltale pointer, which at all times indicated the position of the rudder, and was accordingly normally used as a check that the steering engine was doing its job.

Behind the telegraph standards was a clear passage of five or six feet wide. This stretched between the doors at each side of the house and formed the continuation of the bridge. The rest of the gear was behind this passage. In the centre was the wheel, small and of brightly polished brass, with before it the brass binnacle. Through a little glass window in the latter could be seen the delicately poised compass card, illuminated by hidden lighting and with a lens enlarging the divisions in front of the lubber's line or mark showing the centre line of the ship. At each side of the compass were the great balls of soft iron, used to neutralise the magnetic distortion due to the steelwork of the ship, with behind a separate bundle of iron rods to counteract the effect of the funnel.

The wheel and its attendant fixtures was the largest single object in the room, but spaced at convenient points was a variety of other apparatus. On the back wall at the starboard side were the indicators showing which of the watertight doors were shut and which were open. Close by were the light repeaters. If any of the ship's essential navigating lights went out, a bell would ring and an indicator show the defaulter. At the port side was a battery of half a dozen speaking-tubes to reinforce the telegraphs. Above them were the "rev" indicators, two dials in which pointers recorded the exact speed at which the two propellers were turning. In the back wall was a door leading to the chart room and the captain's cabin, and forward was a desk bearing a chart of Cadiz harbour, on which lay a large pair of parallel rulers.

By force of habit, Claverton rapidly took in the room and everything that was in it. All was clean, tidy, and in order. As the quartermaster took up his position behind the wheel, Claverton saw that he looked competent and alert, as also did the attendant cadet standing back at the port side.

Satisfied in that quarter, the first officer turned back to the starboard cab to watch the approach of the ship's boat. It was now within a cable or two, and the Spanish launch had cast off and was circling a hundred feet away, so as to clear the landing platform for the newcomer. Claverton was satisfied with what he saw. The men who should be there were all in position. They were good men who knew their jobs, and in a very few minutes the ship would have its complement of passengers aboard and the packed boat would be empty and swinging at the falls. Then once the Spanish officials had left, they could get away. And with the falling tide, the sooner the better.

The boat came alongside, and the passengers began to stream slowly up the ladder. There was a little swell, not very much, but enough to make it necessary to time the step on to the platform. This was being done for the passengers by the officers in charge. At the correct moment they gave an arm, an assisting and compelling arm: in fact, the more elderly found themselves practically lifted off their feet. Done competently, but with restrained jokes and hearty good will. Done in a way that inspired confidence, that banished the nervousness of those unaccustomed to boats. "You don't think about it," Claverton had once overheard an elderly lady explaining to a friend. "You feel you have nothing to do yourself and that they will manage." A fine compliment, Claverton had considered it, as indeed it was.

As the last of the passengers reached the landing platform the captain appeared on the lower bridge with the Spanish officials. Polite farewells were in progress, but the captain found time to make a signal to Claverton. This Claverton knew meant "Get your anchor up", and he passed back into the wheelhouse and rotated the handle of the fo'c'sle telegraph till it pointed to "UP ANCHOR". With the clanging of a bell the repeating pointer took up the same position, as the officer forward operated his handle. Immediately the clank, clank of the forward windlass began, and the great links of the anchor chain began to crawl slowly across the deck from hawsehole to locker.

Claverton turned to the helmsman. "Have you got steam?" he demanded.

"Not yet, sir," the man answered. He was rotating his wheel and watching the wheel position indicator move through its arc, from centre to starboard, then from starboard right over to port, and back again to centre.

The first officer moved to the nest of speaking-tubes and blew down one labelled "Engineer". "Get steam on the steering engine, will you," he directed. "We're ready for her."

The reply was evidently satisfactory, for Claverton plugged the tube, and after his habitual comprehensive glance round the wheelhouse, returned to the starboard cab. The windlass was clanking steadily forward and the anchor chain coming in. Below, the ship's boat had fallen aft from the ladder and was hooked on to the falls, while the Spanish launch was just coming up again to the platform. The captain and the Spaniards had disappeared. Probably he was accompanying them to the head of the ladder.

As he waited the two or three minutes before the anchor was likely to break out, Claverton glanced round the horizon. Unlike most of the Spanish coast, the ground about Cadiz was low and unimpressive. They were lying far up the estuary, well above the city, their bows upstream as if heading for Puerto Real. To port was El Trocadero, little more than a dock, railway station and fort, with Puntales on their starboard quarter. Cadiz itself lay fine on their starboard quarter, an attractive-looking white jumble of buildings with the towers of the cathedral projecting upwards from the mass. All along their starboard side was the narrow strip of land connecting the city with the mainland. On their bow it was little wider than the road and railway it carried, and over it could be seen the sea. The great estuary appeared completely landlocked, the sea opening being screened by the town. Claverton thought neither of the history nor the artistic possibilities of the place: to him it was a shallowish fairway with mudflats to either side, which with a low tide had to be navigated with care if a grounding and its attendant troubles were to be avoided.

But now the Spaniards had taken their places in their launch, which was pushing off from the ladder. Claverton moved back to the wheelhouse, to be in touch with the telegraph from the bows. As he did so, the captain came up the bridge steps, followed by the pilot, a small man in a blue lounge-suit with a dark red face, a close-clipped white moustache, and hands deeply buried in his trousers pockets.

"Got steam yet?" Claverton asked the quartermaster at the wheel.

"Yes, sir." Again the man tested his helm to full port and starboard respectively, and Claverton watched the telltale pointer on the emergency steering telegraph jerkily following, indicating that the rudder was moving to correspond.

The captain looked in. "Tell them I shall want plenty of steam for that port turbine," he said.

"Aye, aye, sir," Claverton answered briskly, and going once more to the engine-room speaking-tube, he passed on the message.

A bell rang sharply. The pointer of the fo'c'sle telegraph had moved to "ALL CLEAR", indicating the anchor had broken out of the ground. Captain Goode nodded to the pilot.

"Hard aport," the latter said unexpectedly.

"Hard aport," repeated Claverton, and the quartermaster spun the wheel to the left. Claverton watched the two pointers, and when both had moved to the end of their travel, he repeated to the captain and pilot: "Hard aport, sir."

"Half ahead starb'd machine," went on the pilot, looking forward over the canvas dodger just outside the wheelhouse door, and burying his hands still deeper in his pockets.

Claverton was ready at the engine-room telegraph. He swung the starboard handle backwards and forwards through its whole arc, then stopped it at "AHEAD – HALF". The bell rang, the repeating pointer from the engineers traversed the same arc and came to rest at the same point.

"Half ahead starboard engine, sir," Claverton reported.

No result was apparent. No sound was heard, no tremor passed through the ship; nothing whatever seemed to have happened. The whole business was extraordinarily detached. The judgment of an expert – reinforced by the tacit approval of two other experts – had, after mature consideration, decided on the moving of a handle. The handle had been moved. And that was all.

And so for some time the situation apparently remained unchanged. The three men stood patiently watching. Then gradually it became clear that something was happening after all. Very gradually the landscape had begun to move. Miraculously the harbour was rotating about the ship: at first almost imperceptibly, then unmistakably. Cadiz was now dead astern. El Trocadero was sidling forward towards the port bow. Drawing slightly closer too, was it not?

The pilot evidently thought so. "Half astern the port machine," he called suddenly.

Claverton manipulated the telegraph, ending up with his cadenza, "Half astern port engine, sir." Still there was no result apparent to the senses, save that the swinging motion grew more accentuated. But the dock at El Trocadero was still slowly growing closer.

The pilot mumbled in broken English to the captain and danced impatiently on one leg. "Full astern, the port machine," he called, followed by the usual ritual from Claverton.

A few moments later El Trocadero had drawn fair ahead and *Patricia* was lying right across the channel, milky water surging away in all directions from her stern. Very slowly also she was moving seawards, broadside, with the current. Down the estuary, some half-mile away, a steamer was coming to meet them. A five-thousand-ton freighter, she looked, and she was obviously going to pass them and go on up higher.

"There's a steamer coming up, sir," Claverton called out warningly, lest the others, who were looking ahead from the starboard side of the wheelhouse, might not have seen her.

The information galvanised the pilot into action. He ran nimbly across through the wheelhouse to the port side of the bridge and stood looking at her.

"Better give her two blasts," the captain intervened quietly from his place on the starboard side.

"Yes, two blasts," the pilot added, remembering that he was in charge.

Claverton stepped outside the wheelhouse door and there moved a large lever which was fixed to the wall of the building. It was the one piece of apparatus about the ship, that lever, which seemed somehow out of the picture, as if it might have been designed by Mr Heath Robinson. However it worked. Two short but raucous blasts came from the horn, a signal to the other: "I am going to pass on your port side."

There was no reply and the other ship kept on her course. But before she was up to them *Patricia* had swung till El Trocadero was on her port beam and the telegraph had been altered to show full speed ahead with both engines. Presently the hard aport helm was eased, and soon the ship was heading down the estuary with helm amidships.

"Better start your fishing," said Captain Goode suddenly.

On receiving this somewhat cryptic order, Claverton hurried into the chart room at the back of the wheelhouse, and going up to a large box or case against the back wall, turned a switch. Immediately a whirring sound issued from it, and a large metal arm like a pendulum began swinging backward and forward behind a glass pane. Beneath the arm was a sheet of paper which moved slightly downward at each swing. On the left side of the paper appeared a dark mark. At this the first officer peered earnestly.

"Six fathoms," he called, going to the charthouse door.

"Keep your eye on it," directed the captain, and Claverton returned to his scrutiny of the mark.

This apparatus was the echo sounder, with which, to the secret pride of both officers, *Patricia* was fitted. It was an extraordinarily ingenious machine. A bell fixed to the ship's bottom sounded every two seconds. The sound waves from it passed down through the water to the sea bed and were reflected up again to the ship's bottom. There a microphone picked them up. An electrical impulse was sent to the machine in the chart room both on the departure of these waves and on their return, and the time between them was marked on the moving paper over a scale which showed the corresponding depths. Thus an indication of the depth was given to the ship's officers every two seconds, and as refinements of design had made the affair extremely accurate, its value was enormous. Not only could it be used in shoaling waters, as in the present instance, but when its readings were compared with the chart, it was a valuable guide to position in foggy weather.

"Five fathoms," called Claverton suddenly, the dark line having slightly shifted to the left.

Five fathoms were thirty feet, and *Patricia* was drawing something like twenty-four. However that proved the shallowest point and the depth soon increased first to six and then to seven fathoms.

Another anxiety in the officers' minds while navigating the estuary was the curious fact that a large ship steers somewhat erratically in shallow waters. She will suddenly and without any warning yaw away to the side, as if thrown over by the water banking up against the ground. And no one can tell when or in which direction she is going till she actually swings over. The passing of other vessels in a shallow and confined area is therefore at times nerve-racking enough.

But here, once they had met the tramp, they had the estuary to themselves, and though speed was reduced while traversing the narrower parts of the channel, they were soon opposite the city and crossing the mouth of the inner harbour. A short slack to drop the pilot and then full speed ahead again in a great curve with Cadiz as centre and a distance of some two miles as radius. From their moorings south-east of the city, they drew in turn to east of it, north of it, west of it, and then easing up the helm on a southerly course to Trafalgar and Gibraltar, they grew more and more nearly south of it.

Meanwhile in the great steel box containing the engines, some sixty feet deep and wide by thirty long, work had settled down into routine. Here also the period of the start was a time of anxiety for all concerned, but now that they were under way, this was over. The Chief, Mr Mackintosh, wiping his hands on a sweat rag and satisfied that all in his kingdom was well, was just ascending the steel ladders which led to the corridor of B Deck, off which was his office and cabin. Just nice time for a bath before dinner, he thought with the consciousness of duty well done and relaxation earned. Below the second was in charge. He stood near the door leading to the stokehold, his eye watchful upon the multitudinous batteries of gauges and tell-tales, his ear attuned to the dull roar of the moving machinery, ready instantly to record the slightest variation in that almost solid stream of sound. Most of it came from the gears, for *Patricia* was turbine driven, with reduction gears between turbines and propellers. These gears were supposed to roll on one another, and no doubt did so, but they could not be made to roll in silence. On each side of a wide alleyway were the great turbines, their ends only a few feet from the stokehold bulkhead: two vast metal masses, like two great tuns from Heidelberg turned on their sides. Beyond them and closer together were the twin propeller shafts, with casing housing the gears which connected each shaft to its turbine. Round the room, spaced in every conceivable position, was the auxiliary machinery, of which the chief items were the dynamos and pumps. Pumps were everywhere, and were used for all kinds of purposes, from those sending oil at enormous pressure into the bearings or bringing the liquid fuel forward to the furnaces, to those which threw up salt water for the baths or pumped out the various holds in the case of disaster. Some of these pumps worked under water and could be operated from the deck above, in case the engine room itself should be flooded. Here and there men were working: cleaning, greasing, testing the heat of bearings, carrying out minor repairs. Leaving his colleague in charge near the controls, the second engineer moved about, seeing what was being done, seeing that nothing else required to be done, seeing that everything was right, listening, always listening for undesired noises in that cataract of sound.

His tour of inspection led him at last into the tunnel, through which the sixteen-inch shafts of polished steel ran beneath the after part of the ship from turbine gearing to propeller. In the very stern, where they disappeared out into the sea, he could hear the roar of the water, sucked along the ship by the great propeller blades, so near to him and separated from him only by that wall of comparatively thin steel plates. Sixteen feet across were *Patricia*'s propellers, and they pushed her ahead through the water with the force of many thousands of horses.

The second continued on his round, past the workshops, the smithy, the pumps, the great turbines, and so to the stokehold door. With a word to his colleague he passed into the stokehold.

Here were the five huge oil-fed Scotch boilers that gave *Patricia* her motive power. Two were single ended and three double, and all had three furnaces in the end. That made twenty-four furnaces in all. The second passed from boiler to boiler, noting water and pressure gauges and glancing in through the spy holes at the roaring jets of flame which spurted from the burners. The atmosphere was pleasant enough: comfortably cool and free from unpleasant smell: an almost incredible improvement on the old coal burning method. Instead of a dozen or more half naked firemen, sweating in an inferno of heat and flame, there were only two or three cool efficient-looking men. They swung no great shovelfuls of coal into the white hot maws of the furnaces, but calmly took readings and with delicacy adjusted wheel valves. But *Patricia* could burn coal also if needs were, and only a few hours would be required to make the change over in the furnaces.

So in this wonderful entity of a ship at sea, this moving cosmos, work went ceaselessly on, each pigmy mortal contributing his quota after his kind. The officer of the watch, looking out into the night from the bridge; the helmsman, his hand on the wheel, his eye on the lubber's line; the captain, dressing for dinner, his immediate anxieties over; the lookout man in the crow's-nest half way up the foremast, keeping his eyes skinned and fighting his natural enemy, sleep; the radio operator with his earphones; the engineers in their steel cavern of sound, watchful, concentrating on the one great task of keeping the revolutions of the propellers to the required speed; the cooks, sweating over their pots and pans, almost ready for the coming dinner; the dining-room stewards, the cabin stewards, the deck steward putting away his chairs and the library steward his books; the stewardesses, the doctor, the nurse, the photographer; deck hands; clerical staff; the band, tuning their instruments; the laundry women, knocking off work for the day; all these, and many more, functioning that *Patricia* should continue her advance across the sea, so that the holiday makers she carried should eat meals and see sights and grow strong and wise above their fellows.

Much ado surely about a very little!

– 11 –

THE DEBARKATION OF MANT

After dinner Katherine hurried Jellicoe on deck to obtain their last glimpse of Cadiz, now far astern and visible, only from its galaxy of lights. She had had a glorious day and was enjoying herself more and more as the trip progressed. Her health was improving, her surroundings were delightful, and a wave of optimism was gradually displacing the depression from which she had so long suffered.

The others, too, were obviously better for the change. Her uncle had regained some of his former alertness and seemed less pessimistic. He held himself more upright, there was more spring in his step, and his eyes were brighter. Physical reflections of a mental change, Jellicoe said to Katherine. The new scenes and interests had taken him out of himself and there now seemed every chance of a complete recovery.

Mant also had improved. Much to Katherine's surprise he developed an interest in deck games and in a short time became extremely expert at quoits. Deck tennis was still too much for him, but he watched the players with interest and said that he hoped soon to be able to join. Another thing which surprised Katherine, and which she felt ought not, was his sporting attitude. Sporting in the best sense, she meant. His play was scrupulously fair and he was always ready to give doubtful points to his opponent. She felt ashamed of herself for thinking it, but somehow she had expected he would have done anything to win. For Katherine had never really got to like Mant. Always she felt some reservation in her mind where he was concerned. That was why, in spite of herself, she felt that if Jim and he quarrelled, her sympathies would be with Jim.

Jim and Eva and Luke were also growing more like their old selves. The party did not stick together. Even Katherine and Runciman Jellicoe, who were practically inseparable, had made many friends among the passengers. This applied in greater measure to the others. Each appeared to have found congenial acquaintances and Jim in particular was becoming popular on board.

Jellicoe struck up quite a friendship with the man who shared his cabin. This was a young Scot named Farquharson, a student of forensic medicine at Glasgow University. He was a nice lad, and he and Jellicoe had deep technical discussions to which Katherine listened with a good deal of interest though with only partial comprehension. If the subjects seemed rather morbid – they were principally concerned with revolting physical details of murder – they at least in most instances related to cases of which she had read. Farquharson seemed a walking encyclopaedia of crime, and his exposition of the Roxton case in particular was masterly.

Mant had paired off with a New Zealander named Bradstreet, a retired farmer who had come over to settle in England and who wanted to see something of the Mediterranean. To Katherine he seemed a rather forbidding person, though in his short way he was polite enough to her.

Only William appeared to have picked up no special crony. At times he seemed to Katherine a lonely old man, a rather pathetic figure. She did what she could to keep him company, but he did not appear to mind being alone, and would sit for hours, wrapped in rugs and lost in his own thoughts.

There were quite a number of well-known people on board, men and women distinguished in various walks of life. In one day Katherine met no less than three famous novelists, and a very pleasant and unassuming gentleman with whom she played shovel-board, turned out to be one of the world's best-known black-and-white artists. Members of Parliament were common and so were titles, but the profession chiefly represented was the scholastic. The church too was well to the fore, with two bishops, three deans, and many lesser lights in the ecclesiastical firmament.

One feature which seemed to Katherine to promise a good deal of interest was the lectures. On the evening before they reached Cadiz there had been a talk about Spain in general and the district of Cadiz in particular. In this they were told what they would see on the next day when they went ashore. On their conducted tour of the town the lecturer went with them, and on the various sites amplified what he had said on the previous night. Katherine found this made the excursion much more interesting than if they had attempted to cover the ground alone.

And now their first day ashore was behind them and here they were sailing down the Spanish coast, en route for Gibraltar. Katherine had wanted to remain on deck, in the hope of seeing the Cape Trafalgar light, but a cold fog had come down which quickly drove them below. For a couple of hours speed was reduced and the fog-horn boomed out at two-minute intervals, but it stopped after Katherine had gone to bed, and she supposed the weather had cleared.

Next morning she hurried on deck to get her first view of Gibraltar. They were at anchor in the Bay, lying outside the harbour mole. The ladder was rigged and a shore launch bobbed at its lower end.

"Good morning, Miss Shirley," said a voice. "Is this your first visit to Gib?"

It was Captain Goode, whom she had already met more than once. He was a short, tubby man with one of those mouths which turn up at one end and down at the other. He had light blue eyes and a manner which inspired trust.

"Yes," she answered. "I'm feeling awfully thrilled."

"Not to spoil your anticipation," the captain went on, "but it's a dull hole of a place. You'll enjoy some of our later calls more."

Katherine smiled. She remembered overhearing his comment on one of the show places of the Grecian Archipelago, one of those spots usually referred to as a dream of almost unearthly beauty. "Ah," he had said with a familiarity which had bred its usual offspring, "if you've seen one of those places, you've seen the lot; and the anchorage is no so good."

She told him that when she had seen Gib as often as he had, she would probably agree with him.

"Are you taking the excursion?" he went on.

"Two excursions," she said. "In the morning round Gibraltar and in the afternoon to Algeciras. Is that right?"

He thought it was absolutely right, and began to give her shrewd advice as to what she should look out for, advice which showed that, in spite of his depreciatory remark he himself took a good deal of interest in the place. He was up in its history, too, and told her of ships and sieges, of covered wooden boats designed to land attacking troops and of red-hot balls setting these on fire, of caverns, of waterworks and of monkeys.

Katherine liked the captain. He was pleasant and kindly and she was sure absolutely trustworthy. She had heard of him from some of the stewards and crew, and though none of these had attempted any criticism, it was evident that they liked and respected him. She had the feeling that, if disaster overtook the ship, there was no one she would rather have on the bridge. Anything, she was sure, that would be humanly possible, would be done.

She also liked the chief engineer, a tall man with a stoop, a peering air, and an expression of hopeless melancholy. Runciman Jellicoe had scraped up an acquaintance with him, and she had joined them on various occasions. Besides being an engineer he was a reader and a thinker, and she delighted in hearing the two men discuss the European situation, the theory of government, and other isms of our time. He was kindly also. He had read about the poisoning and displayed a genuine interest in the party's recovery.

Presently Jellicoe came up and Captain Goode passed on down the deck.

"A thorough good man, that," Jellicoe said when they were alone, "and well liked by his crew. You can tell it by the way they speak of him. I always think captains of liners are not nearly well enough treated. They have a very responsible job, particularly if anything goes wrong. They have to be technically quite first class, as well as tactful and socially presentable. And they don't get much out of it. They have comparatively little money, no family life, a very lonely job on their ships, and no tenure of office. Do you know that they're engaged for each trip separately and are not regular employees of their companies?"

"You don't say so? Do you mean that they could be out of a job at the end of any given trip?"

"Yes, I do. They are out of a job at the end of each trip. It is only custom and mutual interest which guarantees them another job in the same line: not any legal agreement."

"It doesn't seem fair."

"Then if they make a mistake, or even if some disaster happens for which they're not in the slightest degree to blame, they're done: finished. When there are dozens of first-class men walking the streets, no one will employ a master who has had his ship ashore. No, ships' officers are a magnificent lot of men, generally speaking, and they don't get their due."

Jellicoe seemed quite upset by the thought. Katherine wondered what had roused him. Some story he had heard, she suspected, and she was just going to ask him to explain when Jim drifted along and they went down together to breakfast.

Katherine enjoyed the two excursions of that morning and afternoon. With Jellicoe at her side she began by walking up through the rock galleries and peeping out through embrasures beside the muzzles of ancient cannon. Below them was British ground, gardens, racecourse, and cemetery, then came the neutral area with beyond it the Spanish village of La Linea, and in the distance thinly populated land stretching up to a hilly horizon. Then they drove down to the south end of the peninsula through the clean but rather uninteresting town, past the harbour and gardens and villas to the lighthouse at Europa Point. From there they looked straight at Africa, across some dozen miles of perhaps the most important waterway in existence. This rock of Gibraltar on which they stood and that near Ceuta over across the channel, formed the two pillars of Hercules, which the ancients conceived must be the absolute end of the world.

The drive to Algeciras, calling at the old world village of San Roque, was another pleasure for Katherine. As she looked out over the country from the excellent road along which their cars were hurrying, she remembered what the captain had said about the Greek Islands: "If you've seen one you've seen them all." Certainly countries were very like in essentials. She remembered as a child she thought seas would be different one from another. She recalled the thrill with which she had obtained her first glimpse of the Mediterranean, and her shock of surprise when she saw that except for a slightly brighter colour it looked just the same as that which was to be found round the English coast. And then she had realised that all other seas must look the same too. What a thrill to sail the Caspian or the Yellow, or the Banda or that dreadfully sinister sounding sea, the Timor! And yet, having crossed from Dover to Calais, she had, to all intents and purposes, been on them all!

During that night *Patricia* crossed the Straits, and when Katherine came on deck in the morning she found they were at Ceuta. They were lying up against a modern, though rather deserted wharf, with a large, reinforced concrete shed stretching along its further side. At the bottom of the ladder stood a group of what seemed to be Arabs, with postcards and leatherwork for sale. No one else was to be seen on the wharf, though some taxis waited a little further down.

Katherine crossed the deck. On the starboard side lay the open harbour, a large sheet of water, with the town rising on low hills to the right and a rocky promontory, also bearing houses, stretching out into the sea to the left. The scene was quite European – again Katherine thought how like all countries were – except that most of the buildings were white and that a larger proportion of them had flat roofs than she was accustomed to. There was not much shipping of size in the harbour, though vast numbers of small boats. Along the shore, in front of the houses, a black locomotive was shunting.

The excursion here was for the whole day: a motor-coach drive along the twenty odd miles to Tetuan, with a walk through the old Moorish city and lunch in an hotel in the European quarter. Katherine was looking forward to the visit as one of the star turns of the entire trip. She said so to Jellicoe, who agreed with her.

"I'm not sure it's not too much for your uncle," he went on. "He hasn't been very well for the last day or two. I advised him to consider giving Tetuan a miss and spending a quiet day on the ship."

"He won't do that if he's able to go," Katherine returned. "I know he was looking forward to today."

William had, so far, proved an inveterate excursionist. He had even taken the Jerez drive at Cadiz, which Katherine had thought too much for her. To her protests he had replied that on his previous cruise he had missed the excursions, and as long as he was physically able he did not mean to repeat the mistake. In particular he had said he wanted to visit Tetuan, which someone had told him was more eastern than the East.

The day came quite up to her expectations. The whole party enjoyed the drive along the splendid new road which wound first along the hills by the shore, and then turning inland, came to the ancient city, its whitewashed houses creeping up over a hill at the entrance to a valley in the low range of mountains backing the coast. For a couple of hours they traversed its narrow streets and bargained with wily traders in small and ramshackle shops. They saw certain stock sights: the house of a wealthy Moor, the Caliph's bodyguard, one of the new schools and the modern part of the town. In the afternoon they drove back to tea on board, well pleased with all they had done.

William, however, had not been very well. He had not walked round with the party, but had rested in the hotel during the middle of the day. But on the return journey he seemed better, and told Katherine he was all right again.

After a rest between tea and dinner a good many of the passengers found that their ardour for sightseeing had again risen to normal strength. *Patricia* was not leaving until midnight, and the suggestion was made that those who wished might go ashore again after dinner and have a stroll through Ceuta and see the cafés and such night life as there was in the place. Katherine thought she had had enough, but the other members of the party decided to go.

"I shall not be long," Eva said to her as they discussed the proposal. "I feel I'd like a little fresh air and a walk, but I'm not going to cafés or anything of that sort. But you can go if you want to, Luke, that is provided I get someone to come back with me."

So it was settled. Even William said he would like a short walk. Some fifty or more people decided on the outing, though the majority preferred books and bridge and chat.

Jellicoe, it need scarcely be said, stayed on board with Katherine. They settled themselves on a sofa in the after promenade deck lounge and fell into a desultory conversation.

Less than an hour later one of the stewards came up to Jellicoe.

"You're Dr Jellicoe, sir?" he asked. "I'm steward to Mr William Carrington. He's not very well and he's gone to bed. He sent me to ask you if you'd be kind enough to look in and see him?"

"I'll go at once," Jellicoe said, and with an apology to Katherine he left the lounge.

Katherine was a trifle upset about her uncle. It was probably just part of the little indisposition he had had off and on for the past two or three days: some kind of mild ptomaine. The poisoning had no doubt made him more susceptible to that kind of attack. Then she remembered all the stories she had heard of people on cruises getting digestive upsets. It was due, some said, to the keeping of food too long, even though refrigerated, others held that Mediterranean fish were to blame. She had heard Runciman and his young friend Farquharson say that some of the local fish contained arsenic. She herself, on the advice of Runciman had avoided fish, but she didn't know if the others had followed her example.

Presently Jellicoe returned. "He's got a bit of an upset right enough," he declared. "It's not very serious, but he'll have to take things easy for a day or two. I've given him some stuff that will help him."

"What do you think it was?" she asked.

"I don't know. Something in the food. Of course, he's specially sensitive at present. You all are."

As he spoke Eva came in. She had gone ashore with Luke and they had had a stroll through the town. It was not very thrilling and an hour had been more than enough for her.

Luke had gone on for a further short walk, but would soon be back.

"I shall go to bed soon," Katherine declared. "I'm tired, and we've another excursion tomorrow."

"Tomorrow's Malaga, isn't it?" said Eva. "We don't go to Granada?"

"No, we don't go to Granada. Runciman thought it was too long a day for us. But we go round the town in the morning."

Eva stood up. "I'll go to bed too," she decided. "I've got a lovely book out of the library and the light's splendid for reading." She waved her hand. "See you in the morning."

Most people went to bed early on board, and by eleven Katherine had switched off her light and composed herself for slumber. Mrs Ingram was already breathing gently with her eyes closed. For a little Katherine thought lazily about their day and their tour and Runciman, then gradually her mental images grew blurred and she also was asleep.

It was not more than an hour later that she was wakened by a touch on the shoulder. She sat up quickly, instantly wide awake. Eva, with an electric torch and in her dressing gown, stood looking down at her with pale and frightened face.

"Katherine," she whispered urgently. "Mant went ashore and hasn't come back, and the ship's due to sail. They're making enquiries. They want to know if he said anything to you. Put on your dressing gown and come out and speak to them."

Instantly Katherine's imagination sprang into vigorous life. For a moment she could scarcely move. Mant! Again!

Was this what in her most secret mind she had feared ever since she had learnt the full details of the poisoning: that as the first attempt had failed, there might be another?

Though Runciman had never said so, she believed he had feared it also. It had been one reason why he had agreed so readily to join the party that he might be able to prevent anything happening, or if anything did happen, that he would be there to do what could be done. With all the old dread back again, she silently put on her dressing gown and followed Eva from the cabin.

– 12 –

THE INQUISITION OF GOODE

The ship was very still as Katherine followed Eva along the alleyway and up the main staircase. They went to the drawing room, which was lighted up. On entering she found a little circle seated at one end. Facing it was Captain Goode. He stood up as the two women entered.

"Please sit down, Miss Shirley," he said. "I'm sorry to disturb you, but, as no doubt Mrs Dugdale has told you, Mr Mant Carrington went ashore this evening and has not come back. Before sailing we want to find out if he said anything as to his intentions."

As she moved to the chair he indicated, Katherine glanced round the little gathering. All the party were there, William looking old and ill in a deep-blue dressing gown with Chinese dragons embroidered on it in white silk, Luke and Runciman also in dressing gowns, though of more sombre colours, Jim still in evening dress and with a rather wild look in his eyes, and herself and Eva obviously having been called up out of bed. But, however differently dressed, all were alike in their expression of anxiety and concern. Beside the captain, and looking as if he also had been roused from sleep, was Major Artt, one of the two cruise managers. He was obviously worried, though his expression showed more annoyance than fear. Only Captain Goode, who was fully dressed, appeared entirely normal.

"Mr Carrington said nothing to me, if that's what you mean," Katherine answered. "The last time I spoke to him was when we met on the way down to dinner, and he didn't mention his plans. I didn't see him at all after dinner."

"Thank you, that is really what I wanted to know," the captain returned. "Now I'm afraid I shall have to ask that question of each of you in turn. Did he mention his plans to anyone?" He looked round the little assembly.

"Yes." Luke and Eva spoke together, while William nodded. Then Luke, who had not seen William's nod, told his wife: "You go on."

"Yes, Mrs Dugdale?" the captain turned to her.

"Before we went to dress, the question arose as to what we should do after dinner. Someone said it was a pity when we were lying in an African port, not to see some more of it. Several members of the party then said they would like a stroll ashore and some wine or beer or coffee if they could find a decent café. Mant, that is Mr Carrington, was one of the party and he said he would go ashore for a short time, but wouldn't stay late."

"He said he wouldn't stay late?"

"Yes, he said so quite distinctly."

"Who was in that party you speak of?"

Eva thought. "You were there, Luke, and you, Uncle William. That's all who are here, I think. But there were some other people, the Robinsons and Mr Miles and the Jepsons. I think that was all. Any others, Luke?"

"No, I think you've mentioned them all," Luke agreed.

The captain looked at him. "You heard Mr Mant say he wouldn't stay late?" he asked.

"Oh, yes, I heard him. We all heard him."

"I heard him and we had a talk about it," William put in. "We turned aside a little, I think out of earshot of the others, though I'm not sure." He paused, glancing interrogatively at the captain.

"Yes, Mr Carrington?" Goode returned.

"I said that if he only wanted a stroll, so did I, and should we go together? I said I didn't want to look for cafés, but only to get a breath of air. I hadn't felt very well at Tetuan and had been sitting in the hotel all day. Before dinner I felt better and thought I would like this little walk."

"Quite so. And did he agree to this?"

"Yes, he said it would suit him nicely, that a short stroll was all he wanted, and that he would like to get back early to go to bed. You understand that we're all a little shaky from our illness."

"I understood that, Mr Carrington. And then?"

"We agreed to meet in my cabin after dinner. We sit at the same table of course, but he wanted to do something after dinner: leave films to be developed, I think."

"And he went to your cabin?"

"Yes, in about fifteen minutes he turned up. Unfortunately dinner had brought back some of my unpleasant symptoms and I asked him to sit down for a minute, hoping I should feel better. He did so, and we chatted for perhaps another fifteen minutes. But, instead of getting better, I grew worse. I felt I should be unwise to go ashore, and I told him so and apologised for having kept him so that he had missed the others. He was very nice about it: said he quite understood. He said he would go ashore by himself for half an hour and that he hoped I'd be better. Then he left me. I went to bed, but I still felt badly, and I presently rang for the steward to ask him to call Dr Jellicoe."

"And that was the last you saw of Mr Mant?"

"Yes, that was the last."

Captain Goode looked round. "Did anyone else see Mr Mant after dinner?"

"I saw him," said Jim. "About five minutes after I left the dining-saloon. I was in A Deck lounge. He came in. Dropped a roll of films in photographer's box. Then he met Bradstreet. They chatted. Heard him ask Bradstreet if he was going ashore. Bradstreet said he'd had enough of it for one day. Mant said he was going for a stroll with his uncle. Said he must go, as his uncle would be waiting."

"Then," said Captain Goode, "it would appear that he went ashore direct from your cabin, Mr Carrington. The purser's officer on the gangway checked his number card. He was alone, and so far as the officer can remember, it was just about the time indicated by you."

"He left me intending to do so," William answered.

"Then that's the last thing we've heard of him. He has not returned. As you know, we were to sail at twelve, and when twelve approached the purser's officer advised his cabin steward that he had not come aboard and they searched the ship. Then they advised me, I called up Major Artt, and when there was still no sign, I had you all called. We must now decide what to do. And first I should like to ask you, Dr Jellicoe, as his medical attendant, if you can tell us anything which might throw light on the affair. Was he, for example, subject to fits of giddiness or anything of that kind, in which he might have fallen and hurt himself?"

Jellicoe moved uneasily. "Mant Carrington has been very seriously ill," he answered slowly, "and he's still by no means fit. I cannot say that fits of giddiness are to be expected, but on the other hand, with a person in his weak state such would not be surprising. The possibility you suggest cannot therefore be altogether overlooked."

"Can he speak Spanish?" Major Artt asked suddenly.

The captain nodded. "I was coming to that," he declared. He looked round.

"Not a word," Katherine answered. "He told me so at Cadiz."

"Then," said Jim, "if he got giddy and had a fall and was picked up, he mightn't have been able to explain where he came from."

"He could surely have said *Patricia*," Eva suggested.

Luke shook his head. "Saying *Patricia* mightn't convey a lot to a Spaniard or an Arab."

"He had his numbered landing card," Goode pointed out. "It had *Patricia*'s name printed clearly enough on it."

"That is so, of course," Luke admitted.

Katherine's vivid imagination was already working at full pressure. It was clear, she thought, from the captain's manner, that he believed that something serious had happened to Mant.

But what?

Happily nothing which had been said supported that fearful idea which had flashed into her mind when Eva had wakened her. There was no suggestion of anything but accident. Suppose Mant had had an attack of giddiness and had fallen down some cliff or steps or precipice? Or more likely – a thrill of horror shot through her – suppose he had slipped off the wharf into the harbour? In her mind's eye she seemed to see him walking along the stretch of mole between ship and shore. It was lonely enough in the day-time and at night would doubtless be quite deserted. She pictured the sudden unsteadiness in his gait, the few halting steps forward, and then – the small and almost silent splash, for in this tideless sea the water came to within three or four feet of wharf level.

Or again, had he been robbed? She had read tales of these native cities. A cloth thrown round the mouth from behind: robbery: and – and – She could scarcely bring herself to contemplate what would probably follow robbery. A knife in the back – or something equally effective.

Suddenly Katherine wished her imagination was not quite so powerful. Not only had she been frightening herself unnecessarily, but she was losing Captain Goode's remarks. "I don't think we need fear robbery," he was saying. "The natives are not so bad as they are painted, and in any case the Spaniards have them well in hand. No, since you put it to me," and he looked at Eva, and Katherine saw she had missed some suggestion, "I should fear an accident."

He was continuing, but Katherine interrupted him. "If he got giddy, might he not have fallen into the harbour?" she blurted out.

The others looked distressed by the idea. Captain Goode nodded gravely.

"I didn't want to suggest that," he declared, "but I have to admit it was in my mind. Now we must decide what to do? I don't mind saying that if the case was in my hands alone, I should inform the police. But I don't want to do that without consulting you, his relatives. I'm afraid that in the last resort the responsibility is mine, but if I can act in accordance with your wishes, I should prefer it."

For a moment no one spoke. Then Katherine glanced quickly round. "I think the police should be told, and at once. What do you say, Uncle William?"

The old man nodded. "Yes, yes," he said impatiently. "Certainly. There's nothing else for it."

"I think so too," Jim added. "It's not likely he'll turn up of his own accord now, and the police would have to be consulted sooner or later."

The others made signs of assent. "Very well," the captain agreed, "then we shall send at once." He looked at Artt. "Would you go, major? You're good at the language, you know."

Major Artt agreed readily. "Yes, I'll go," he answered, "but I think I should have some member of the family with me. What about you, Mr Musgrave?" He looked at Jim. "And you also, doctor? You two between you should be able to answer any questions the police may ask. Say in five minutes outside the cruise office?"

The three men rose, but Captain Goode stayed them with a gesture. "A moment," he said, and they sat down again. "We've got to settle about the ship. We were due out of this at twelve, half an hour ago. When are we going to get away?"

"It's a short run to Malaga, isn't it?" Artt answered. "We can afford to be a bit late leaving here."

"I know all about that," Goode answered with a faint smile. "What I want to be sure about is the latest time your Granada people can leave the ship in the morning?"

"Half past eight," said Artt.

"Then to get our port formalities through we should be in not later than eight. Very well, we'll leave here at three. That'll give you two and a half hours to make your arrangements with the police."

"It'll not take so long."

William made a sudden move. "One other point," he said, speaking with a nervous hesitancy which showed Katherine how far he still was from his normal state of health. "It has been suggested that Mant may have fallen into the harbour. Would it not be well to make a search?"

Captain Goode looked doubtful, and William went on. "I have been looking at those fishing boats from the deck. It seems to me that if half a dozen of them would row about the harbour that is all that would be required. As far as the cost goes, of course I would bear that."

"Oh, yes," Katherine broke in. "Don't you think that should be done?"

She also had seen the boats before turning in, dotted like fireflies over the sea. They were, most of them, rowing boats, and each carried six brilliant lamps, three at each side projecting over the sea and with the beams directed downwards on the water. These lights attracted the fish, which then fell victims to their curiosity.

The others nodded, but Captain Goode was not enthusiastic. "I'm afraid," he said, "you must either handle the affair yourselves or leave it to the police. Even in England the police wouldn't be too ready to accept amateur help, but here I don't think you could attempt it at all. No harm to suggest the boats, and if Mr Carrington will pay for them that will have a powerful effect. But I doubt you can do more than suggest."

"What might help would be a reward," Major Artt put in. "I don't mean the police wouldn't do their best in any case, but human nature should be considered."

"I'll agree to that," William announced at once. "How much should it be?"

Artt looked at the captain. "Oh, I don't know," he muttered. "A thousand pesetas?"

"Somewhere about twenty-eight pounds," Goode explained. "That too much, Mr Carrington?"

"Good Lord, no!" William replied. "I shouldn't have thought it was nearly enough."

"It's heaps," Artt declared. "You don't want to make them suspicious."

"That's right. A thousand pesetas will bring you all the information that's available, and won't do any harm." Goode looked round. "I think that's an important point."

Artt rose again, but this time Katherine stopped him. "There's just one other thing," she said. "Should we not go ashore here? I mean, leave the ship and go to an hotel?"

There was silence for a moment and then Eva asked, "Just what do you mean, Katherine? What do you think we should gain by it?"

Katherine hesitated. "I don't suppose we should exactly gain anything by it," she said slowly. "But if anything has happened – well – wouldn't it seem heartless to go on with the cruise? Suppose Mant had met with an accident and had to go to hospital? Shouldn't some of his own people be here to visit him?"

Though Katherine felt herself compelled to make the suggestion, she did not at all relish the idea of remaining in this African town, attractive though in many ways it no doubt was. Nor did she want to give up the cruise. Besides, there was always that feeling of instinctive dislike to Mant, which made her less anxious to be with him than she otherwise would.

No one spoke at once, then William slightly hesitatingly gave his view. "It's very nice of you, Katherine, to suggest it, and just what we should expect of you. But I really don't think you are right. We did not come on this cruise as a matter of pleasure. We came by our doctor's orders," he glanced at Jellicoe, "to try to regain health after our illness. Probably Mant will be found before the ship sails, but if not, I suggest we go on as far as Malaga and see what develops. We can return from Malaga if we wish to, I suppose quite quickly?" He looked enquiringly at Goode.

"You mightn't get a ship back at a moment's notice," the captain answered, "but you could always get a car from Malaga to Gib, and a launch across the Straits. I agree with you, Mr Carrington, that you would be wiser to come on at least as far as Malaga."

"And so do I," Jellicoe said, decisively. "As Mr Carrington has pointed out, you are here for the sake of your health, and as things are, your health is your first consideration. And I don't agree," he went on, looking round, "with what is so evidently in most of our minds, though no one has put it into words. I don't agree that there is any reason to assume the worst. There are a dozen explanations of Mant's not turning up without assuming he is dead. I suggest we go to Malaga and reconsider the question there."

To this there was general approval. Katherine felt relieved. She had made her proposal because she thought good feeling demanded it of her, but she was glad it had been rejected.

"Then we should be going," Artt said, getting up. "In five minutes at the cruise office?"

He left the drawing room, followed by Runciman Jellicoe and Jim. The captain rose to follow them. "If I may make a further suggestion, ladies and gentlemen," he said more deprecatingly than he had yet spoken, "it is that you go back to bed. Nothing will be gained by your sitting up." He bowed, and with a few words of encouragement disappeared.

"I'll go to bed," William said, also getting up. "I haven't been well all evening and this business has upset me. But I should like to hear what happens. Will you send Jim to my cabin to tell me when he comes back, Luke? He's sure to tell you."

"I'll ask him now," Luke answered, rising hurriedly. "We'll all want to know."

"Yes," Eva added. "And I'll come and tell you, Katherine."

After some further conversation they separated. Katherine was prepared to slip into bed quietly and in the dark, so as to avoid waking Mrs Ingram. But when she reached her cabin she found the light on and the lady reading. She put down her book.

"Oh, my dear," she said, "I heard you being called and you've been away a long time. I do hope nothing's wrong?"

Katherine had to tell her. She asked her to keep the details to herself and then told her everything. She found it indeed a relief. Mrs Ingram was sympathy itself. And while she seemed fully to understand Katherine's suggestion that they should go ashore, she was comfortingly reassuring that they had done the right thing in deciding not to.

Though Katherine presently turned off the light and composed herself to sleep, she could not do so. Now, in the darkness and silence, the affair seemed to her to look much worse than it had done while discussing it in the drawing room. That Mant was incapacitated and unable to return to the ship or send a message, was obvious. If so, he was surely either alone and helpless or the victim of foul play. If an accident had happened, he could scarcely have been found by law-abiding persons, as his landing card would indicate where he had come from, and these persons would have sent a message.

Then she thought again about that idea of the harbour. *Patricia* was the only ship berthing at that particular mole. At night when the itinerant merchants and taxi-men had gone it would surely be deserted. If Mant had fallen in, he would have been neither seen nor heard.

Thankfully she saw that at least there was no suggestion that her first hideous idea was true. Ever since she had seen that look of hate on Jim's face, she had been uneasy in her mind. But thank heaven since then Jim's relations with

Mant had improved. Why, they were sharing the same cabin and seemed to be getting on splendidly. No, she needn't worry about Jim.

Then suddenly she remembered that of all the party Jim alone had been in evening dress – at half past twelve on a tour on which everyone went to bed early. And he had certainly looked upset: more upset than the others. Katherine grew a little cold as she considered the point. Then once again she rallied herself. No, she was imagining things. Jim was all right.

In spite of herself she dozed a little and then Eva was there once again. She began to whisper, but Mrs Ingram called out that she was awake, and they turned up the light.

"Mrs Ingram knows," Katherine explained, as Eva hesitated.

Eva nodded and went on. "They've just come back. The police were very civil and routed some superior officer out of bed. They have heard nothing, but have promised to do all they can. They did not express any opinion, but they were going to have an immediate search made of the cliffs and harbour as well as to make enquiries among the natives. Jim and Runciman both say they seemed businesslike and efficient. So we must let it go at that for the present."

"Did they suggest our staying on here?"

"Jim suggested it, but the officer said it would serve no purpose: that we could do nothing. He promised to wireless the ship directly they learnt anything."

It was too late to reconsider the matter now at all events. As Katherine listened to Eva she also heard the sounds of getting under way. A few minutes later *Patricia* was pitching gently in a long swell coming up from the east.

– 13 –

THE APPREHENSION OF KATHERINE

When Katherine went on deck next morning they were lying at anchor in Malaga Bay, well outside the harbour. From there the town looked attractive, as it stretched along the shore behind the moles, the green of trees showing behind the white buildings. Above the roofs projected the single tower of what she thought was the cathedral, and to the right on a rocky hill were long buildings like military barracks. The country rose behind the town into hills, range after range climbing into the distance. To the left of the town was a wide valley through which a river evidently entered the sea. On a higher hill towards the right Katherine could see zigzag markings, and a man who stopped to speak to her said these were on the road to Granada.

"We should see the Sierra Nevada over there," he went on pointing to the right, "but unfortunately it's too misty. They're a wonderful sight from the sea. I've seen them, going round this coast, just hanging in the sky. No apparent connection with earth. Sort of white ethereal ghosts. Wonderful."

"They must be," Katherine agreed. "I've read of mountains looking like that. They hang in the sky, as you say, and no matter how far you go towards them they don't seem to get any nearer. Shall we see the Sierras?"

"I'm afraid we pass them tonight. It'll be dark. That's the worst of travelling: you'd like to see everything and you can only see part."

Katherine found it hard to concentrate enough on such matters to reply intelligently. Her thoughts were back in Ceuta. What about Mant? Had he been found? Was he alive or dead? She wondered when they would know.

That morning the travellers were unusually early astir. Breakfast began at seven-thirty, and those who were taking the excursion to Granada left the ship an hour later. Several boatloads of them went ashore. Then at nine the second party started, those who were to spend the morning driving round Malaga. Katherine and most of the Carrington party had booked on this shorter excursion, but all of them cancelled their bookings and stayed on board.

About ten a boat returned from the shore and in it was Jellicoe.

"I went ashore with Artt," he explained, as he settled two chairs in the sun and out of the wind. "I got him to ring up the police in Ceuta. But there was no news."

"Oh, Runciman, was there not?" Katherine shook her head. "I'm afraid it looks awfully badly. Did they say what they had done?"

"Yes. They had searched along the shore and cliffs and also very thoroughly in the harbour. They found nothing. Nor did their enquiries through the town lead to anything."

"It is extraordinary, isn't it? What *could* have happened?"

"Well, that's just it. Of course I'm afraid we mustn't assume that because they found nothing in the harbour there wasn't anything there. But so far as it goes, it's hopeful."

"Do you mean – a body would sink?"

"Yes. But, of course, it would float again later, so that if anything of that kind had happened, we should know in time."

"Tell me," she went on, "do you *really* believe that about the attack of giddiness: what we were speaking of last night?"

He hesitated. "I think it's certainly possible," he said at last. "But I confess I don't think it's very likely. Of course I may be wrong."

She also was silent for some moments. "I'm afraid it's looking worse and worse," she presently declared, "more and more like – foul play. Do you think some of those natives?…For robbery, you know?"

"There again it's possible, though not very likely. That coast is different since the Spanish took charge: it's now quite a law-abiding place. If Mant had fallen, let us say, over a cliff and had been found by some of the lower type, they might, of course, have robbed him and tipped his body into the sea. But then what could he have been doing on the edge of a cliff in the dark? Besides, the cliffs are a considerable way from where the ship was lying, and he said he was only going ashore for a short time."

"An attack by robbers?"

"Very unlikely, I should say, and the police agreed with me. No, it does seem a puzzle." Jellicoe puffed slowly at his pipe, staring vacantly in front of him.

"Tell me exactly what you did last night," Katherine said presently. "I haven't heard in detail."

"There's not much to tell. When Jim and I met at the cruise office Artt was there. He asked what photographs of Mant we had. I had brought two snaps, both rather poor, but Jim had a fairly decent one in a group. We went ashore and had the devil's own job to find the police station. No one seemed to be about. However we got it at last. There was a sleepy policeman in charge: I don't know what he was, a civil guard or something. He was quite polite, but when he heard of the reward, he undoubtedly did wake up. He said he would call his superior, and he phoned for him. Presently the chief officer turned up. Artt apologised for disturbing him and all that, and then he told our story. The officer took down details very quickly and efficiently. He asked at once for photographs and a description. We did our best. Then he wanted to know what clothes Mant was wearing, and if he had valuables in his pockets. We didn't think he had valuables, but, of course, didn't know for sure. He inspected our go-ashore cards, and noted the number of Mant's. It was all very thorough. Artt tried to get his opinion, but he wasn't committing himself. He asked me through Artt about Mant's health, and about attacks of giddiness or paralysis, or if he ever took too much to drink. Showed what was in his mind."

"Was anything actually done while you were there?"

"Oh, yes, he sent us round with a policeman to some cafés. In three of them we had to knock up the proprietors. In two of these people from the ship had been, but no one like Mant. One where there was dancing was where Jim had been, but again there was no trace of Mant."

"Did the officer seem hopeful?"

"Well, he thought they would find out what had happened. He said that for some years there had been no case of a disappearance of a European, and that he didn't think the natives were likely to be responsible, though of course he couldn't be sure."

Once again silence reigned. That dreadful doubt which had before entered Katherine's mind was again clamouring for admission. She tried to banish it, but at last heard herself saying: "What was Jim doing last night? He must have come home late. You remember he was still dressed at half past twelve."

Runciman puffed away deliberately at his pipe. She wondered if he purposely avoided looking at her. "I asked him that," he replied. "He said he went ashore with the Tremaines and they wandered about for a time, finding it cold and dull. Then they saw a café with native dancing and went in for a little. But the Tremaine girls got bored, and soon wanted to go back to the ship. They walked back together part of the way to the harbour. But Jim thought it was too soon to go aboard, and he left them and returned up the town. He went into the café again and stayed longer than he intended. I think he took too much native spirit: in fact he said so. He didn't get aboard till nearly midnight, and then he felt hot from the drink and decided to stroll about on deck and watch the start. Then the stewards began to ask about Mant, and of course he didn't go to bed."

"Was he alone in the café?" Katherine tried to make her voice careless.

"Yes, so he said. When the Tremaines left he couldn't find anyone else from the ship."

Katherine tried to reassure herself, but it did look horribly badly. Suppose when he had left the Tremaines, he had met Mant...But no, she wouldn't suppose anything of the kind. Jim might be passionate, but he could never bottle hatred up in his mind for a long period, as she was suggesting.

And yet...Jim had been drinking native spirit. Could it not be that...

No! Desperately she strove to put the horrible thought out of her mind. No; she mustn't even think of Jim in such a connection.

"By the way," she said suddenly, "what about Uncle William this morning? Is he better?"

Jellicoe seemed relieved at the change of subject. "Indeed, he's not at all well," he answered. "He's got a nasty enough internal attack. He was very sick when I was in with him this morning and seemed to be in pain. I can't make out what he's eaten, because he seems to have had the same as the rest of us. However, since he was sick he's easier. I've kept him in bed."

"Lucky you came with us, Runciman."

"Oh, I don't know. The ship's doctor seems a nice fellow and is thoroughly qualified. Your uncle would have been all right with him."

Presently Eva made her appearance, followed by Luke and Jim. "We're going ashore," she announced. "I don't see what good we're doing by staying here, and we may as well see something of the town. Come along, Katherine. Put your hat on and join us. Don't you think she should, Runciman?"

Jellicoe got up. "I really do," he agreed. "As you say, we're doing no good here, and to see the town would take us out of ourselves."

Katherine also stood up. "I'll go," she said. "Somehow at first it didn't seem decent, sightseeing and all that. But I think you're right. Let's all go."

"We have a couple of hours before lunch," Luke pointed out. "I think a walk would be quite pleasant, and it's not too hot."

Boats were constantly running between ship and shore, and soon they were rising and falling over the long smooth swells. These seemed quite large when they were down close to them, though *Patricia* lay steady as if rooted to the bottom. The harbour, which they soon entered, was larger than Katherine had expected, and much busier. Three quite big steamers lay alongside the wharfs or at anchor in the outer harbour, while several tramps of moderate tonnage were loading or discharging. At the steps where they landed was a small crowd of loafers, who wanted to supply them with postcards and flowers and seats in phaetons or taxis.

"Let's take a taxi and drive round," Luke suggested. "There are just five of us and these are decently large vehicles."

"No," said Katherine, "a taxi goes too fast. We'd run through the entire place in about ten minutes. Let's take two of these phaetons. It'll be quite an experience to drive again behind a horse."

Eva smiled slightly as she agreed, and Katherine and Jellicoe got into one vehicle, leaving the second for the other three. The drivers required no instructions, but started off to the cathedral as a matter of course. A service was in progress, and the party tiptoed about, admiring the carving of the choir stalls and silently resisting demands for money from choirboys. Katherine thoroughly enjoyed the excellent playing of the fine organ. Then to the bullring, where Luke's halting Spanish and a fee gained them ingress. Katherine was interested and rather shocked to find that the first thing they were shown was a small hospital with thoroughly up-to-date operating theatre. It threw, she thought, a rather vivid sidelight on Spain's national sport. Then they saw the enclosure itself, with its sandy floor, its surrounding barricades, and the tier after tier of seats stretching up, the lower ones open to the sky, the upper ones, in two storeys, covered with a roof supported internally on pillars. Next they were driven through the residential area to the east of the town, and back to a new and apparently endless garden city along the river at the west. Finally they visited a huge wine-exporting concern, where they sipped samples and from which they could have ordered barrels to be delivered "free of duty" at their several homes.

They returned to the ship for lunch, and from a hurried enquiry learnt that there had been no news. It did not seem worthwhile going ashore again, so they made themselves comfortable on deck, and read and chatted and thought the afternoon away.

In time for a late dinner that evening, the two parties arrived from Granada, those who had left the ship at Cadiz and gone overland through Seville and Cordoba, and those who had started that morning. All were tired but enthusiastic, and Katherine wondered whether her party had done the right thing in sticking to the ship. Before these late diners had finished, *Patricia* had weighed anchor and was steaming eastward on her two-day run to Marseilles.

The question of whether the party should leave the ship at Malaga had been discussed and rediscussed. While on the previous night there had been little doubt that they should go on to Malaga, they found it much harder to decide about continuing to Marseilles. To return from Malaga to Ceuta in case of need was a matter of a few hours, but once they left Malaga, they could not get back under several days. However, the balance of opinion had been in favour of carrying on. Now the die was cast irrevocably. *Patricia* was once more at sea.

Next morning they were off the coast of Murcia, with Cartagena hidden somewhere at the base of the blue hills and Cape Palos coming up on the port bow. They studied the chart on the main staircase, on which their course was laid down in pencil and a tiny flag marked their eight o'clock position. During the day they would pass Alicante and Cape Nao, and before sundown would see the outline of Iviza, of the Balearic group, away to port.

But before long they had something other than geography to think about. Presently a steward came along to offer Captain Goode's compliments and to ask if they would kindly see him in his cabin.

They went forward and up the companion marked "Officers Only" to the lower bridge. There the captain met them and with ceremony ushered them into his sitting room. It was small but comfortably furnished, with a well-padded armchair and sofa, a writing-desk, an electric fire, a fan, and other fittings. Major Artt was already there, and there was some little difficulty in fitting all the party in. However, at last a seat was found for everyone, and Goode began to speak.

"I'm sorry for disturbing you all and squeezing you like this," he apologised, and Katherine could not but think how grave both he and Artt looked, "but some news has come in that I think you should hear. I regret to say it's bad news: about Mr Mant Carrington."

He paused for a moment and looked round. Katherine could not refrain from doing the same. Without meaning to, she found herself contrasting the contours of the seven faces in her view. The captain's, round and chubby, with his mouth like the f-hole of a violin, up at one corner and down at another, Major Artt's a trifle hatchety, William's pale and a little haggard – he was better today, though not yet quite well – Jim's dreamy with his small red moustache and heavy-lidded eyes, Luke, heavy-cheeked and bulldoggish, already slightly blue where he shaved, Eva, so charmingly pretty even with her distressed appearance...And Runciman! So good, so strong, so kindly, so – so – noble-looking. How infinitely superior he looked to all the others! Such a man! In a moment of time Katherine took them all in, each so individual and unlike the others, and yet each with a similar grave and anxious expression. In the case of Artt and the captain, worried; in the others, sorrowful and apprehensive. It was indeed what she felt herself. Sorrowful and apprehensive.

For a moment Captain Goode seemed doubtful as to how to proceed. Then, making up his mind, he spoke, quietly and decisively.

"We got this information late last night, but there was nothing to be gained by waking you up. I regret to tell you that Mr Mant Carrington is dead."

Katherine felt as if a hand had clutched her heart, though the news was no surprise. It was, indeed, what in their secret hearts they had all expected. For a moment no one spoke. Then Runciman Jellicoe asked in a low voice, "Tell us the particulars."

"I'm going to do so," the captain replied, "but I'm afraid you will be distressed. The first thing we had was a wireless from Gibraltar" – he picked a paper up from his desk, waved it in the air, and let it fall again – "saying that on Sunday morning the dead body of a man had been picked up from the sea some miles inside the Straits by a British tramp. The body was landed at Gib, and was identified by the Gib police as that of Mr Mant Carrington."

There were looks of bewilderment and incredulity, but again no one spoke.

"I'm afraid," Goode went on, "there's worse to come. The skull had been fractured and the police believe it was not an accident."

"Murder!" exclaimed Luke in a small voice.

"They think so."

Once again the hand gripped Katherine's heart, and she felt panic rising within her. Mant murdered! An attempted murder in Bromsley: a successful one at Ceuta! Oh, no! Dreadful! There could be no connection. This was some native who had killed Mant to rob him.

"Any further details?" Luke asked presently, also in a low and rather hoarse voice.

"Nothing, I think," the captain answered, though he made no attempt to pass over the message.

Again there was silence and then Jim moved suddenly. "We should go to Gib, shouldn't we," he asked, looking round. "Or some of us should?" He turned to Goode. "Could you transfer us or put us ashore, or what do you recommend?"

Goode shook his head. "I'm afraid you'll have to come on to Marseilles now," he returned. "If you then think it necessary you could return at once, either by steamer, or if there was no steamer, overland. But you'll have to consider whether you'd really gain anything by going. You couldn't be in time for the funeral, you know. That is, if you bury at Gib. You can, of course, get in touch with the authorities by wireless at any moment."

"Yes, it'll take a bit of thinking over," Jim agreed and relapsed into silence.

"Oh, isn't it *dreadful*?" Eva whispered with a shudder. "*Poor* Mant. Even if we didn't all like him as much as we might, this is horrible beyond words. Oh, dreadful!"

"Dreadful indeed," William agreed. He moved uneasily. "I think we ought to go to Gibraltar," he went on. "We must see that everything is done."

"I agree," Jim declared. "Sure, captain, you can't do anything for us? Transfer us to another ship, eh?"

"I'm sorry, Mr Musgrave, but I'm afraid that's out of the question," Goode said with decision. "But, if I may say so, I think you may trust the police. You're in their hands in any case. You see, if their fears are well founded, you will unfortunately have no say in what is done. They'll take charge."

"The captain's right, Jim," William agreed. "The matter isn't in our hands. We couldn't do anything."

Then at last Luke asked the question that had been hanging on Katherine's lips ever since she heard the news. "Have the police any theory as to what might have occurred?"

"No," Goode answered; "or if they have, we haven't been advised."

"I suppose nothing can be deduced from the fact that the body was picked up in the Straits?"

"I'm afraid not. You see, we don't know exactly where it was found. Of course there's the obvious suggestion that it was taken out in a boat and put into the sea. As to its being found inside the Straits, as you know, a current flows inwards from the Atlantic to the Mediterranean. Anything put into the sea off either Ceuta or Gib would go east."

There was really not much more to be said, though for some time the anxious little party discussed the affair with the captain and Major Artt. The Gibraltar authorities had promised to wireless the ship if and when they had further news to communicate, and Captain Goode undertook to pass this on directly he received it.

The conference looked like coming to an end, when William made a suggestion. "If we can't go to Gibraltar, don't you think we ought to wireless them that everything proper is to be done about the funeral? I don't know whether we can wireless money, but I think they should know that all expenses incurred in connection with the funeral will be met. What can you do for us, captain, about that?"

"No difficulty there, Mr Carrington. If you hand what you think right to our purser, he'll wire it to our agents, who will pay it over to the authorities. I needn't say that we shall all be only too glad to help in any way possible."

William's suggestion was unanimously approved and the old man went off to get the money. This move broke up the party, and the others returned to their chairs, though still discussing the affair in undertones.

On the whole, Katherine was relieved by what she had heard. It was dreadful of course about Mant, but she had already come to believe that he was dead, and the confirmation scarcely came as a shock. But she was relieved about that hideous fear which had occurred to her directly she had heard that he was missing. Immensely relieved. It couldn't have been Jim. For Jim couldn't have arranged the boat. He could only have obtained one by hire, and he would never have dared to take such a risk.

At first the general view was that the whole party should return as soon as possible to Gibraltar to pay a last tribute at Mant's grave. But after discussion this opinion was revised. After all, what good could such a visit do? William, however, was insistent that some member of the party should attend, if only to indicate their feelings and to see in person that everything suitable had been done. He wanted to go himself, but Jellicoe vetoed that. Then Jim offered, and it was finally decided that he and Jellicoe should go together. They would see to everything, then if they could pick up *Patricia*, they would do so, if not they would complete their holiday in Spain or North Africa.

"It will be at my expense, whatever you do," William declared, and though at first they protested, the offer was finally accepted.

But once again their plans were changed. Shortly before they were due at Marseilles a steward, for the second time, presented the captain's compliments and asked them if they would step up to his cabin. Once again they assembled, to meet both Goode and Major Artt. Both looked even more worried than before.

"I'm exceedingly sorry," said Goode, after apologising for calling them together, "but I've got some further news and I'm afraid it will also distress you. I pass it on with great regret. But first let me tell you about Gibraltar. I have had information from our agents that the inquest is over and that the funeral has taken place in a most reverent and seemly way. Everything appears to have been done as you would wish it, and I don't think, had you been there, that you could have had things better. That is the first thing."

He paused for a moment. William nodded appreciatively, but doubt as to what might be coming kept everyone silent.

"My distressing news is this," Captain Goode went on slowly, apparently having some difficulty in choosing his words. "As I informed you, the condition of the remains suggested that death had been due to foul play. The chief of police at Gibraltar says that, as the murder did not take place there, his men could not investigate it. He points out also that enquiries would have to be made in various other places. In his opinion the work could best be done by sending out an officer from Scotland Yard. He said he had so reported to London. Well, that was the police view. But there was also the view of my owners and" – he looked at

Artt – "of Messrs Cunn, who are responsible for the cruise. We put the facts before them by wireless, and they have decided that however distressing the publicity would be, an unsolved mystery would be still worse. They have been to Scotland Yard and urged the sending of a man. It appears this has been agreed to, and a chief inspector is travelling out with the cruise party and will come on board with them tomorrow."

The captain paused and a little babble of conversation broke out. But it was Luke who voiced the general question.

"You say the police officer is coming on board here," he said. "But surely it's to Ceuta he ought to go?"

"He will have to go to Ceuta, I imagine," Goode answered, "but it appears he wants to begin on the ship with the circumstances under which Mr Mant went ashore. However, I don't really know about that. All I have heard is that he will join at Marseilles as an ordinary passenger, and will come along with us to Athens. It is not to be generally known who he is, but I didn't think it would be fair to you not to tell you what was being done."

"We all appreciate that," said William, amid murmurs of approval.

"And of course," the captain continued, glancing round his little audience, "you must please keep the secret."

"Well, what do you think?" Jim said rather bitterly. "None of us exactly want the thing broadcast."

"Quite so, Mr Musgrave. Then there is only one other point. The officer sent a special request that you would all remain aboard, as he particularly wishes for your help."

Jim looked at Runciman. "Dr Jellicoe and I had decided to go to Gibraltar from Marseilles. Does this mean that we can't?"

"No, there's no compulsion whatever. But I think you'll admit the chief inspector's request is reasonable. Also I really believe you may be satisfied with what has been done at Gib."

Jim looked at William. "I take it we should stay?" he asked.

William looked round the little circle. "I don't see what else can be done," he said. "What do you all think?"

There was unanimous agreement. Katherine indeed, on selfish grounds, was relieved. She had hated the idea of Jellicoe going off and leaving her to complete the cruise without him, and she knew he felt the same about leaving her. He had offered to go only because he thought it right to do so. But also, now that she was satisfied about Jim, she was not displeased at the idea of having the affair cleared up. It was so obviously a native crime, since that point about the boat had become known. But wasn't the whole affair distressing! As Katherine walked back to her place she shivered at the thought of what might still be to come.

– 14 –

THE DISQUISITION OF KIRBY

While *Patricia* was rolling gently through the waters of the Mediterranean between Malaga and Marseilles, Chief Inspector Joseph French was having a hectic time in England.

For some months he had not been feeling up to the mark. About a year earlier he had had an attack of influenza, the effects of which he had seemed unable to shake off. When recovering he would have liked a change to complete the cure, but a wave of crime had so increased business at the Yard that he had been unable to get away. All the time he was working at that petrol affair in Northern Ireland he had been feeling seedy, and his week's holiday in Portrush and Donegal at the end of that case did not do him the good he had hoped. Then an attack of toothache had led to the relinquishment of a fine molar, and hey presto! his debility had disappeared and he had become once again his old hearty self. Delighted at again feeling fit, he had thrown himself more energetically than ever into his work. Once more, to a large extent, his business was his pleasure.

On that Monday evening, when *Patricia* was passing between Spain and the Balearic island of Iviza, French was returning to town by a late train from Arundel. He had had a tiring day there enquiring into the suspected murder of a woman whose body had been found in the Arun. When the time came for his return train one small item of evidence remained to be obtained, and he had waited on till the 8.7 train to get it. And he had got it. With all the proof required to ensure a conviction for murder, he had left for home, weary but triumphant.

He reached Victoria a few minutes before ten and drove home. Then it was that once again in his life he realised the truth of the old proverb that it never rains but it pours. A message from the Yard was waiting for him saying that a new case necessitated his going to Birmingham that night, and on to France next day for a cruise to Athens and possibly Istanbul. He was to get ready as quickly as possible and go to the Yard, where further instructions would be given him.

This news was so utterly unexpected that for a time French could only gape at his wife and emit slightly blasphemous expressions of wonder and delight. "Bless us all, Em!" he exclaimed. "A cruise in the Mediterranean! I would have as soon expected a cruise to the moon. Athens and Constantinople! Good Lord!"

"Aye," grunted his wife. "Did ever you hear the like of it? as your friends in Northern Ireland would say. Well, look here, it won't help you in the Mediterranean to starve to death now. When did you have your last meal?"

"Oh, I had something before I left Arundel," he explained. "But I could do with a peck now all the same."

"What did you have?" Mrs French asked sceptically. She knew her husband. While he liked his meals as much as anyone, if he was keen on a case he would forget about them, and she didn't want to have him ill again.

He told her and she snorted. "I just thought so," she declared. "Well, your supper's ready now. And you'll not go a step to any Yard till you've eaten it, so you needn't think it."

Mrs French was one of those women who hold the theory that men are only large boys, not fit to deal with the really important matters of life.

He was very willing to agree, for he had only had a light afternoon tea and was hungry. But he didn't know the hour of the last train to Birmingham and he was afraid of being late.

"I must pack my things," he expostulated.

"Didn't you see them packed and ready in the hall?" she retorted. "You're a nice observant detective."

"Look up Bradshaw like an angel," he adjured her as he began to eat, "and see when the last train to Birmingham goes."

"Euston or Paddington?" she asked as she took down the book.

"I don't know. Try both."

Satisfied that he had time for all he wanted to do, French ate and enjoyed his supper. During the process they talked about the cruise. He began by insisting that she must go also. But of this she wouldn't hear. First of all it was business, not pleasure, that he was going on, and she supposed that even on a cruise he would do *some* work. Then she declared that an Olympic cruise was not the type which would suit her, "with lords and ladies all over the show." If he liked it she would join him on another occasion. This matter disposed of, they turned to the question of a cruising outfit. "You can't get anything in the time," she complained. But he said it didn't matter. "My flannel bags and pullover and brown coat are all I want," he declared, "with those rubber soled shoes I got last year." In the end a list was made and she promised to pack the stuff and meet him with it at Victoria if he telephoned the train by which he was leaving.

Though married for more years than he liked to remember, French and his wife remained profoundly attached to each other. If at times they appeared to spar, it was only to keep up a sort of joke which had become traditional. They were pals in the best sense and were entirely happy in each other's company.

French dealt handsomely with his supper, though he did not spend much time over the job. By a few minutes after eleven o'clock he had reached the Yard. Sir Mortimer Ellison, the Assistant Commissioner, had just returned to have a word with him about his new case.

"It seems a complicated affair," the AC began, leaning back in his chair and languidly lighting a cigarette at the smoke of which he gazed with his heavy-lidded eyes. "Briefly, a party of seven persons booked for two successive Olympic cruises, the first from Glasgow to Marseilles, and the second, from Marseilles round the Eastern Mediterranean and back to Marseilles. They sailed from Glasgow. At Ceuta, which an explorer like you will know is on the African coast just opposite Gibraltar, one of the members disappeared. The evidence is that he went ashore alone after dinner and never came back. Next day his body was picked up in the Straits and brought into Gibraltar. There were certain wounds on the body which indicated murder. By the way, won't you smoke?"

He pushed his still open case across the desk. This was one of those small courtesies which made Sir Mortimer so popular with his men. Not that their liking for him rested on these alone. Much more important was it that he was about as just as a human being can well be, that he stood up for them when he could, and that when they made mistakes he remembered that he also was human. Only in cases of carelessness, crookedness or deliberate slacking was he implacable. He had not to deal with many of them.

"The usual complication arose as to who was responsible for the investigation: with the usual result that everyone actually concerned has shuffled out and left it to us. And so you're off to the Mediterranean."

"Yes, sir," French returned primly, though he would have embraced the various officers who had done the shuffling.

"I know," said the AC, answering his thought. "It's an ill wind, isn't it?"

French grinned. "I don't deny that I'm very grateful to you for sending me, sir," he admitted.

Sir Mortimer shrugged. "Tell you the truth," he confided, "if I could have gone myself, I would. So 'grateful' is not exactly the word. Now there's an interesting feature in the case. It seems that the reason that this party took the cruise is that they had all recently been ill from poisoning. We didn't deal with it, but perhaps you saw about it in the papers? It's the Carrington family, of Bromsley near Birmingham."

"By Jove, sir, yes!" French exclaimed. "I read about that, and a very interesting case I thought it. In fact I wondered it hadn't come our way."

"You suspected foul play?"

"Well, I had hardly enough evidence for that, sir. But I did think it fishy looking."

"Fishy is the word. It was fishy, distinctly fishy. I rang up the Bromsley police this afternoon, and they say it was undoubtedly attempted murder of one member of the family by another. But so far they have not been able to fix the responsibility."

"And you think the two affairs are connected?"

Sir Mortimer smiled. "Ah, there you're going too fast for me. I don't know. But at first sight and on the face of it, and so on, it doesn't seem impossible."

"So you wish me to begin by going to Birmingham?"

"Don't you think it would be wise?"

"I do, sir. Quite necessary."

"Very good then, that's all I have to say to you. Everything is arranged. You go from Euston by the" – he consulted a paper which lay on his desk – "eleven fifty-five to Birmingham. There you will be met, and during the night you can mug up the case. I asked them to let you have copies of the evidence and photographs. Then tomorrow you will come up to town by the" – again he looked at the paper – "seven thirty from New Street, getting to Euston at ten. This will leave you oceans of time to catch the 11 a.m. Golden Arrow service to the south. How you're to eat and sleep between this and then I don't quite know, assuming you're unreasonable enough to want to do so. But from 11 a.m. tomorrow you'll be all right. You'll live on the fat of several lands, drink ambrosial compounds and sleep on down, or more likely, steel springs. However, I expect you'll like it all right."

French smiled dutifully as he stood up. "Right, sir. Thank you very much. I'll manage to exist."

"I should, if I were you. By the way, I'm not sending Carter with you. On this eclectic cruise you might deceive even the elect, but Carter, I fear, never could. We shall run no risks."

As French settled down in the Birmingham express he looked forward with a more than usually keen interest to his new case. First as to its locus. That it should be out of London was good, but that it should involve a cruise to the Eastern Mediterranean was so infinitely better as to be almost incredible. Nothing within the bounds of possibility that French could have imagined would have pleased him more. And it was not only that he was going on a cruise to the Eastern Mediterranean: he was going in his department's time and at its expense! This delightful change would not in any way curtail his holidays. Of course, he would have to work while he was on it, but that he did not mind. He had never been afraid of work, and he had seldom found it irksome.

His only regret was that his wife could not accompany him. But that again was tempered by the knowledge that a cruise was not her form of pleasure. But why, he now thought, should she stay alone at home? She had talked for ages about going to see her youngest sister, who was married to the harbour master of one of the smaller Yorkshire ports. Now was her chance. He would mention it to her tomorrow, or rather that day, for it was already Tuesday.

Then apart altogether from its setting, the case was one about which he had read with a good deal of interest. The full details had not been given in the papers, but it had been hinted that while the poison was arsenic, neither doctors nor police could trace how it had been administered. To French the whole circumstances had looked suspicious and he had felt that the investigation could scarcely have been sufficiently thorough. He now wondered whether he himself would do better.

Presently he felt that he was wasting his time reprehensibly. He had had a heavy day and was going to have to work all night. Here were a couple of heaven-sent hours of enforced idleness. It was his bounden duty to sleep.

He tried, with such success that a few seconds later he found the train had stopped at Birmingham. Refreshed, he soon identified the constable who had been sent to drive him to Bromsley. Before three o'clock he was shaking hands with Inspector Kirby and Sergeant Scarlett and apologising for keeping them out of their beds at so ungodly an hour.

"Don't mention it, sir," Kirby returned, smiling politely. "We understand you have to leave London for the Mediterranean at eleven, so you could scarcely come here at any other time. We didn't know if you had any supper before you left, so we have a cup of coffee ready."

"That's really kind of you," French returned heartily. "I'll be glad of it. Nothing like it when you're working at night. Won't you smoke, inspector, and you, sergeant?"

He passed over his cigarette case and soon the three men were smoking and imbibing fragrant cups of coffee. The stimulant removed the last traces of French's weariness. He felt a new man, and said so.

"And now," he went on, "as you know, I've not got a great deal of time. Suppose we get ahead with the business?"

Kirby was very willing. He pointed to two thick files of papers as material he had prepared for French. "Luckily we had spare carbons of the statements and so on," he said. "I've put them up here together with copies of the photographs and other details. I think you've enough here to give you all the facts. However, if you'd like a verbal account of the affair in addition, I'll do my best."

"That's fine," French approved. "You're certainly doing me proud. But I should like your own account as well. In fact, it was really for that I came down. Those files will be a magnificent help, but there's nothing like a personal statement to start with."

"What about turning round to the fire, sir? It's not very good, but it's better than nothing."

They made themselves as comfortable as possible and then Inspector Kirby began to speak.

"First of all, about these seven people who have gone on the cruise. Six of them belong either to the Carrington family or are connected with it by marriage; the seventh is the family doctor. But we might almost call him a member of the family too, for he has recently become engaged to the old man's niece.

"This old man, the head of the family, is William Carrington," and Kirby went on to give a brief résumé of his history, mentioning his illness, his cabling for Mant and Mant's arrival and taking over of the works. Then in turn he dealt with Mant himself, Jim and Katherine, following on to Luke, Eva and Runciman Jellicoe. "There are their photographs," he continued, and when he had finished French felt that he already knew the party intimately.

"Now we come to the matter of the poisoning," Kirby went on, and he told of the family dinner, the illness of the party, the rise of suspicion through Mant's being so much worse than the others, and the report of the analyst that while all the sufferers had had arsenic, Mant Carrington had had eserine as well.

"Oh," said French, much interested. "That didn't come out in the paper."

"No. We thought it wiser to keep our knowledge dark. Well, it seemed clear this was an attempt to murder Mant Carrington, and that the other five had been doped as a blind. The idea apparently was that ptomaine would be assumed. But, if suspicion were aroused, arsenic might be found in the analyses. If so, it would be supposed that it had done the damage – having got into the food accidentally – and the other poison would not have been looked for."

"A smart enough idea, too."

"Yes, and the whole thing might have worked only for two points. First, the maids had eaten some of all the food, and they remained well. That was bad luck for the murderer" – Kirby gave a twisted smile – "for it showed us that the poison couldn't have got into the food accidentally, but must have been put there by a trick."

"That's right. A good point, if I may say so."

Kirby made a gesture dissociating himself from the praise. "Unfortunately it didn't help us. Anyone of the family, and goodness knows who else besides, could have got hold of both poisons. There was weed-killer in the garden and eserine in a cupboard in the bathroom. So, on the face of it, anyone who had the entry to the house could be guilty."

"It looks like it," French agreed. "But look here, one point puzzles me. If this was really murder, why didn't the murderer give a fatal dose of the eserine? It's not a poison I know much about, but I understand a little kills."

Kirby nodded his appreciation. "Quite so, sir: I asked the same question myself. But we can't make anything of that. He did give a fatal dose."

"Then why didn't Carrington die?"

"He escaped for a cause that one would scarcely guess: because of the arsenic. The arsenic made him sick and he got rid of the eserine before it did him serious harm."

"H'm. That looks as if the murderer, for all his cleverness, didn't know quite enough about these poisons."

"Either that, or he made a genuine mistake. Well, the next thing was to find out how the doses could have been given," and Kirby described the reconstruction which led him to suspect the glasses. "I can show you one of them," he added. "Get it from the back room, Scarlett."

The sergeant vanished, reappearing immediately with the glass in his hand. French examined it curiously.

"The lighting of the dining-table was dim," Kirby explained. "Only four small-power electric candles, and we found it possible to have as much as five drops of liquid in these glasses unnoticed by some of our other men. We therefore assumed that a few drops of some arsenical solution had been put into all the glasses, and the little pellets of eserine into Mant's as well. The doctor tells us they would have dissolved at once."

"Very good," French approved again.

"It seemed the only way out. Then the big question arose: Who could be guilty?"

French nodded. All this was admirable: exactly the way in which he would have carried on the case himself had it been in his hands. An investigation, not directed by chance or whim, but proceeding in ordered sequence from step to step, each new step developing logically from the last. That was the way to achieve results. Why, he wondered, had such good work failed to get a conviction?

"If we were right so far," Kirby continued, "it seemed to confine the guilty person to someone in the house, either one of the party or one of the maids. Of course there was the possibility that some stranger had entered the house and done it, but this didn't appear likely. All the lower windows were bolted, and the evidence of Miss Shirley and the maids was that they had been bolted all the afternoon. Then the front door could only have been opened by someone with a key, and no such person was known. Besides it would have been very risky for any outsider to have entered the dining room. If one of the guests had been found there he could have made some excuse, but no stranger could. After thinking it over, we decided the guilty person must be one of the party, though I admit it's not absolutely proved."

"I agree it sounds likely."

"Yes, sir. Then we found that every single person in the house could have got into the dining room alone before dinner, for a period of at least two minutes. But here again there was no evidence which it was."

"Not to be wondered at. If anyone had gone in, it would be secretly."

"Quite. It then became a question of trying to find motives, and as you know, sir, that's not so easy, particularly among a family party."

"I know it only too well."

"But we did find motives, in three cases. Whether any of them were strong enough, we don't know.

"There was first Mrs Dugdale. She's a very beautiful woman, Mrs Dugdale, and it seems Mant Carrington was pestering her with unwanted attentions. He would go to the house in the late afternoons after dark, and also in the evenings when the husband was away, as he had sometimes to be on the firm's business. We got that easily enough from various people who had seen him here and there, as you'll know yourself, sir. But it wasn't so easy to find out whether the lady had encouraged him. But from pumping her daily help and so on, we got to believe she hadn't."

"Not very convincing, that part of it," French suggested.

"No, sir, I admit that. All the same if Mant was bothering her and she objected, she would be in a nasty position.

Mant was the boss of the firm, and the jobs of both her husband and her brother depended on him. And she's reported to be very fond of both. Mant could have brought a lot of pressure to bear on her, and the only way she could have really safeguarded herself was by getting him out of the way. And she had ample opportunity to get both the poisons and put them into the glasses before dinner. In fact, you might almost say she got rid of Miss Shirley, who had gone upstairs with her, when she was taking off her things."

French whistled. "You've made a case there all right, but it's not proven."

"No, sir, it's certainly not. And her getting rid of Miss Shirley upstairs might be simply thoughtfulness, to let her see to the serving of the dinner."

"She couldn't have know that Miss Shirley wouldn't have gone into the dining room when she was dropping in the stuff."

"She could, sir. She could have followed Miss Shirley to the head of the stairs and watched her into the sitting room. She would know she would be unlikely to come out again before the meal."

"I suppose that's so. Well, you said there were two other suspects?"

"Yes, sir. There was the husband, Luke Dugdale. If he knew what was going on he'd be tempted to do Mant in from two points of view. First, if he was in love with his wife, and he's supposed to be, he'd want to kill Mant out of jealousy. Then, secondly, he'd know that if there was a burst up, he'd probably lose his job. So that he'd have a double motive."

"Also not proven."

"Admitted, sir. But there it is. Then there's Mrs Dugdale's brother, Jim Musgrave. He's a man with a grievance. He's a member of the family, and yet he has only a subordinate position in the works. It appears he has always felt this keenly, and when the old man retired, he thought he should have got the job. When Mant was brought over from Australia, he hated him from the first. And by all accounts he and Mant haven't got on too well. Then again if Mant was out of the way, there would be no one for the job but himself. There's no doubt Jim Musgrave had a motive, real or fancied, to kill Mant."

"And again no proof?"

"No, sir; none whatever."

"Then the other two?"

"We've no reason to suspect either. Miss Shirley's a woman of excellent character, very kindly and all that, and not the type to turn to murder. Besides, we've found no motive. And old Mr Williams, besides being ill, had himself brought Mant over to do just what he was doing. He had no grievance and, from all we've heard, they got on well together. Besides, I doubt if the old man was in good enough health to have carried through the job."

"And you've learnt nothing to make you suspect anyone outside the family?"

"No, sir; nothing whatever."

For some moments French sat thinking over what he had heard. Up to a point these men had done extremely well, but for all that they had certainly left the case in the air. Three suspects known, other possible suspects admitted, and no proof about any of them.

"Then there's this new development," French went on. "What do you think of that? That whoever it is has got Mant at last?"

"I don't know the details, but it's certainly what I'd think."

French nodded. "You may be right: I don't know. At all events I'm grateful to you for your help. Now I'd like to have a look through these folders before I go, so that if any question occurs to me I can ask it. What time must I leave here?"

"About seven, sir."

"Right then, just leave me here. And will you come back a bit before seven?"

Kirby hesitated. "My missus wondered if you'd come home and have a lie down? It's none too comfortable here."

"Very good of you, I'm sure. But half the night's gone, and it's not worth it. Besides, it'll take me the rest of the time to look over these."

Murmuring regrets, Kirby and Scarlett left him, and settling down as comfortably as he could, French set to work to make up the dossier so that he could ask any needful questions before leaving.

– 15 –

THE PEREGRINATION OF FRENCH

When French had finished his breakfast in the seven-thirty train from Birmingham to Euston he lit his pipe and settled down to consider what he had learnt of the case. He felt he ought to try and sleep while he had the chance, but his coffee had been strong and his brain was active. And it was certainly true that the more thought he put into the affair now, the better able he would be to deal with the new development when he reached the ship.

It seemed to him that the Bromsley police were right on two points: first, that the poisoning was a case of attempted murder, and second, that the arsenic and eserine had been administered by being dropped before dinner into the glasses. So much he thought he might take for granted. No other explanation that he could see would meet the facts.

What, he wondered, could he deduce from these conclusions? One thing at least was obvious: that the criminal was an extremely able person. That idea of giving poison to everyone who was at the dinner, was brilliant. It in itself was well calculated to rule out the suspicion of murder and supply a strong suggestion that what had taken place was accidental. And then the actual carrying out of the scheme postulated ability of no mean order. A person not only of inventive genius, but of coolness and nerve.

Kirby was right when he said that had the maids not had identically the same food and drink without ill effect, suspicion might never have been aroused.

Next there came that vital question: must the job have been done by someone from within the house? Kirby had believed so, but had admitted that there was no absolute proof. French examined once again the plan of the building, the photographs of the fastenings on the various windows, and reread the statements of those concerned.

It seemed clear that no one could have opened those windows from the outside when they were latched, or latched them from the outside after he had passed out through them. And the evidence was fairly conclusive that all the downstairs windows were latched. To have attempted an entrance by a ladder through an upstairs window would have been so risky that French thought he might eliminate the possibility. If he were right, an outsider could therefore have entered and left only through the front door. But this meant a key of the door. Who could have had one?

Here again the evidence was that no one could, but though this might be an honest opinion, it was not necessarily a correct one. A person wishing to commit such a crime could doubtless have obtained a key secretly.

But what did seem certain was that such a criminal would have to be very intimate with the family, not only to obtain a pressing of some member's key unsuspected, but also to have that detailed knowledge of the household which would have enabled him to carry out his plan. He would have to be thoroughly acquainted with the arrangements for the birthday party; the hour of the dinner; the dim lighting employed; the fact that tinted, goblet-shaped glasses would be used which would enable the drops to lie in them unnoticed; the hour at which secret access to the dining room would be possible; and last, but by no means least, the place at the table which Mant Carrington would occupy. Could anyone, not actually a member of the family, have all this information?

The more French considered it, the less likely it seemed, particularly when he read Katherine Shirley's evidence that normally they had few people to lunch or dinner. No, Kirby was probably correct in his opinion that the criminal was one of the party who had sat down to dinner on that tragic night.

Either old William Carrington, Katherine Shirley, Jim Musgrave, or Luke or Eva Dugdale, that was. One of five persons! If that were true, it would surely be an easy matter to learn which.

Kirby had not found it so, however. French shrugged. These local police were good, but they couldn't be expected to have the knowledge or experience of the men of Scotland Yard. When he himself got going, he was sure he would have no difficulty in clearing the thing up.

His thoughts turned to the development Sir Mortimer Ellison had outlined. Of this he did not know the details, but Mant Carrington had died and it was evidently believed that he had been murdered. If so, was it a case of the second attempt succeeding?

It might well be, and if so, it should greatly simplify the investigation. Only persons common to both situations need be considered. But that meant these same five persons, and so far as he knew, no one else. But steady! There was another person whom he had overlooked. That doctor! Jellicoe was now practically a member of the family. Kirby had thought the engagement was subsequent to the poisoning, but how could he know? It might easily have been in existence, but unannounced. And though Jellicoe was not at that dinner, he might well have obtained a pressing of the front door key, and have had the details of the household arrangements necessary for the attempt. And Jellicoe had gone with the others on the cruise.

There was, of course, no evidence incriminating Jellicoe, but it was obvious that he must be included in the list of suspects. That brought them up to six. Well, six was a small number compared to what he had been up against in many of his previous cases. He would soon eliminate five, and then his job would be done.

But not too soon! He would do his level best of course, but he hoped the investigation would take long enough to let him see Athens and Istanbul at least!

At the Yard French was handed a copy of all the messages which had passed between the ship and the owners and cruise agents, as well as a special passport, travel tickets, reservations, and money. He also took a large suitcase of professional apparatus, aids of various kinds to the art of detection. There was not time to go home and change, as he would have liked, but at Victoria he found Mrs French standing guard over another enormous suitcase.

"My word, Em, I'm doing myself proud," he exclaimed, looking at the two huge pieces. "Might as well be one of those lords or ladies you're so fond of."

"I hope I've forgotten nothing," she answered. "But if I have, there's a shop on board, or so I've always heard."

"The thing I'll want most will be a way of getting the murderer, but I don't suppose they'll sell that."

"It is a murder case, is it?"

"Supposed to be. I haven't heard much about it yet. And now, old lady, I want to talk to you. What are you going to do while I'm away?"

"I don't know," she returned. "A trip to Paris with that nice Mr Sedding, I suppose."

"I was just afraid of that," he declared, "and I'm going to run no risks. You're not to stay at home at all. You're to go to Yorkshire," and he outlined his plan for her holiday.

She was obviously pleased, though at first she demurred. But he would listen to no objections. "I've been sitting up half the night to write a cheque," he concluded, "and here it is. You can't turn me down after that."

She glanced at the paper. "Oh, Joe," she murmured, "it's too much. You mustn't."

"It's not too much," he assured her; "we can afford it well. Now have a good time and take Rose on excursions. And my best respects to Tom."

The Olympic party was going by special train, ten minutes in advance of the ordinary. While French and his wife were talking they had passed through the barrier and French had pushed his way into a second class near the engine. The train was practically full and he got one of the last seats. Porters were still hurrying up with vast truckloads of luggage, which was being hastily stowed in the front van. The driver with true Olympian calm looked superciliously down on the struggling forms, then glanced forward where a bloodshot eye which had been menacing him had suddenly vanished and an innocuous green one had appeared in its place. A moment later the last of the luggage had been swallowed up, various officials had raised their arms as if in valediction, and the platform with Mrs French's figure upon it, began slowly to move away in the direction of St Paul's.

In spite of his years French felt like a boy leaving school for a particularly promising holiday. As he looked out and saw sober Father Thames also on the move after the platform, he could have hugged himself or sung aloud.

Presently he began to look at his fellow passengers. In front was an elderly clergyman with a posse of daughters; or so he thought at first. Then he saw that not all of the girls were daughters. They were talking of books and he overheard one say she had read the clergyman's new book with great interest. Not a daughterly remark, that. On the other side of the corridor was a middle-aged pleasing-looking lady zealously nursing a round hat case, and opposite her a strong-faced young man with a pretty woman. These were obviously two separate parties, but they were already making friends. Immediately opposite himself was a young man, a schoolmaster French imagined. He thought he might as well follow the example of his neighbours. He therefore told the young man that it looked as if they would get it calm in the Straits.

The young man knew this for himself, and so was able to agree. He asked French had he done this particular cruise before. French hadn't. It appeared that neither had the young man, but some of his friends had, and had been greatly delighted. It appeared also that it was very well run, which explained why the young man had chosen it. So the conversation artlessly progressed, till they reached the subject of football and became interested.

On the *Canterbury* French made the acquaintance of a number more of his fellow travellers. One, a tall ramrod of a man with a repellent manner and a rough chiselled face, whose luggage French noticed was labelled "Brigadier-General Mulholland", turned out to be a very agreeable man whose chief interest seemed to be in the growing of roses. He lived near Cowes, on ground which French knew well from his visits in connection with the Chayle-Joymount cement case, and the two were soon friends.

In the train from Calais he met still others. Here he got into conversation with two men, who with their wives and families occupied the remainder of the compartment. They were, he learnt, a doctor and a solicitor respectively, both from Edinburgh, but apparently strangers before the trip. The solicitor had been on a similar cruise some three years earlier, and gave his impressions at length. They were all very friendly and French found himself temporarily absorbed in the party.

The train went round the Ceinture, and after a long and slow journey, they found themselves in the Gare de Lyon. By this time it was dark, and soon they followed their conductor, an emissary of Messrs Cunn, up the stairs to the restaurant. Dinner followed, with the making of still more friends, and then came a slight hiatus in their progress. They were to go on by special train, and as this train had not yet put in an appearance, they strolled about, keeping an occasional eye on the vast pile of luggage which formed a sort of island on the concourse. French spent the time following in imagination the great trains whose destinations, placarded up at the ends of the various platforms, so intensely thrilled him. To Rome by the Mont Cenis, Turin and Genoa; to Milan by the Loetschberg –Simplon; to Cannes, Nice and Ventimiglia; to Narbonne; to Geneva; to Venice and Trieste via the Rhône Valley, Simplon, and Milan; to Port Bou for Barcelona: all wonderful and intensely exciting. How fine to be travelling by any of them!

Then he thought that the notice of his own train, which had now just been put up, was as thrilling as any of them. "9.25. Spécial. Marseille Maritime." "Marseille" was delightful enough, but it was the "Maritime" which gave it just that something extra which was needed for real perfection.

Presently the coaches backed slowly in, and French rescued his suitcases from the island and found a place. Then, remembering his experiences at the Whitness Widening on the Southern Railway, he put a book on his seat and went forward to see the engine. Immense, he found it, judged by British standards, and showing a good deal more of its internal economy than was considered proper on the Southern. Dirty, too, he was sorry to notice. Little heaps of sand and coal dust and patches of congealed oil showed where they ought not, and tiny wisps of steam blew about the joints of pipes, giving it a slightly unkempt appearance. However, it was a magnificent machine. He walked forward to get a head-on view and was duly impressed.

They ran well for some three hours, and then some slow train appeared to have got in front of them, for they were checked at block post after block post. They crawled through the long tunnel under the high ground before reaching Dijon, then stopped again and again. And during these stops French was rather shocked to find that the weather had changed for the worse. A wild wind had suddenly risen which screamed over the silent train, blowing sheets of rain against the windows. Less glowing thoughts of the Gulf of Lyons occurred to French, and he began to wonder whether the motion of a 15,000-ton boat would be trying.

Presently whatever was holding them up departed, and they began once more to make good time. French fell asleep and missed the stops at Dijon and Lyons, only waking after they had passed Orange. The wind, he was glad to discover, had died down, though the morning remained damp and foggy. He went along the corridor to breakfast as they swung inland from the river at the approach to Avignon, and though he missed seeing where the famous bridge had been, he was interested in the glimpses of the old city's walls and portals.

There was a pleasant man in his compartment with whom he compared notes. Those extraordinary hedges of trees across the valley! What a suggestion they gave of the force of the terrible mistral! Then Tarascon and over the pair of points, which if moved some four inches one way or the other, would send the train to Italy or Spain. In the grim castle at Tarascon, still used as a prison, the pleasant man had seen some dreadful medieval dungeons. Then on to Arles, with its Grecian women, its old theatre and its arena, and down on the Camargue, past Miramas and Rognac and so on to their first glimpse of the Mediterranean. A few minutes later they drew up in the shunting yard at Marseilles.

Here they delayed for some time, then suddenly began to move again, out to the right of the main line to St Charles, and downhill towards the sea. Ah, here were ships at last. But once again they stopped, lying for quite a long time beneath a huge motor freighter, designed more like a long narrow biscuit box than a ship. Then at last they started off in the opposite direction, hauled by a small shunting engine, and after grinding round an extremely sharp curve, drew down to the wharf alongside which *Patricia* was lying.

To French she seemed a big boat as they climbed a long gangway to a door high up in her tall black side. In the room at the top passports were handed over, and French followed a steward to his cabin, an outside one on C Deck, which he was to share with one other man. To his surprise and satisfaction this turned out to be the pleasant man with whom he had travelled from Paris, and he felt that here again he was in luck.

By the time he had settled down it was after twelve, and almost at once the bugle went for the first lunch. Though the ship was not leaving till six o'clock, no one without special business was allowed ashore. French filled the time by learning his way about the ship and making some more acquaintances. He called on the captain after lunch, but Goode said he was sorry he would be too busy to discuss the Carrington affair till they had left port. He invited French to his cabin after dinner.

From no less than three of his new acquaintances – people who had taken the cruise from Glasgow and were going on to the Eastern Mediterranean – he heard the story of Mant Carrington's disappearance, though none of these told him any more than he already knew from the messages. But he managed to have a good look at all six members of the party, though without introducing himself. He recognised them instantly from their photographs, and did not require the hints and nudges so freely given by his informants.

It was dusk as *Patricia* cast off and slowly nosed her way out of the harbour. French was disappointed not to have seen the coast more clearly, but the lights dotted along the shore and over the surrounding hills were perhaps even more beautiful. By the time these were beginning to die back and merge into a general glow, the first bugle sounded.

Dressing was optional on this first night, but as everyone had had time to unpack, most of the passengers changed. French was glad he had done so when he saw the gorgeousness of the ladies who sat down at the table he had rather diffidently chosen, the final seats not yet having been allocated. But, like everyone else he had so far met, they proved pleasant and friendly.

It was close on nine and the lights of France had long vanished beneath the horizon when French climbed the steps to the bridge and asked for Captain Goode.

"He's in his cabin, sir," the cadet on duty answered. "Are you Mr French? Then please come this way."

French passed in through the wheelhouse and chartroom and down a steep flight of steps to the captain's room. Goode was writing at his desk, but he got up and motioned French to a chair.

"Have you had coffee?" he asked, holding out his cigarette case. "No? That's good. Neither have I. We'll have it now." He touched a bell, then went on to ask how French had fared on his journey out.

"Fine," said French, "though when I heard the wind howling last night on the way down from Paris, I scarcely hoped we'd be going along as steadily as this."

"We didn't have wind at Marseilles, though we had thunder and lightning pretty badly. This is the first time you've done one of these cruises?"

French answered that it was, but that he didn't know whether he could be said to be "doing" it now, though he declared that in spite of his job he was going to see all he could.

"That's right," Goode agreed. For a while they chatted on various subjects, but as soon as the steward had gone Goode turned to business.

"This case that you've come down to look into, chief inspector, is a curious one from several points of view. First, it wasn't altogether easy to say whose business it was to investigate the crime, because there doesn't seem to be much doubt that there was a crime. But if the crime took place, as we suppose, in Ceuta, and if the body was found on the high seas and taken into Gib, whose job is it to act? The Ceuta police have already been asked to do so, and the Gib police have arranged the inquest and so on, and now here's London putting a finger in the pie."

"At your request, I understood, captain?" French smiled.

"Well, that's a fact in a way. But we could hardly help ourselves. Here was one of the members of our cruising party apparently murdered at one of our ports of call. For the sake of our trade we were bound to have it cleared up. I mean we couldn't hope to continue running these cruises unless we could offer our passengers a safe conduct."

"I follow."

"It's only business. Of course I don't mean that we've no feeling for the man himself and his friends. I'm simply showing why we felt it necessary to apply to Scotland Yard."

French nodded.

"And it wasn't so easy to get help either," the captain continued. "As you doubtless know, it wasn't a question of asking for it and getting it. Oh no, we couldn't do that. We had to approach the Gib police – very tenderly, I may say – and get them to apply for it, on the grounds that enquiries would have to be made aboard this ship and that they had no opportunity of making them. A ticklish business, working with police," and the captain shook his head disparagingly, though a twinkle showed in his eye.

French laughed. "Well, you couldn't expect us to be at the beck and call of any Tom, Dick or Harry that chose to ring us up, could you?"

"I don't know," Goode returned. "I thought it was Tom, Dick and Harry that paid for the whole outfit. If so, they ought to have a say in the tune."

"Not they! They don't pay enough for that: just the very least they can get off with. And we're very good with the three gentlemen. In spite of being grossly underpaid, I've turned up."

"So you have, and I suppose we'd better quit talking like a pair of fools and get to business. How much do you know about the affair?"

"So little that I think I had better say, 'Nothing'. Perhaps you'd tell me the story from the beginning."

"I'll do so, as far as I know it. Have you seen the messages?"

"Only those from Gib, and they only asked for help. Also I've seen letters from your owners and the cruise agents, but there was little information in either."

"Then I'd better tell you all I know. Got all you want? There are cigarettes in the box."

"Thanks, I'm all right."

Goode settled himself more comfortably on his settee and began to speak.

– 16 –

THE NARRATION OF GOODE

"On Saturday last," said Goode, "we put into Ceuta in the morning and lay there all day. There was an optional excursion by road to Tetuan, and most of our passengers took it. They got back about five. We were not due out till midnight, and after dinner some of the passengers decided to go ashore again and see something of Ceuta. We had about a hundred and fifty aboard, and of these some fifty went ashore.

"Among them were Mant Carrington and some members of his party. Those of the party who went were" – Captain Goode swung round to his desk, picked up a paper and glanced at it – "Jim Musgrave and Mr and Mrs Dugdale. Old Mr Carrington, Miss Shirley, and Dr Jellicoe remained on the ship. Mr and Mrs Dugdale didn't stay very long ashore: Mrs Dugdale about an hour, and Dugdale about an hour and a half. Jim Musgrave was late: it was nearly midnight when he came aboard. Mant Carrington didn't turn up at all."

"Did he go ashore with anyone or alone?"

"Alone. He had intended to take a short stroll with Mr William Carrington, but at the last minute old Carrington felt unwell and remained aboard. Mant, therefore, had to go alone, as the others had all by that time left the ship."

"There's no doubt he went, I suppose?"

"None. We have a check by means of numbered cards. These take the place of passports, and no one can go ashore or come aboard without showing their cards. Mant Carrington showed his going ashore. Besides, the man on the gangway recognised him."

"I follow."

With equal brevity Captain Goode described the steps taken on board, his enquiries from the members of the party, William's offer of a reward, and the reporting of the affair to the police, and handed over the wire from Gibraltar telling of the discovery and identification of Mant's body.

How seldom, French thought, did he listen to a statement of this kind, giving the facts directly and concisely, and nothing but the facts. With some witnesses it might have taken an hour or more to obtain so much information, and even then it would have been hazy and inaccurate.

"The Gib police," went on Goode, "had had the remains medically examined, and as a result they had come to the conclusion that the death was due to foul play. The wireless message was not particularly illuminating, but it said that the body had been terribly injured. In the first place the back of the skull was fractured, and this the doctor said was the cause of death. But in addition some frightful blow had been struck on the left leg, for it was torn or cut off between the knee and the ankle. And round the other ankle was tied a piece of rope, so tightly that it had almost cut down to the bone. These injuries obviously could not have been self-inflicted, and as accident could not have knotted the rope round the ankle, there seemed nothing for it but murder."

Captain Goode paused, glancing at French as if to see how he was taking the story.

"A very interesting case, Captain," French declared, feeling appreciation was due. "I've never heard anything like it before. What did you do?"

"Well, there wasn't very much we could do. I discussed the situation with Artt and Mortimer, that's the second cruise manager, and we all agreed that matters could not be left as they were. Eventually we decided to suggest to our respective employers that Scotland Yard should be called in. As a result, a high official of that honoured institution is now being worried with the tale."

"Much to his secret satisfaction. Olympic cruises don't come to us every day at the Yard."

"You may thank your stars for that," Goode said with a crooked smile. "That, I think" – he slowly turned over the papers on his desk – "is all I have to say. Perhaps you would now tell me what happened in London. By the way" – he passed over a sheaf of papers – "here are the messages which passed, in case you'd like to look them over."

French took the bundle. He did not suppose they would be helpful, but he would have to read them.

"Nothing very interesting happened in London," he answered. "Your owners and the cruise agents sent representatives to the Yard and saw the AC, and the Gib police cabled. Their combined efforts persuaded him to send someone along. He sent me. I had to go first to Birmingham to get details about the poisoning affair, in case it should prove that there was a connection between them."

"Ah," said Goode, "I wondered about that. Do you think there is?"

"I don't know enough to say," French admitted. "Speaking without thought, it doesn't seem from what you tell me that there could be."

"Just my conclusion. And yet it's suggestive. I wonder if some time you'd tell me what really did happen about that poisoning? Not, of course, that I've any right to ask. It's just curiosity."

"I'll tell you all I know with pleasure," French returned. "Glad, in fact, to be able to talk to someone about it. It occurred at a family gathering"; and he repeated Kirby's statement, though omitting the inspector's suggestion that Jim Musgrave and the Dugdales had a motive for Mant's death. Goode appeared much interested and made such shrewd observations that French decided to take him fully into his confidence in the Ceuta affair, if only for the sharpening of his own wits.

"Now," said Goode, when their talk seemed to be drawing to a close, "is there anything I can do to help? As you know, we lie all tomorrow at Ajaccio: that is Thursday. Friday we're at sea, then on Saturday we get to Malta and on Monday to Piraeus. From Malta, if you want to, you can get back to Gib and Ceuta. Or if you like you can wireless Gib and Ceuta to have further details sent to one of these places. Just think it over, will you, and if there's anything you'd like, let me know." He got up to indicate the close of the interview.

French had been a couple of hours with the captain and when he reached his cabin he found the pleasant man asleep. He undressed quietly and got into bed. But he couldn't sleep. In spite of his last two disturbed nights, he had never felt more wakeful in his life. Something potent about the captain's coffee perhaps, or was it the novelty of his surroundings? *Patricia* was very steady and very silent. There was no vibration and scarcely a sound other than the deep soft murmur from the engine room. French could not have told whether or not the main engines were going: a dynamo, he thought, would produce all the sound he was hearing. And the sea was evidently very calm. The ship was neither pitching nor rolling. Only sometimes she seemed to edge gently a little to one side or the other.

It was inevitable that after a few minutes of sampling his sensations his thoughts should return to his case. Certainly it was a strange story that the captain had told him. Incomplete also. He wondered, for instance, whether Mant Carrington had had money in his pocket when leaving the ship, and if so, whether it was still there when the body was found. Also whether the Ceuta police were searching for the boat which presumably had been used to get the body out into the Straits.

One thing, however, was clear. He must get more information for himself. On no point had he sufficient to enable him to come to a conclusion; not even on such a major matter as the cause of that terrible injury to Mant's leg. He needed details. What was the best way of getting them? He began to regret not having gone direct to Gibraltar.

Then he saw that had he done so he would have had it in his mind that his real investigation lay on board: into the actions of Jim Musgrave and the two Dugdales. As it was, he could ask for a more comprehensive report from Gib. It could be sent to Malta to await his arrival.

Silently he got up, and by the light of his torch wrote a message to the chief of police at Gib. Then he let himself out of his cabin and went back to the bridge. Yes, the officer in charge would certainly get it wirelessed at once.

French lingered for a moment looking out over the canvas dodger into the darkness ahead. It was a clear night with bright stars and rather cold. The sound of rushing waters was in the air and patches of foam showed ghostly on the black sea at each side of the ship. There was nothing in sight save, before the beam on the port side, a white and a red light: some vessel passing back towards Marseilles.

Next morning a reply to French's message was brought to his cabin. The Gibraltar authorities would send all known details to Malta. Luckily a RAF plane was going the next morning, and they had arranged with the officer in charge for the pilot to carry the parcel. It would therefore be waiting for French on his arrival.

This was satisfactory, and French decided to begin as soon as possible the first stage of his investigation: the interrogation of the members of the party as to their doings in Ceuta.

When he went on deck he found they were lying in the Bay of Ajaccio, a mile or two from the shore. Opposite was the town, looking attractive with its white buildings buried in the green of its trees. Behind rose hills, ascending into a more distant range of low mountains. French felt that if at all possible he must go ashore and see it all.

The chief excursion was, he learnt, a drive along the coast towards Calvi, and as there were not sufficient vehicles available to take the whole party of some three hundred and fifty at once, this was being run twice, in the morning and afternoon respectively. If he could find out whether the Carringtons were going with the first or second party, he could do the same, and when they were resting aboard would be a good time for his interrogation.

Accordingly he waylaid Jellicoe and introduced himself. "I don't want to interfere with your shore excursions," he explained, "but as soon as conveniently possible I want to get statements from each of you. I thought perhaps if you were taking the drive this morning, we could have the afternoon, or vice versa."

"That's quite easily arranged, chief inspector," Jellicoe returned. "We're going on the drive this morning, and we think we can see all we want of the town on returning and before we come aboard for lunch. We intended in any case to remain on board all the afternoon, so we would be at your service then."

This suited French exactly. He also obtained a voucher for the morning drive, and after it he had a quick walk round to see Napoleon's house, his relics at the Hôtel de Ville, and some of the other sights of the town. There was a frequent service of boats, and he reached the ship with the Carrington party, but little late for the second lunch.

After the meal he asked Jellicoe to join him on the deserted forward well-deck. There, lolling in deckchairs and with cigarettes drawing, he began to ask his questions.

He was very thorough in his examination, not only about the events which had taken place on board, but also on those connected with the poisoning affair. Jellicoe appeared anxious to tell what he could, but practically all he said had already been mentioned by Kirby or the captain. One point French hadn't heard was how they had come to take the cruise. "I had been urging on them all to go away for a proper change," Jellicoe continued, "and I had obtained an agreement in principle, as they say in international affairs. Then Messrs Cunn sent an advertisement of this cruise to old Mr Carrington. I happened to see it in his hand and seized on it. 'That's what you should do,' I said. 'All of you go on that cruise. It's just what you want to put you right.' I could see that Mr Carrington was impressed, and presently I found the reason. He had taken the first of the pair, from Glasgow to Marseilles, on the previous year, as it had seemed the easiest way to make business calls at Cadiz and Malaga. This had fired him with an enthusiasm to do the rest, and now seemed an opportunity. At last he agreed, and he invited the others as his guests. He's very well off, of course. Then very kindly he extended his invitation to me, ostensibly that I should go as his doctor, really I think because at this time I had become engaged to Miss Shirley. I don't mind saying I couldn't have afforded it otherwise."

With regard to the Saturday evening in Ceuta, Jellicoe explained that after dinner he had gone to the smoke room with Katherine. Some forty or fifty minutes later William's steward had turned up to say that William was ill and would Jellicoe go down? "I went to his cabin at once and gave him some medicine. He had had an attack of some kind of food poisoning two or three days before, and I had wanted him to stay on board instead of taking the Tetuan excursion. However he would go. He was not very well during the day and sat in the hotel in Tetuan instead of walking round. Then he had been better, but dinner had brought back his symptoms, as often happens. He's very fond of a plunge in the swimming bath, and later I found out that he had had one on his return from Tetuan, and he may have got a chill. At all events he was very sick while I was with him, then he settled down. But I had to keep him in bed most of the next day."

"Can you put times on to all that?" French asked. "What time was dinner, to start with?"

"Since the extra people came aboard at Marseilles, meals, as you know, have been doubled: we dined at the second dinner at eight o'clock. We finished, I suppose, about quarter to nine and went then to the smoke room. Perhaps it was half past nine or twenty to ten when old Mr Carrington's steward came. I was with the old gentleman for, say, another fifteen or twenty minutes. I can't tell you exactly, but I should think I returned to Miss Shirley about ten."

"That's good enough, thank you. Was Miss Shirley still in the smoke room?"

"Yes, she was reading."

"She hadn't gone ashore?"

"No."

"And then, Dr Jellicoe?"

"That was really all that happened, until of course the alarm was raised about Mant Carrington. We went to bed shortly, Miss Shirley a few minutes past ten, and I a little later, after a smoke on deck. Most people go early on these cruises. I was asleep indeed when the steward came to say the captain would like to see me."

After hearing about Captain Goode's enquiry and the visit to the Ceuta police, French turned to another point.

"As you can understand, doctor, a man with a job like mine is anxious to know all he can about his witnesses. I wonder if you'd describe the members of the family from a medical and perhaps psychological point of view?"

Jellicoe smiled. "You're not asking much," he declared. "If I did that I could only give you opinion. That wouldn't be much use to you."

"It would be great use," French insisted. "You've already told me something about old Mr Carrington's health. Can you do the same for the rest, particularly Mr Mant?"

With some difficulty French obtained the doctor's views. It was of neither old William's nor Mant's health that he wanted to hear, but to get a sidelight on the dispositions of Jim Musgrave and the two Dugdales. Probably the information would be quite useless, but some illuminating fact might come out.

But none did. According to Jellicoe all the members of the party were normal, a quite good lot of people who in any circumstances which might present themselves could be counted on to act in an ordinary and decent way.

French took to the doctor personally. He thought him capable and kindly, and on every point but one he was satisfied he had been straight. But that one point left French vaguely disquieted. All through the interview Jellicoe had seemed uneasy. And when it was over he was obviously relieved. Did the man after all know more than he had told? Was he afraid of French finding out something which up to now had been kept secret?

Could it be about Mant's death? Instead of smoking on deck after Katherine Shirley went to bed, had he gone ashore? Had he met Mant there? French did not believe, from his apparent personality, that Jellicoe had murdered Mant, but he might know something about the murder. If he did, there might be a strong reason for his keeping it secret. If Jim Musgrave or the Dugdales were involved, they were relatives of Miss Shirley, members indeed of his own future family. The point was one which could by no means be overlooked.

Proof of Jellicoe's innocence of the murder, should at least be easily obtainable. It was only necessary to find out from the purser's staff whether he had gone ashore that night – owing to the disappearance all records had been kept. But to find out whether he had well founded suspicions would be a more difficult matter.

With Katherine, whom he interrogated next, French received a precisely similar impression. Undoubtedly she also was uneasy. In her case it was even more suggestive of knowing or suspecting something which she was afraid he might learn. He tried all his arts to trap her – but without success. All the same he remained dissatisfied.

Katherine had nothing to tell him that he had not already known. She corroborated Jellicoe's statement of how she spent the evening in Ceuta. She had, it was quite obvious, been in touch with people all the time from dinner on. In the smoke room she was with not only Jellicoe, but other passengers, and she went straight from the smoke room to bed, where Mrs Ingram, her cabin mate, had already arrived. French had never suspected Katherine of the murder, but here at all events was proof that she was innocent. From this did it not look as if her uneasiness, supposing it to be connected with the murder, was due to the suspicion rather than knowledge? French thought so.

Old William Carrington was French's next witness. He had little to say except to confirm Jellicoe's account of his indisposition. But he was the last to see Mant alive and for that reason French was more detailed in his enquiries than he would otherwise have been.

William repeated what he had already told Captain Goode about his arrangement with Mant to go ashore for a short walk. Neither was very strong and neither wanted to make an evening of it. They were to meet at William's cabin some ten minutes after dinner. Mant had turned up, but by then William was feeling ill again; the same complaint that he had had earlier, brought back, he believed, by eating a dinner for which he was not fit. He had hoped to recover, and Mant had sat with him in the cabin for perhaps fifteen minutes. Then he had felt he could not face going ashore, and Mant had gone on alone. He had apologised to Mant for keeping him back, and Mant had been very nice about it and had said it was of no consequence whatever.

During their conversation Mant's manner had been perfectly normal. He had been in his usual spirits, neither high nor low. He had not said nor done anything which suggested he had a premonition of his fate, and had definitely stated he would not stay more than half an hour ashore.

This seemed to be all that French could get. He thanked William and asked him if he would send on one of the others.

Presently Eva Dugdale came along. French up till then had only seen her at a distance, and he was very much impressed with her appearance. He felt that in her looks alone there might well be motive for murder. If Mant really were making her life a burden to her, and if Dugdale got to know of it, a jealous hatred would almost certainly spring up which might lead to anything. And Eva herself? French thought that in spite of her beauty she looked a trifle ruthless. More than ever he felt he must satisfy himself as to the movements of husband and wife during the critical period.

He opened politely. "I'm sorry for giving you this trouble, Mrs Dugdale, but as you know, I have been sent from London to investigate the death of Mr Mant Carrington, and I have to ask all of you for your help."

"Of course, chief inspector," she answered in the same key; "we all understand that and are only too ready to give it. We all want this dreadful affair cleared up. But I'm afraid I've nothing to tell you that can help."

"Well, I can't expect you to do more than your best, can I?" he agreed. "And now first of all, can you give me any suggestion or theory which might help to explain Mr Mant's fate?"

She couldn't. She was completely puzzled by the whole affair. Just as much puzzled as horrified.

"Then we'd better begin at the beginning and follow the events through. When did you last see Mr Mant alive?"

She proved a good witness. She answered his questions readily. But she did not tell him much.

She had, she said, seen Mant last at dinner: they sat at the same table. After dinner she had gone to her cabin to put on a wrap. She had been ten or fifteen minutes getting ready. Then her husband had come in for his hat and coat, and they had gone ashore. They had intended to go with some people named Glasgow, but after looking round they had not seen these people, and so had gone together. So far as she knew, none of the other passengers had seen them going.

They had walked into the town, and for perhaps half an hour had strolled about. It was not, she thought, extremely interesting. Presently they came to a café and her husband suggested a drink. They went in and found the Glasgows there. They had some drinks, some local wine which she hadn't cared for. She soon grew tired and suggested returning to the ship. The Glasgows agreed at once, but her husband thought he would like a little further walk. They accordingly separated and she returned with the Glasgows while he went on alone.

"That's all very clear," French declared. "Now if you could put approximate times on it, I think I need trouble you no more."

She didn't think she could give any times; however, by dint of questioning, French obtained a reply. She thought she and her husband had gone ashore about nine. They had strolled about, say, till half past. They had been in the café for perhaps a quarter of an hour, and it had taken them another quarter to walk back. That would mean that she and the Glasgows had reached the ship about ten, which she remembered was correct.

French considered asking her about Kirby's story of Mant's unwelcome attentions, then he thought it would be better to keep this information to himself. If Mrs Dugdale were telling the truth, she was not guilty of Mant's death, and it would be time enough to bring the other matter forward if and when doubt were cast on her statement. He therefore contented himself with thanking her for her help and asking her to request her husband to come and speak to him.

French didn't particularly take to Luke Dugdale. He seemed conceited and self-opinionated, and his manner was patronising when not overbearing. But French could not complain about the replies he received to his questions. Luke also answered readily everything he was asked, and if he were telling the truth, he also was innocent.

He confirmed his wife's statement on all points up to where he had parted company with her and the Glasgows. He had then, he said, gone for a smart walk along the shore in the direction of Tangier. But it had not proved interesting and after about a mile he had turned and gone back to the ship. He had reached it at about half past ten and had gone at once to his cabin. His wife was already in bed. He had not seen Mant ashore, and knew nothing of what had happened to him.

It remained only to take a statement from Jim Musgrave and then this first item on French's list would be complete.

French had not spoken to Jim before, and he was agreeably surprised by his pleasant manner. Jim, he imagined, was the sort of man who might get drunk or fly into a rage about very little, but he did not seem to be the type who would harbour a continuous grudge.

Jim also made no difficulty about answering his questions. He also had last seen Mant at dinner, and he also had gone ashore for the evening. He had left the ship some five or ten minutes after dinner with some people called

Tremaine – a brother and two sisters. They had strolled about for a while, looking for a native café to sample the drinks and if possible see some dancing. They had found such a café and for half an hour had sat watching. Then they thought they had had enough. They left and the Tremaines said they were tired and would go back to the ship. Jim had walked with them part of the way, but he had felt that he didn't want to go to bed so soon and he had left them. He had strolled about alone for a time, then he had found himself back at the café and had gone in again. Unfortunately he had drunk rather too much of the native spirit, or it was more potent than he had expected, and he had got slightly fuddled. As a matter of fact it was more by good luck than by good guidance that he had remembered the hour the ship sailed and got on board in time. On reaching the ship, shortly before twelve, he had stayed on deck to walk off the effects of the spirits, and it was for this reason that he was still in evening dress when the captain called the conference shortly after twelve.

This brought Jim's statement to an end. French indeed now believed he knew all that he was likely to learn from the sextet. If any of them were keeping back information, they would continue to do so. Unfortunately, their stories were not very illuminating. However, their interrogation was only the first of the many enquiries he saw stretching out before him. He could scarcely expect to succeed at this early stage of the investigation. As he had told himself on more than one previous occasion, patience was the detective's greatest virtue.

– 17 –

THE RUMINATION OF FRENCH

When Jim left him, French sat on in his chair on the forward well-deck, considering the statements he had heard and trying to assess their various values. But unhappily the more he did so, the more he saw that they left him pretty much where he had been before they were made.

Assuming for the moment they were all true – and he did not doubt them: in any case a few enquiries would quickly settle the point – it was obvious that Dr Jellicoe, Katherine Shirley, and old William Carrington were innocent. He had never suspected either of the last, though he had wondered if the doctor knew more than had come out. However, now he was sure. Quite definitely, not one of the three had left the ship. Mant had gone ashore, alive and well – though this was a matter he had still to confirm. But almost certainly he had gone, and if so, the fact completely cleared these three.

It was quite otherwise with the second trio, Jim Musgrave and the Dugdales, the three whom Kirby had suspected in the poisoning affair. So far as French had learnt up to the present, any one of those three might be guilty.

He considered them in turn. Eva Dugdale had said that from about nine to ten she and her husband were on shore together but otherwise alone. Suppose they had waited for

Mant on the mole: from all accounts it was deserted at the hour in question. Suppose, while Eva attracted his attention, Luke had got behind him and killed him by a blow on the head. Suppose a boat had been tied up somewhere to the wharf. What would have been easier in the dark than for them to have "borrowed" it and rowed outside the harbour? Once thrown into the water there the body would be carried east by the current, doubtless to the point at which it had been found. There would have been plenty of time for the guilty pair to row ashore again, replace the boat, and for Eva to be back on board again when she had said. Yes, it was undoubtedly a possibility.

But Luke Dugdale had admitted being ashore alone during the additional half-hour between ten and ten thirty. Suppose after the murder the body had been hidden behind something on the deserted wharf or dropped into the sea attached by a cord to a bollard. Suppose the boat were not available close by and had to be brought from a distance. This half-hour might have given Luke the necessary time to borrow and return it, and he might have disposed of the body alone. This was a second possibility.

A third was that Mant might somehow have been delayed ashore, and might have been murdered by Luke alone in that half-hour after Eva had returned to the ship.

Then there was the question of Jim Musgrave. Jim had admitted being alone during part of the time he was ashore. He had parted from the Tremaines about ten or a little earlier, and had not returned to the ship till nearly twelve. Almost two hours were unaccounted for. Of course, enquiries at the café might confirm his statement that he was there, but from the information French had so far received, Jim could well be guilty.

One point, however, tended to incriminate the two Dugdales rather than Luke alone or Jim. This was the probable hour of the murder. If Mant had gone ashore for a short time only, it looked as if he must have been killed almost immediately after leaving the ship. If so, only the Dugdales could have done it. Jim was in the company of the Tremaines until after the hour at which Mant had intended to be back on board.

French was pleased with his theory of the Dugdales' guilt. At worst it was possible, at best likely. It was the first constructive explanation of the facts which had been reached, and so far as he could see, it was the only one possible.

Then a difficulty occurred to him. If the Dugdales had known Mant was going ashore, they must have learnt at the same time that William intended to accompany him. In this case the murder would have been impossible, and it was therefore inconceivable that arrangements should have been made to attempt it. It was William's unexpected illness which rendered it feasible. But as the Dugdales couldn't have foreseen the illness, they would not have prepared for the crime. And it was impossible to believe that so skilful a murder had not been thought out beforehand.

But stay! Was it so utterly impossible that the Dugdales had foreseen the illness? Suppose they had brought it about? Suppose as soon as they had heard of his arrangement to go ashore with Mant, they had dosed the old man? They sat at the same table, and one of them could undoubtedly have slipped a little powder on to his food, while the other attracted the attention of the rest of the party. The doctor's keen eye, moreover, was not upon them. He and Katherine Shirley were at another table.

French pondered over this. The idea didn't seem very likely, but he supposed it was possible. At all events it was one which he must consider further.

But here he was once more, theorising before he knew his facts. This would never do. He took out his notebook and looked up the next item on his list. "Check that Mant C. went ashore."

Yes, that was an important point. Getting up from his chair, he went along the deck to the main staircase and down to the embarkation room at the top of the ladder.

From his experience going ashore that morning, French had learnt at first hand the numbered card system by which it was known at any given moment which passengers were aboard the ship and which were not. He, like all the others, had been given a card bearing a number, and he had had to show this card – not merely mention the number – but show the card on going down and coming up the ladder. Two officers on the purser's staff were in charge of the check. One saw the cards and reported the numbers to the other. The second, seated at a desk, was provided with a sheet bearing all the numbers in sequence, and as each was called out, he marked it off on the sheet. The sheet therefore showed at any time who was on or off the boat.

Obviously this was a perfect check, if only it were adequately carried out. But was it? That was what he had now to find out.

As he reached the hall some passengers were coming aboard. He stood and watched what was done. The officer on the ladder, he noticed, saw all the cards for himself. As each passed he called out its number to his colleague. The latter marked it off on his sheet, repeating the number. It was done with great care, and French felt he might depend absolutely on the result.

When the passengers had passed he got into conversation with the officers. They had been, they told him, on duty after dinner on the Saturday night in question. All the passengers had come aboard for dinner, but as several wanted to go ashore after dinner, they had taken a new sheet and made a fresh check. They showed French this sheet, and he saw the mark indicating Mant had gone ashore, and the absence of the further mark which would have shown he had returned to the ship.

The officer on the gangway further remembered Mant. He remembered him because first, he was the only passenger to go ashore alone, and second, because he went later than the others. He knew Mant's appearance, having seen him once or twice before. When Mant failed to turn up at the time of departure, the officers had reported the circumstance, and they understood a search of the ship had been made before the relatives were informed.

All this evidence seemed to French quite convincing. He had not doubted that Mant had left the ship as the captain had said, but now the matter had been put beyond question.

French next went in search of Mant's cabin steward. It was unlikely this man would have anything to tell him, still he might reveal something which might help.

But here once again he was disappointed. Andrew M'Leod proved a smart young man who seemed to know his job and who answered French's questions promptly, but he had nothing to tell which very much advanced French's knowledge.

It appeared that the cabins of five of the party – Mant, William, Jim, Eva, and Luke – were close together. All were outside cabins, close to the stern on the starboard side of B Deck. Leading off the second transverse passage from the stern were cabins 217 and 209, occupied by William and by Mant and Jim respectively. The doors of these cabins faced one another, and William's was a single berth and the other a two-berth. The adjoining outside cabin, No. 203, was also a two-berth one and was occupied by Luke and Eva. It was reached from the next transverse alleyway. Katherine and Jellicoe, French learnt later, occupied the halves of two two-berth cabins on the port and starboard sides of A Deck respectively.

M'Leod, it was evident to French, thought well of the five members of the party he had attended. He said all were pleasant spoken and gave no unnecessary trouble. Old Mr William, of course, gave more than the others, but that was because he had been ill and he couldn't help it. Mr Jim was a very pleasant gentleman: he liked Mr Jim. Mr Mant was "all right" also, but it was clear that about him the steward was less enthusiastic. He appeared to be also benevolently disposed towards Luke Dugdale, and was obviously overwhelmed with admiration for Eva.

About the evening of the disappearance M'Leod had little to say. He had laid out the clothes and brought the hot water before dinner as usual, and while the party were at dinner he had cleared up the cabins and left them all ready for the night. In the normal course he would not have had to visit them again that night, but Mr William had rung for him shortly after half past nine. He had gone to the cabin to find Mr William in bed and the old gentleman had told him he was not well, and had asked him to fetch Dr Jellicoe. He had done so. Later, Mr William had been sick, and he had done what was necessary. The doctor had told him to watch out in case Mr William rang for him again, but he had not been required. He had seen nothing which threw any light on what had occurred, nor had he found anything unusual in the cabin.

Owing to the evening turning cold, M'Leod had closed the portholes of the cabins in his charge. He had finished up about eleven, but about twelve he was called up by the cruise manager and asked to find out if Mr Mant was in his cabin. Later, he was sent to call Mr William and Mr and Mrs Dugdale to a meeting in the drawing room. Mr Jim was not in his cabin at the time. Mr Mant was wearing a soft black hat and a thin black overcoat when he disappeared.

French's next business was in the dining-saloon, and there he found the waiter who attended the party, or rather the same five members, for Katherine and Jellicoe sat together in another part of the room. The five sat at a six-seat table, one seat remaining vacant. It was a narrow table with three seats along each side, and William and Mant faced each other in the middle seats. At the end next the door Eva sat opposite to Jim, Eva beside William, and Jim beside Mant. Luke occupied the seat on the other side of William.

French was a good deal interested in the seating. The arrangement was natural enough, but it happened to lend itself to what he had had in mind. William on the door side of Luke, who sat alone at that end of the table. If Eva had suddenly called attention to someone entering or leaving the saloon, all would have turned in that direction, and nothing would have been easier than for Luke, in following suit, to have slipped some powder over William's food. Nor, as it happened, was it likely that anyone could have seen Luke do such a thing, as in front of him was the side of a staircase and not another table.

It seemed scarcely likely to French that such doping had been done, and yet it was possible and must therefore be kept in view. He wondered whether Jellicoe had noticed anything suspicious, and decided to ask him. It was impossible to do so at the moment, as the first bugle had gone and people were already dressing for dinner. All French did, therefore, before knocking off was to put a notice on the board asking anyone who had seen Mant after dinner on the night of his disappearance kindly to inform the purser.

Next day *Patricia* was at sea, running between Ajaccio and Malta. When French went on deck he found the morning was fine, with a bright though rather thin sunshine pouring down from a sky of the lightest and clearest blue. A gentle breeze blew from the south, slightly rippling the sea. Except for this there was a flat calm and *Patricia* floated absolutely steadily, even her forward movement imperceptible save when revealed by the passing water. Neither land nor other vessel was in sight: nothing but the sea bounded in every direction by the hard clear line of the horizon. French congratulated himself as he looked forward to a day of such ideal travel.

But business could not be entirely neglected. After breakfast he waylaid Jellicoe and inveigled him to the deserted forward well-deck.

"I wanted to ask you confidentially a little more about Mr William Carrington's illness on last Saturday evening," he began. "Would you tell me whether you were entirely satisfied about it?"

"I don't follow you, chief inspector," Jellicoe replied sharply. "How do you mean, 'satisfied'?"

"Was it quite natural?"

The doctor stared. "Natural? Still I don't know that I understand."

"Yes, you do, doctor," French returned good-humouredly. "Look here. If Mr William had gone ashore with Mr Mant, as was intended, the murder could not have been carried out. Was it therefore necessary to someone that Mr William should stay on board? Now you see?"

That this was a new idea to Jellicoe seemed clear to French. For a moment the man continued staring, then his expression grew uneasy and he said, "That never occurred to me, but I do see what you mean. A very disquieting suggestion, I'm sure. And you really think that someone – well, doped him?"

"I have considered the possibility," French admitted, "but I have come to no conclusion. I wondered could you help me?"

"I help you?" He shrugged. "No, I know nothing about it."

"It would be a help to me to know whether you thought Mr William's illness that night quite natural."

Jellicoe hesitated, while his uneasiness grew more pronounced. "Rather a nasty question," he said at last. "I admit, since you put it to me directly, that I was not entirely satisfied about it, though I never suspected what you suggest."

"You suspected something else?"

"No, I didn't. I supposed it must have been natural. Mr Carrington had been ill off and on for two or three days, but that evening after tea he seemed all right. Then after dinner this attack came on. I confess it surprised me. Not that he should be a bit knocked up after dinner: he ought to have had special food, and apparently just took what was on the menu. But I was surprised how ill he was. He was actually sick two or three times and very much upset. I admit I was unable to account for it."

"But if he had been given something to prevent him going ashore?"

Jellicoe was now evidently acutely distressed. He shook his head. "I can't tell you any more, chief inspector. I really cannot. I believe it possible that his upset may have resulted from his dinner and from nothing else."

"Though not very likely?"

The doctor shrugged and sat staring silently before him.

"It's too late to make any tests now, I suppose?" French went on.

Jellicoe roused himself. "Oh, yes," he agreed. "I can't do anything now."

French smiled suddenly. "Right, doctor; if you can't, you can't. Thank you very much. What you've told me has been a help."

It was clear to French that Jellicoe was more than suspicious. But he had no proof and therefore wouldn't commit himself. But French thought his suspicion supported his own theory powerfully enough to make its truth a practical certainty.

He was settling down to reconsider its bearing on the case as a whole when a steward came up, followed by one of the passengers, a tall man with a spiky nose whom he had seen several times, but never spoken to.

"The purser's compliments, sir," the steward said, "and he thought you would like to meet Mr Rodgers."

The newcomer nodded, as the steward discreetly vanished. "I've heard who you are, Mr French," he said. "I went to see the purser about the notice which was posted last night, and he told me. I had no idea the affair was looked on so seriously as all this."

"Won't you sit down, Mr Rodgers?" French got up and drew forward the chair Jellicoe had pushed back. "We don't know how serious the matter is, except that the possibility of murder cannot be excluded. And the murder of a passenger on a cruise must be cleared up. Both owners and cruise agents think it would be bad for business to leave it a mystery."

Rodgers nodded, his nose sawing the air like the jib of a cutter in a head sea. "And so it would," he agreed. "Perhaps I shouldn't ask, but have you – have you any idea of what – er – happened?"

French smiled. "None," he declared heartily. "Why, I've only just got on the job. Very nice of you to think we work miracles at the Yard, but I assure you we don't."

Again the cutter pitched. "Of course; of course. I was perhaps premature. Still – murder, you know."

"Quite," agreed French, and indicated that he would be interested to know in what way Mr Rodgers thought he could help him.

"Not at all, I'm afraid," the man answered, "but the notice asked anyone who had seen Mr Carrington after dinner on the evening of his disappearance to communicate with the purser. I had seen him and therefore I did so."

"Thank you," said French cheerily. "I wish everyone acted as you have. Now perhaps you'd tell me just what you saw."

"Nothing of any importance unfortunately. My daughter and I were going ashore after dinner, but she wasn't ready at once and I had to wait for her. You know what ladies are." He shrugged delicately and French indicated that he too…

"She had to throw a wrap round her shoulders," Rodgers went on, "and it took something like half an hour. When at last she was ready and we were walking to the ladder to go ashore, we met Mr Carrington, or rather when we turned into the alleyway from the main staircase he was just coming along the alleyway. I had spoken to him once before – just to say good morning. So I called 'Good evening. Are you going ashore?' just like that. He said, 'Yes, just for a short stroll.' 'So are we,' I said, and made as if to join him. He at once dropped in beside us and made some remark about a breath of air before bed being pleasant. I agreed. By this time we had reached the embarkation room, and my daughter went in. I stood aside to let Mr Carrington follow her, but he suddenly put his hand to his chest and said, 'By Jove, I've forgotten my landing card. So sorry. Don't wait,' he went on, 'I shall overtake you.' He gave a short nod and turned back the way he had come."

"And did he overtake you?" French asked.

"No, that was the last we saw of him."

"Which alleyway did he come along?"

"The one on the port side of B Deck. It's not really a passenger alleyway at all, though you can get to it from aft on B Deck. I expect you know it; just the steel plates painted a sort of dull brown and no carpets."

"I know it. The engineer's and purser's offices are off it."

"That's it."

"Then you were with Mr Carrington only for a few seconds? It's not many feet from the main staircase to the embarkation hall."

"Yes, that's all."

French felt that Rodgers was right in saying that his story would be of no use to him. He was about to thank him and bring the interview to a close, but he thought he recognised a certain hesitation in the man's manner, as if there was more to come.

"And what did you think of all that, Mr Rodgers?" he asked.

Still the other hesitated. "Well, you know," he said at last, "I thought, and my daughter agreed with me, that it was simply a polite shake off. As a matter of fact I happened to look at his chest when he put his hand up, and I distinctly saw the bulge of a pocketbook on the cloth."

"It mightn't have contained the landing card."

"Of course I realise that. But I thought it from his manner as well. And so did my daughter. She hadn't seen him put his hand up, and she spoke to me about it first."

The story, French thought, was suggestive, though unconvincing. Rodgers might easily have been mistaken about that bulge. And Mant might well have forgotten to transfer his card to his evening clothes. Or he might have had it in his pocket and simply not have wished for company on his stroll. There was probably nothing whatever in the affair.

Yet this was not certain. Did Mant really wish to be alone for some definite reason? And – a further idea – had he worked out a plan to ensure it, first, by arranging to go with William in order that he would thus be separated from the others, and secondly, by himself, giving William the dose to prevent him accompanying him?

Here was another possibility, and one which would have to be looked into pretty thoroughly. It was easy to suggest a motive. Had Mant arranged an interview with someone ashore? If so, that someone would have, if possible, to be found. French suddenly grew rigid. Could it have been Eva? Or if Mant were that sort of man, some other woman on board? Or again, some woman whom he had met during the excursion to Tetuan?

French lay back in his chair and gave free rein to his imagination. Suppose Mant had met some woman at Tetuan? Perhaps even a native: some of them were very attractive? Suppose he arranged a further meeting for the evening? Suppose the woman's husband or brother got to know? Suppose they laid a trap for Mant? Would that not account for the whole thing?

French thought it would. Whether it was very likely or not, he thought it was a possibility, and as such must be gone into. If he were right about a native woman, she would probably have been done in also. One matter for the Ceuta police to find out would be whether any woman had disappeared about the same time.

And if it had been Eva or some woman on board? Well, if it had, he would find it out himself. That was what he was here for.

He made it his business to ask each member of the party privately whether he or she knew anything of an appointment which Mant might have made ashore.

All denied such knowledge, Eva as convincingly as the rest. All the same French felt that with a woman you could never be quite sure. They were all, or most of them, born actresses.

During the remainder of that day several people sought French out and told him they had seen Mant in the A Deck saloon after dinner. He had dropped films into the photographer's box, and had talked to the New Zealander, Bradstreet. The photographer also came forward to say that he had found a roll of films belonging to Mant in his box. None of this testimony, of course, advanced the case in any way.

When he went to bed French remained puzzled and with a completely open mind as to what really had taken place.

– 18 –

THE SUGGESTION OF MACKINTOSH

French had something of a thrill next morning when he went on deck and found they were lying at anchor in the Grand Harbour at Valetta. Malta was a place he had always longed to see, and here at last his dream was being realised. Eagerly he walked round the deck, gazing first at one side and then at the other.

The harbour was much finer than he had anticipated, and the town was larger and had better buildings. It was indeed a splendid sheet of water that was fringed by the low quays with their rows of clean looking flat-roofed buildings, backed by the huge cliff-like walls of what seemed to be forts. There was a deal of shipping in the port, but what he admired most were the rowboats, which had their stem and stern posts carried up some three or four feet, the stem post higher and cut off at an angle, and the stern post square. They looked to him like embryo gondolas and were rowed by the oarsman standing and pushing forward. He had attended the lecture on Malta on the previous evening, and was now hoping against hope that he should have time to go ashore with the party to see at least the cathedral and some of the streets of steps, even if he could not manage the longer excursions.

The mail had just come aboard and he was presently handed a carefully sealed package. He retired to his cabin to open it.

The Gibraltar police, he soon saw, had done their job well. There were seemingly exhaustive reports, admirable photographs, as well as a short length of rope. He settled down to study the lot.

The first report was from Captain Holmes of the *Tyne Maiden*. He was proceeding from Alexandria to Gibraltar in ballast, and about 8.30 a.m. on the Sunday had noticed the body of a man in the sea. He was then some thirteen sea miles east-by-north of Europa Point. He had stopped and picked up the body, brought it into Gib, and handed it over to the harbour authorities. The left leg was missing from half way below the knee.

The next was a document headed "Preliminary Report" from Inspector Costello of the Gibraltar police to his superior officer. "At 10.45 a.m. on Sunday, 1st March," wrote the inspector, "as a result of a telephone call, I proceeded with Sergeant Gordon to the Harbour Office. I was there shown the body of a man which, I was informed, had just been landed from the tramp steamer *Tyne Maiden*." Here Costello gave particulars of the *Tyne Maiden* and of the finding of the body in the sea.

"The remains," the report went on, "were those of a well-built man of about thirty-five, six feet one inch in height, with strongly marked features, blue eyes, and light coloured hair. They were clothed in evening dress – a dinner jacket and black tie – covered with a thin black overcoat. There was no apparent injury to the body except to the legs. The left leg was missing from a little below the knee. It had been taken off as if by a sloping cut, which had also torn away the trouser leg. Round the right ankle was a fairly loose loop of rope, the knot of which had been drawn very tight, and the two ends torn off some nine inches from the knot. The loop seemed to have been at some time drawn tightly against the ankle, for it had cut into it on the outside almost to the bone. The rope was about one inch circumference, of fine and very good quality hemp. Photographs as follows: Exhibits 17, 18, and 19 – the body; Exhibits 20 and 21 – the end of the cut off leg; Exhibit 22 – the rope mark on right ankle.

"I may mention here that I had the remains examined by Dr Duncan, and he informed me that the cause of death was the back portion of the skull being fractured. The skin was not broken and the injury was not apparent to observation. Dr Duncan's report is attached hereto.

"On the left wrist of the body was a watch, which had stopped at nine thirty-one. I took this watch to Messrs Venables, watch-makers, Clokey Street, and Mr John Venables examined it and informed me that in his opinion it was stopped by immersion in water, and that it would have gone for perhaps five to ten minutes after immersion. This watch is Exhibit 7.

"The following articles were found in the pockets:

Coins amounting to 6/2d. English and 27 pesetas, and two 10/- Bank of England notes. Exhibit 8.

A bunch of seven small keys. Exhibit 9.

A pocket handkerchief. Exhibit 10.

A small penknife. Exhibit 11.

A pink cardboard ticket about 3 in. square with the following lettering: On the upper half a large 23. Below this the words 'This card must be produced at gangway for debarkation and embarkation at all ports.' Below that printed in large letters 'TSS *Patricia*.

Cruise No. 72,' and at the bottom 'Name' in print and 'Mr Mant Carrington' in writing. The writing was blurred by the water, but was decipherable. Exhibit 12. A small pocket-book in the breast pocket of coat. Exhibit 13.

"I was aware that the *Patricia* had called at Gibraltar on Friday, 28th February, two days previously. I proceeded to Messrs Jones & Jamieson, the agents, and was informed that the *Patricia* had spent the previous day, Saturday, at Ceuta. I accordingly communicated with the Ceuta police and was informed that the disappearance of a gentleman of this name had been reported to them on that evening. The description given them by the relatives made it clear, if there had been any doubt, that the deceased was Mr Carrington.

"A further report to follow in due course.

"Yours obediently,
"MATTHEW COSTELLO."

The report of Dr Duncan, police surgeon at Gibraltar, was also enclosed. Parts of it were rather technical, but French understood the essentials. It appeared that death was not due to drowning or to the injury to the leg, but to the fracturing of the skull by a blow on the back of the head, evidently by some soft though heavy weapon such as a sandbag or bar of metal wrapped in cloth. The skin was not broken and there appeared to have been no bleeding as a result of the blow. Otherwise there were no injuries except to the legs. The left leg had been severed after death, as if by a glancing blow of some heavy tool, such as a hatchet or chopper. The right ankle was cut from the drawing tight of the rope which was tied round it. This was not tied tightly round the ankle: the loop which it formed was quite loose and easy. But it had been pulled with great force towards the left, and while the skin was uninjured on the left or inside of the ankle, that on the right or outside was cut almost to the bone. The organs showed the deceased had been in good health, though some debility was apparent. The writer could not state with exactitude the hour of death, but it was likely to have occurred between eight o'clock and midnight on the previous evening.

The further report of Inspector Costello, if any had been made, was not enclosed, but there was a note to say that the inquest had been opened and adjourned for further enquiries to be made by the police.

The loop of rope had been cut from the ankle so as to leave the knot intact. French next examined it. The knot was an ordinary one such as a landsman would probably make. It was drawn extraordinarily tight, and two ends, each about nine inches long, came from it. These ends certainly did look as if they had been snapped from a sudden pull, and not cut or frayed.

There were here some very puzzling circumstances. As French sat considering them he felt the discoveries of Inspector Costello by no means helped to clear up the situation. He could imagine how the body might have got into the sea, but these injuries to the legs were harder to account for.

And what, he wondered, could have been the purpose of the rope? To tie the legs together? It seemed unlikely. Why should the murderer do such a thing? If Mant were dead, he could neither struggle nor escape. No, this would scarcely explain it.

But what about a weight? Could this rope have been used to attach a weight to the ankles, so that the body would sink? Ah, that was more likely. A weight would have been an obvious necessity in any such scheme. If the body were not weighted, it would float. The only sure way to prevent its being found would be to keep it at the bottom of the sea.

And the fact that it had floated was no argument against this conclusion. The rope had been torn apart and the weight had therefore dropped off.

French slowly filled and lit his pipe, his hands moving automatically as his mind grappled with his problem. Could the breaking of the rope and the injuries have resulted from the same cause? It must have taken enormous force to cut through the leg. What could that force have been?

Suddenly French remembered an extraordinary case which had occurred three or four years earlier in Australia, in which a shark had bitten off the arm of a man who was believed to have been murdered. Could he be investigating a somewhat similar event? Had this terrible injury been caused by a shark?

At once he felt that he had insufficient information to say. That sharks were to be found in the area in question he believed, but he had never heard of their being a menace, as was the case in more tropical waters. Sharks, he knew, came as far north as the coasts of Britain, but he wondered if these were not of some innocuous kind, as he had never heard of their causing fatalities. However Goode would put him wise there.

All the same, the more French thought over the idea, the more probable it seemed to grow. If a weight were tied to the ankles, the shark in biting the leg, would certainly have bitten the rope too. Sharks are tremendously powerful creatures, and a sudden swing away of its head might easily produce enough force to do all that had been done.

There was just one difficulty – or was it a difficulty? If the legs were tied together, would not one expect both to have been bitten off? For a moment French considered the point, then he saw that there was no evidence that they had been tied together. The weight might have been tied to the right ankle only. It was likely, he thought, that the average person would tie the weight to both ankles, but if the length of the rope were limited, he might tie it to one only. Here again a discussion with the captain might be useful.

Presently his thoughts switched over to a different part of his problem: what his own action should be. This really was rather baffling. After the despatch he had just received, it did not look as if anything would be gained by visiting Gibraltar. The real explanation would seem to lie at Ceuta. What had happened there between the time Mant Carrington went ashore about nine-fifteen and eight-thirty the next morning, when his body was found floating in the sea?

Here the evidence of the watch struck French. It had stopped at nine-thirty-one, and as it would have gone for from five to ten minutes after immersion, it suggested that Mant had met his death almost immediately after going ashore. French saw that this would work in extremely well with his earlier theory as to the guilt of the Dugdales.

Indeed the more he considered it, the more he found himself forced to the conclusion that only the guilt of the Dugdales would explain what had happened. If Mant had met with his death directly after going ashore, it must have been while he was walking along the mole. At this time Jim Musgrave was with a party, and therefore could not be guilty. That left only the Dugdales as possibles among the ship's complement. And he had already seen how easily those two could have committed the murder at that time, the body being rowed out to sea either then or later, when Dugdale was alone for another period.

Then a further consideration occurred to him. When he had first thought of this possibility he had seen that another explanation could be put forward. Suppose Mant, being the sort of man he was, had made an enemy on shore? The idea of the native woman and her jealous husband was perhaps far-fetched, but it had appeared a possibility. Now, however, he saw that this explanation must be ruled out. Since he had considered it he had learnt of the doping of old William. It was inconceivable that this doping should be unconnected with the murder, seeing that its purpose could only have been to prevent William from accompanying Mant ashore. But the doping could only have been done by someone who knew that the two were going ashore together. This not only ruled out the native woman theory, but once again pointed strongly to the Dugdales.

But if this train of argument were correct, the solution to the mystery lay, not at Ceuta, but on board. Should he, French, not therefore remain where he was? It was true, to do so would get him further away from the scene of the crime, but did this matter? On the other hand did he not know everything that was to be learnt on board? For not the first time by a great many, French was entirely at a loss as to his next step.

Finally he decided to carry out his earlier idea and have another discussion with Captain Goode. Perhaps with his knowledge of ships and boats in general, and of Ceuta Harbour in particular, the captain might see something that he, French, had missed.

He went on deck to investigate the chances of an interview. It was a gorgeous morning. The sun was shining bright and clear, and the air was balmy and warm, though not in the least too hot. Some passengers were just going down the ladder into a launch, bound for the shore, and French felt he would give a good deal to join them. However business must come first. He must settle before evening whether or not he was going on with the ship.

With a half sigh he turned forward. As he reached the lower bridge he met an officer coming down. Captain Goode, the officer thought, was disengaged. He would find out with pleasure.

"Tell him to come in," French heard in the captain's voice, as he waited at the door of his cabin.

"I'm sorry to trouble you," he began when the officer had vanished, "but I think you might be interested to see the reports I've just had from Gibraltar, and if you have time I should like to discuss one or two points with you."

"Delighted," said Goode. "I'm just back from the shore, and as I breakfasted early, I'm going to have a cup of coffee. You'll join me?"

French said he too would be delighted. Goode pressed his bell and they lit cigarettes and chatted about the trip till the steward brought the coffee. Then Goode took the papers and read them carefully through without speaking.

"I've something to add to all that," French continued, and he went on to explain the difficult matter of the doping of William, and the deduction which seemed to follow: that the murderer was on board.

"It's what you'd expect," Goode answered. "If the murderer's not on board, the crime must have been committed by someone ashore, probably natives, and I will say that's not very likely."

"Then we've got it fairly clear so far," French summarised. "Mant Carrington went ashore about nine-fifteen. His watch was found stopped at nine-thirty-one. It was stopped by falling into water, but it might have gone from five to ten minutes after immersion. Therefore the watch, and presumably Carrington, fell into the water at some time about nine-twenty or nine-twenty-five. That could only have been into the harbour, because there would not have been time for him to reach any other place. To get so powerful a man silently into the water, he must have been first rendered insensible. And there we get the blow on the back of the head. I think we're on fairly safe ground in assuming that that blow was delivered on the mole at Ceuta, not very far from this ship. Do you agree so far?"

"I think so," the captain admitted cautiously.

"Now from nine-twenty or thirty, when the body was dropped into the harbour, till eight-thirty the next morning, when it was picked up east of Europa Point, we have no idea what took place. I wondered, captain, with your special knowledge of the sea, whether you could put up any theory as to what might have been done?"

Goode smiled. "Not so easy as you might think," he declared. "What about the injury to the leg? How do you account for that?"

"I can't account for it, except that it must have been done during those eleven hours during which the body was in the sea. What do you think? Could it have been a shark?"

Goode shook his head. "It doesn't look like it to me. I've seen a man whose arm was bitten off by a shark just above the elbow, and it didn't look like that." He picked up the photographs again and examined them speculatively. "You see, there's no doubt the leg was cut in two by a glancing blow by some not very sharp instrument. A shark's bite would have taken it off comparatively square. And another point. If it had been a shark you would be able to trace teeth marks. There are none here."

"Then what could it have been?"

For a moment Goode did not reply. Then with some hesitation he answered. "Well, I think I could hazard a guess. But I'll tell you. We'll have Mackintosh up and put the thing to him. If the same idea strikes him, then it may be worth considering."

French was not keen on taking still another officer into his confidence, but he was too anxious for help to hesitate. "That would be fine, captain. By all means," he said warmly.

Goode picked up his telephone. "Mr Mackintosh there?" he asked. "Oh, it's you, Andy. Could you come up here a minute? The chief inspector's here and there's a point we want to put to you...Right, that'll do fine."

The chief engineer was tall and thin, with a lugubrious expression and a pessimistic outlook on life. But, as French soon found, he was a very good fellow, sound at his job, beloved by his men, and with a vein of dry humour which made him a pleasant companion. He entered in a depressed manner and sat down with a mournful little nod to French.

"What evil are you and the chief inspector hatching now?" he asked gloomily. "I'm telling you in advance I'm not going to be in it."

"You'll be in it up to the neck," Goode assured him. "Look here, Andy, here's a little problem for you." He picked up the photographs. "This is a body which has been picked up out of the sea. You will observe one of the legs is injured. How did that happen?"

"The Honourable Mr Mant Carrington, Esquire, I suppose? Yes, I obsairve an injury to one of the legs, as you say."

"Yes, but that's not an answer to my question."

"Do you not know yourself?"

"Well, I had an idea, but I wanted to see if you had it, too."

"Well, I have."

French chuckled. "Have pity on a wretched landsman," he begged. "What's the idea you've both got? The captain thinks it wasn't a shark."

"Shark? He knows well enough it was no shark."

"Well then, what?" Though French controlled himself and smiled amiably, he felt the canniness of a Scotsman could be infuriating. But at last Mackintosh gave a straight answer.

"I'm thinking there's only one thing would produce an injury of that kind, and that's the propeller of a ship. Ask the captain if that isna right."

"It's certainly what I thought," Goode agreed. "I don't see what else could possibly have done it."

A ship's propeller! This was a new idea to French. And, as he thought over it, a very disappointing one. In fact it got him no further at all. The body was floating in the sea, a ship passed, and the propeller struck the leg. No help there. However, he mustn't seem disappointed.

"Well, it's good to know that," he declared. "All the same I'm afraid it doesn't help us much."

The engineer continued staring at the photographs. "You think not?" he asked slowly after a dozen or more seconds had passed.

"I don't see how it does myself," French repeated. "But then I'm not an expert. If it gives you any light, I wish you'd pass it on."

Mackintosh cast an eye across the table. "Is that coffee you have in yon wee jug?" he asked, adding in response to nothing whatever, "I don't mind if I do, thank ye."

"I stand reproved," Goode said solemnly, as he rang for a clean cup and a fresh brew.

Mackintosh took up the piece of rope and examined it closely. "I wouldna say that it gives me any light exactly, but on the other hand I might say it was a wee bit suggestive."

"It suggests nothing to me," French declared. "I wish you'd tell me."

"Well, you need to conseeder the circumstances: the poseetion of propellers and the action of bodies in sea water. What did you think broke this wee piece of rope?"

"I supposed that whatever had cut off the leg, had snapped the rope."

"Oh, ye did, did you?" returned the chief as if surprised at French's brilliance. "I wouldna wonder but what you're right. What do you say, James?"

Captain Goode said he thought it pretty clear.

"And what," went on Mackintosh to French, "did you conceive was the purpose of the rope?"

"That's just one of the things which are puzzling me," French admitted. "At first I thought it was to tie the deceased's legs together, then I thought, if he was not drowned, but killed before he was put into the water, that would seem unnecessary."

The engineer nodded with a sort of melancholy satisfaction. "I hadna known that. It clears up the seetuation fine."

French felt more puzzled than ever. "I'm very sorry," he said with a rueful smile, "but still I don't see what's in your mind."

"Would it no occur to you the rope was to fix on a weight to sink the body?"

French made a little gesture. "No," he returned. "I thought of that of course, but when you said the injury had been done by a propeller, it seemed to make it impossible. If the body had been weighted, it would have sunk. How then could it have got up to near the surface to get in the way of a propeller?"

"Aye, that's right enough," the engineer agreed. "And there's another thing: the depth of the propeller below the surface. In all ships with normal loading the propeller is well covered."

"And what does that mean exactly?"

"It means that a body floating on the surface would more than likely escape the blades."

"Then – " This seemed to French more puzzling than ever. He tried to collect his wits. "This body, we assume, has been struck by a propeller. If the body were not weighted it would float on the surface and so escape injury. Therefore it was weighted and was not on the surface. But if it were weighted, it would sink to the bottom. And if it were on the bottom it couldn't have been struck by the propeller. It doesn't seem to me to make sense."

"Go on," the engineer encouraged, with a grin to Goode. "You're doing fine. Just one more step and you'll be through. That right, James?"

Captain Goode agreed. "Yes, I see what you're driving at, and I wouldn't wonder but you're right. Go on one step more in your chain of reasoning, chief inspector."

French felt rather like a boy at school, but he mastered his irritation. Why on earth couldn't these two say what was in their minds without all this circumlocution? Come, he adjured himself, he was not being very brilliant. He must do better so as to uphold the honour of the Ya –

"Suppose the weight tied on and consider what would happen," Mackintosh's voice broke in on his meditations.

Ah! That was an idea! Yes, why hadn't he thought of that? The body, weighted, was thrown into the sea. Very good. There on the surface it would be safe from propellers. But it would immediately begin to sink. On its way to the bottom it would pass the level of the blades. If the blades happened to be there at the correct moment it would be struck, the weight would be cut off, and it would then float.

"Ah," he exclaimed, "I see at last. The body would be thrown into the sea, and while sinking, would be hit by the propeller. This would cut the weight off, and it would therefore float. But – but – "

How, French was wondering, could the body have been thrown into the sea so close to a rotating propeller? A boat would have been swamped. And then suddenly he saw what the sailors must have in mind. To meet the conditions the body could only have reached the sea in one way. It must have been dropped overboard from the steamer whose propeller blade struck it.

"By Jove!" he said, and explained his idea. "Is that what you both meant?"

"Aye, but it was better for you to think it out for yourself. You'd likely give it greater weight so. Aye, and there's more than that you can say about it too."

French grinned. "I've had enough guessing," he protested. "Let's hear it."

"Well, it's this. It's no likely the ship was a small coaster, because it would be a fairly big propeller that would do an injury like yon. But if it was a ship of any size, the body would have been thrown over from pretty well aft. Else it would have sunk below propeller level before the propeller reached it."

Captain Goode nodded. "I thought so too," he declared. "You're getting on with your enquiry, chief inspector."

"I should say so. I'm extraordinarily grateful to you both."

French indeed was delighted. Not only had he obtained a theory of what had happened, but the line of enquiry which should give him his proof and finish his case had been revealed. It was evident that Dugdale had agreed with the sailors of some ship to carry the body out to sea and there throw it overboard. It would be necessary only to get a list of the ships which left Ceuta on that evening, and elimination should give him all he wanted. Enthusiastically he put his view to the others.

"A wireless to the harbour people in Ceuta should give me the information," he declared. "Or perhaps better to the police."

"That's right," Goode answered. "You should have an answer in a couple of hours, and meantime if you'll take my advice you'll go ashore and have a look at the town."

French mentally blessed the captain for giving him a clear conscience to do what he wished. He sent off his message and took the next launch to the landing stage.

He had missed the remainder of the party, but he spent an enjoyable couple of hours rambling through the streets of the old town. Then, in nice time for lunch, he returned to the ship.

A reply from the police at Ceuta was awaiting him. It read: "No vessel other than TSS *Patricia* left Ceuta between hours of nine on Saturday evening and nine on Sunday morning."

– 19 –

THE NAVIGATION OF GOODE

French stood motionless, gazing at the flimsy scrap of paper. For once he was genuinely surprised. He had pictured Luke Dugdale paying some low-type sailor to hide the body on his ship till, outside the harbour, he could tip it overboard. Dugdale might have been seen "borrowing" the boat he had intended to use. The boat might have belonged to the sailor's ship. Was it too much to suppose that under such circumstances liberal baksheesh might have purchased assistance?

All this, of course, was pure surmise. The idea had come into French's mind while he was outwardly investigating the streets and buildings of Valetta. He hadn't deliberately worked at his problem: simply he couldn't keep it out of his mind.

But now it appeared that this theory, if theory it could be called, was entirely false. No such sailor existed. There was no steamer to which he could have taken the body.

Because it was out of the question that any of the crew of such a ship as *Patricia* would do such a thing. Even if, incredibly, any member had been otherwise willing, he would never have taken the risk.

Yet if Mackintosh were correct, the body *had* been brought on board *Patricia* and thrown overboard after she had left the harbour.

It was confoundedly puzzling. Indeed, whether Mackintosh were right or wrong, it remained equally insoluble.

French found a solitary chair and sat down with a pipe to worry the thing out. First of all, suppose Mackintosh right and that the body had been brought on board *Patricia*: how could it have been done?

Not with the help of any member of the crew. That was so obvious that he need not spend time considering it. Nor could the Dugdales have managed it single-handed. In fact, no passenger or passengers could have done it. Technical or professional help would have been required.

But if neither crew nor passengers had done it, how could it have been done?

And there was a further difficulty. Suppose in some magical way this problem had been surmounted. Suppose the body had been smuggled aboard. Where could it have been hidden until the time for throwing it overboard arrived? Not in any of the public rooms. Not in any of the cabins, with passengers and stewards about all over the place. Not in supposedly dark or secret parts of the deck. There were none such. Not in any of the parts of the ship from which passengers were prohibited. This would require a wholesale technical assistance which could not have been forthcoming.

There was no place on a crowded ship where the body could have been hidden, free from the chance of discovery. Even if a cabin were available, there was no way of getting a body to it. No, the thing was impossible.

That reasoning of the chief engineer's had seemed unanswerable when French had heard it first. But it must have been unsound after all. The body simply could not have been taken out of harbour on *Patricia*. All that about the propeller was interesting, but there must be some other explanation of the injury.

But then if the body had not been taken by *Patricia*, how had it got to where it was found? Once again French thought of the rowing-boat. The only reason he had given up the rowing-boat idea was because of what Mackintosh had said about the propellers. The rowing-boat must be the solution.

And the injury? How, then, had it occurred?

French swore in exasperation. Once again, it was confoundedly puzzling.

He smoked for some time, then he thought it might be worth putting the difficulties of their theory up to Mackintosh and Goode. They would have either to meet them or admit the theory unsound.

He got up and climbed to the lower bridge. Once again his luck was in. Captain Goode was in his cabin and would see him.

"A scrap of paper to show you, captain," French began, placing the message from Ceuta on the desk.

Goode smiled. "I was thinking that was the answer you'd get," he answered. "That should be a help to you."

French stared. "I suppose it should," he admitted. "But how did you know?"

"I didn't know for sure. But since you were here I've been going into the position in which the body was found. I hadn't known that before."

"But I thought there was no question about that. If the body had been dropped into the sea outside Ceuta Harbour, it would have floated to the position in which it was found? Is that not so?"

For answer Goode stood up. "Come to the chartroom," he invited, leading the way up the half staircase, half ladder, which stretched up from a corner of the cabin. The room was deserted, and Goode searched through the drawers in the large flat cabinet and brought out a chart of the Straits of Gibraltar.

"Now," he said, "let's go into this a bit more thoroughly. And first as to the course of the *Tyne Maiden.*"

He took a pair of parallel rulers, and after scaling a short distance off Europa Point he laid them in the direction west-by-north.

"This is where she came along," he remarked, ruling a light pencil line. "Apart from the captain's report, this is the course she would take from Alexandria to Gib. Very well, he says he picked up the body thirteen sea miles from Europa Point. Let's scale that off. There," he continued when he had done so, "that's the position where the body was picked up." He made a dot and surrounded it by a tiny circle. French watched, enthralled.

"Now look here," went on Goode. He drew another line from Ceuta to Malaga.

French gazed in surprise. This second line crossed the other through the little circle. Goode watched him with a smile.

French felt baffled. He was certainly not showing up to advantage. This seemed more puzzling than ever. However, he needn't pretend to knowledge he had not got. Goode would see through that in a twinkling.

"I'm sorry, captain, but I don't get your idea. I don't understand what this is supposed to show. If the body was thrown over from this ship, it must have been at this position where it was found?"

"That's correct."

"And at about four a.m.?"

"About four-thirty."

"Very well; four-thirty. Now the body wasn't picked up till eight-thirty – four hours later. I was informed that a current ran into the Straits from the Atlantic, and if so, wouldn't that have carried the body to the east?"

Goode nodded. "We'll make a seaman of you yet, chief inspector. You're correct as far as your information goes, but it has not gone far enough. What happens is this:

"There is, as you know, a big tide in the Atlantic and a very small one in the Mediterranean. But there's a lot of evaporation in the Mediterranean. The result of these two facts is, firstly, that there's a strong tide running in and out through the Straits, as the Atlantic level rises and falls above or below the level inside. Secondly, on the balance, there is always more water goes into the Mediterranean than goes out. Your information is correct then, that an object thrown into the Straits will float eastward into the Mediterranean. But if you think it goes steadily, you are wrong. It doesn't. It floats back and forward, going a little further east and less far west each time. You follow me?"

"Clearly."

"Now when we passed this circle" – he pointed to the chart – "the tide was nearly high inside the Straits. It flowed for an hour or so more. Then it turned and began to ebb. The body would be carried east, and then back again west. I needn't go into the calculations with you, but I've worked it out and I find the amount of east and westward travel would be about the same. That is, when *Tyne Maiden* passed, the body would be back where it started from."

"That's certainly strong evidence the body was on board this ship," French admitted, more puzzled than ever.

"Yes, but there's more in it than that," Goode went on. "What I've told you indicates that the body might have been thrown overboard from this ship about four-thirty in the morning. But there's another consideration that practically proves it couldn't have got to where it did in any other way."

"It seems to me, captain, that we should swap jobs," French declared with a rueful smile.

"You'd like the sea, would you? What's the betting you'd have her piled up on the first lee shore you came to. No, every man to his own trade."

"All right," French agreed, "I didn't really mean to pinch your job. What's the other consideration?"

"This," Captain Goode returned. "Suppose there wasn't the evidence of the injured leg. Suppose the body could have been carried out of Ceuta Harbour in a row-boat: it could never have got to where it was found."

In the light of French's recent conclusions, this interested him even more than the first point. "Now just how do you get that?" he asked.

"Once again it's a question of tides and currents. Have a look at this chart again. Now you see that the end of the Mediterranean is semi-circular shaped, like a clock from six to twelve. The Straits are situated at nine o'clock. Now imagine a tide pouring in through those Straits. You can see quite well that all the water will not travel due east. That in the centre of the stream, so to speak, will do so, but that north of the centre will tend to turn north, and that south of the centre to turn south. It will spread out fan-wise. It must, to fill up the wider expanse of water."

"I see that," said French.

"Very well. Now suppose the body had been thrown from a rowing-boat. In the nature of the case it would have been nearer Africa than Europe. But if so, it would have floated to the south of east – not to the north, as it did."

This really did seem conclusive to French. Moreover, all these arguments were cumulative, and cumulative evidence could not be gainsaid.

But though he felt he must now agree that Mant's body had been taken out of Ceuta on *Patricia*, this only left him the more mystified. The difficulties which such a theory involved still remained. How could the body have been brought on board? If it were brought on board, where could it have been hidden? Who could have been guilty?

He put these points to Goode, but here the captain was unable to help him. What had actually occurred was as great a mystery to him as to French.

"All the same, I'm tremendously grateful for what you've told me," French went on. "Though there's a deal that I still don't understand, two points seem pretty clear. The first is that Mant Carrington was murdered by some person or persons now aboard this ship, and the second, that my immediate business is aboard this ship, and not at Ceuta or Gibraltar. And my next job is clear, too. I've got to work out just how the thing could have been done, and then I've got to get proof that it was done that way. Not so easy as you might think, as you said to me some time ago." He smiled at the captain.

"No," Goode returned, "our own job's always the hardest, isn't it? What did you think of the town?"

They chatted about Valetta, and then Goode indicated that he had some business to attend to.

French went back to his chair on the forward well-deck. There once again he lit a pipe and settled down to worry over his problem. He kept a book open on his knee to discourage chance passers-by, but he did not read it. He could see in his mind's eye a great deal of what must have been done on that fatal Saturday evening, but at a certain point the vision grew blank. There was a hiatus in his reconstruction which he was unable to bridge. And until he had done so he need not hope for progress.

He thought it might help to go back to the very beginning and picture what must have happened. Luke and Eva Dugdale were comfortably enough situated at Bromsley with William Carrington as head of the business. They had no special grievance with life and were as happy and contented as most people.

Then William had had his breakdown, and had sent to Australia for Mant to take charge. In this, whatever Jim Musgrave might have felt, Luke Dugdale could have had no grievance, as his was a specialist's job, and he had not the training which would have enabled him to take charge in William's place. Conditions after Mant's arrival ought to have gone on as before.

But owing to the character of Mant they had not done so. Eva Dugdale was an extremely pretty woman, and Mant had begun to pester her with unwanted attentions. So much appeared to be fact. Whether or not Luke knew of the affair was not known, but there were strong reasons for believing he did. Only on such an assumption could the presumed action of the two be explained.

Suppose for argument's sake he did know. The situation as it appeared to the Dugdales must have been extremely difficult. Definitely Luke was not going to allow his wife to be annoyed in any such way, but how could he stop it? Any open breach with Mant would have meant the sack. Somehow Mant would have worked it. He might have used the threat as a lever with Eva. However, it was obvious that the simplest way out of the difficulty for both the Dugdales would be that Mant should die.

But how could his death be brought about?

As French sat dreaming he seemed to see, as on a mental stage, the whole affair in that house in Bromsley being enacted. These two knew the house. They knew where the different members of the family would sit. They arranged an opportunity before dinner. While Eva got rid of Katherine Shirley from upstairs by a pretended thoughtfulness, Luke had managed to be left alone in the cloak room. French could picture Eva coming silently downstairs and halting on the steps so as to warn Luke if anyone approached and to prevent any such person from entering the dining room; and Luke slipping in and dropping two or three drops of his arsenic solution into each glass and in addition a number of the tiny pellets of eserine into Mant's. Their rejoining, separately, the party in the sitting room. The resultant illness, and the wholly disconcerting and surprising fact that Mant did not die, due to a factor which they had overlooked: that the arsenic made Mant sick, and that he thus got rid of the eserine.

What would have been the feelings of Luke and Eva then? They had risked their lives and liberties, given immense trouble and suffering to themselves and their family, and gained – nothing whatever! Their problem remained just as acute as ever. It was necessary to take some new step.

Then came convalescence and the decision to go on this Olympic cruise. No doubt the Dugdales had agreed that their attempt must be repeated, this time with success. No doubt they had been watching for an opportunity of carrying it out, probably devising scheme after scheme. At last they devised one which seemed satisfactory. If they could get Mant alone at night in some deserted spot near *Patricia*, they could see their way. When they reached Ceuta and noticed the long, deserted pier, they felt that this was the place. It was decided – had the Dugdales anything to do with it? – that Mant would go ashore. Here was the chance they had been waiting for.

It now became necessary to arrange that they themselves, and Mant, should go ashore alone but separately. As far as they themselves were concerned, this was easy. But they were faced with the difficulty that Old William proposed to go with Mant. What was to be done? Their former plan of the poisoning occurred to them. By Eva directing the attention of the party away from Luke, Luke was able to lean over and let a drop of poison fall on William's food. Probably this also was arsenic.

After dinner Luke and Eva went ashore and took cover to wait for Mant. He might not, of course, have been alone: he might have accompanied other passengers, in which case the plan would be postponed. But, as it happened, he was alone, and they joined on. Then doubtless Eva held him in talk while Luke slipped behind him and sandbagged him. They had their rope with them, and they made it fast to the body and lowered it into the sea.

So far French could go with reasonable ease. But when he tried to reconstruct the next step he found himself entirely baffled. In the light of his recent discoveries, it seemed clear that the Dugdales had then got the body somehow on board *Patricia*, there hiding it so extremely well that no one suspected its presence. About half past four in the morning they somehow threw it into the sea, removing all trace of what they had done.

All that evening French wrestled with his problem, and that night he lay awake in his berth while *Patricia* rolled over a heavy ground swell which was setting northwards up the Ionian Sea. He could not sleep. He must find some solution. He had got so far with the case that the remainder must be comparatively easy. As had happened in countless instances before, he told himself that what another man had done, he could do. The Dugdales had devised a plan to meet these conditions. Well, he could do the same.

But he didn't: not till daylight was shining in through his porthole. Then suddenly he could have kicked himself. There was a perfectly simple and obvious way out.

Suppose before they went ashore after dinner the Dugdales had hung a rope out of their porthole? Suppose after killing Mant, Dugdale had found a boat and towed the body to the side of the ship. Their cabin was on the starboard side, and the ship was lying facing out to sea, with her port side against the mole. Suppose Dugdale had then tied the body to the rope from the porthole, replaced the boat, and gone into the town with his wife? Suppose on returning to the ship they had pulled in the rope, so that the body was raised out of the water? Or even so that it was left in the water and would be towed along? In either case, in the darkness of the night, it would not be seen. Then when they were out sufficiently far from the shore, all they had to do was to cut the rope, and all trace of their crime was hidden. No doubt before throwing the body into the sea the necessary weight to sink it had been attached.

French was delighted with his theory. It met the facts, and as it seemed to be the only one which would do so, it must, he thought, be true.

Presently powerful confirmation of the idea occurred to him. The chief engineer had pointed out that the time that the body would take to sink to propeller level would be such that, in the case of a ship of any size, it must have been thrown into the water near the stern. Now the Dugdales' cabin *was* near the stern.

But still, French saw, there remained the greatest problem of all: How was he going to prove his theory? So far he had no evidence which would be worth two pins in a law court. No, before his case was finished, he must do a lot better.

Usually he had found that in what seemed at first sight perfect schemes of murder, a really careful consideration showed previously unsuspected flaws. Fortunately for the security of the public, few such plans were completely watertight. Was there in this plan of the Dugdales' any intrinsic or fundamental flaw, which, if he could only find it, would give him the proof he needed?

As he was considering the point he grew sleepy. With a grunt of satisfaction with the progress he had made, he turned over and did his best to recover the sleep that he had lost earlier.

– 20 –

THE DECISION OF WILLIAM

When French woke a couple of hours later he found they were rolling more heavily than they had yet done. He shaved with some little difficulty and went on deck. The morning was fresh and clear and the sun brilliant, but the wind was high. It screamed through the deck fittings and made him cling on to the rail and to his cap. The sea he thought really rough, but the second officer told him it was only "much furrowed", or not more than about eight feet from trough to crest. French would have said the waves were two or three times as high, but whatever their dimensions, their beauty was unquestionable. Delighted to find he was not ill, he watched them with joy. Their colouring was superb: the deepest ultramarine, dancing and scintillating in the sun, and crested with dazzling white. Whole separate series of waves he could trace. On the great fundamental rollers were others, forming on their sides what he would have called an ordinary choppy sea. These bore still smaller waves, and on the smallest were ripples. Fascinated, he felt he could watch them forever.

About a mile to port and moving parallel with *Patricia* was a tramp of perhaps a thousand tons. She was fairly wallowing. She would put down her bow as if she were going to dive to the bottom, then raise it in a smother of white water and foam. French could see her screw come out high and dry at times, while at others the blades slashed the water, throwing up cascades like an irregular and spasmodic fountain. He was glad, as he watched her, of the comparative stolidity of *Patricia*.

Presently matter triumphed over mind, and he went below to breakfast in a sadly depleted saloon. No one had yet arrived at his table, and as he ate alone his thoughts inevitably returned to his case.

In the cold light of day he was more critical of his conclusions than during the more fevered night. That theory he had evolved was very ingenious, but was it true? Almost at once a fact occurred to him which caused him to wonder.

He had assumed that during the night the body had been hung by a rope from the Dugdales' porthole, either above or below water level. But was this a tenable assumption?

It was clearly impossible, he thought, that the body should have been below water level while the ship was moving. To drag a body through water at the rate of fifteen or sixteen knots would require great force. If it didn't break the rope, it would surely injure the body. The clothes would be torn off and the rope would cut deeply into the flesh. Therefore, from three till four-thirty at least, the body must have been drawn up out of the water.

But was this possible either? Would the pressure of the rope not mark the body under these circumstances also? French was certain that it would. Even if the rope had been put round the chest beneath the arms, an hour and a half's swinging on it would have caused post-mortem bruising and discolouration.

But the body showed no signs of such bruising, save for the one mark half round the right ankle. Was it conceivable that the Dugdales had tied the rope to the ankles? French couldn't believe it. Somehow it wouldn't be human nature to do so. To tie a sinker to the ankles was different. But to haul a body up, the rope would be put round the chest or wrists.

But there was a further consideration, and rather a devastating one. If the body had been hauled up by the ankles, certain objects which were found in the pockets would have fallen out. The coins in the trousers pockets might conceivably have remained, but the pocket-book in the breast-pocket of the coat would certainly have been lost. The more French thought over this point, the more convincing he found it.

If then he were right, the body had not been swung from a porthole. And if it had not been swung from a porthole, his theory was false. The Dugdales could not be guilty. French swore beneath his breath.

How he wished he could find out something definite. It was all very well to go on supposing what might have happened, but at best this only produced theory. What he wanted was certainty. Had the Dugdales committed this crime or had they not? That was the immediate question, and he could find no answer to it.

He moved like a brooding spirit about the ship, trying to find a deserted place in which he might attack the problem once again. His own special preserve on the forward well-deck was impossible this morning, not only from the wind, but from the mist of flying spindrift which came up over the side and from which everything on the decks was streaming. He thought he would go back to his cabin, like the majority of his fellow passengers. His berth would be as good a place for rumination as any, and he knew his cabin mate was on deck.

He lay down and began to think. But for a long time he made no progress. The affair seemed insoluble. He had an urge to go and consult the captain again, but he felt that he couldn't depend on Goode for everything and must do some of the work himself.

As he lay looking at the reflections of the sea on the white woodwork a further idea suddenly struck him. That steward who had called the Dugdales to the captain's enquiry! Had he by chance noticed their porthole? Could he say definitely that a rope had not been fixed to it?

Ten minutes later he was interviewing the steward. The man stated he had been in all three cabins occupied by members of the party on that evening, and he had noticed that in all of them the portholes were closed. He knew this because that evening there had been some difference of opinion about the portholes. The night was cold and he had shut them all. Some passengers had opened theirs again. None of the Carrington party had done so.

A glance showed French that a porthole could not be shut if a rope passed through it. Therefore, definitely he was wrong in his theory. He was in fact no further on than when he had started.

He felt baffled and exasperated. The problem had seemed easy and straightforward at first sight, but it was turning out one of the worst he had ever tackled. He knew the man had been murdered. He knew where. He knew how. He knew almost certainly who had done it. And he could obtain neither the complete details, nor proof of the guilt of his suspects. It was not good enough, he told himself severely. He must do a lot better.

But it was one thing to make a resolve, another to carry it out. For two hours he tossed in his berth, worrying over the affair.

Then at last a smile broke on his face. Fool that he had been! His theory had been right all the time, but he had missed just one small part of it.

Suppose the Dugdales had done exactly what he had already imagined, from the moment they left the ship up to the time they returned on board. If so, they would reach their cabin to find the body in the harbour beneath them, but anchored by a rope through the porthole. Why should they not then have pulled it up into the cabin? There would be no difficulty in getting it through the porthole. All these portholes are made, by Act of Parliament, large enough for a large-bodied man to pass through. There was ample space beneath the berth to have hidden the body behind their suitcases. Then at half past four they could have opened the porthole and pushed it out.

French was pleased. This theory would meet the case. At last he could be certain of what had been done.

But could he, after all? He was far from being convinced in his own mind. Then be saw that two tests were available. The first was: At what hour had the steward closed the portholes? If before the return of Luke Dugdale – for Mrs Dugdale could never have got the body in alone – he was still far from the truth. The second was that the body could scarcely have been pulled in without wetting the berth beneath the porthole. Had that been done?

French immediately made a second call upon the long-suffering steward. And then at once he was plunged into a deeper slough of despair than ever. The steward had closed the portholes about ten o'clock, except in the case of old Mr Carrington, who had himself closed his earlier. That was before Mrs Dugdale had returned to the cabin and a considerable time before Dugdale had done so.

The matter was so completely decided by this evidence that it did not seem worth while asking the further question about whether the man had noticed traces of sea water in the cabin. French's general training, however, made him do so.

The reply was unexpected. There had been no sea water in the Dugdales' cabin, but the next day he had noticed slight traces of it in Mr William Carrington's. Mr Carrington had explained that they had been caused by his tripping and falling against the wall behind the berth while wet from a plunge in the swimming pool, which was next to his cabin. French remembered that he had heard that William had had a bathe on his return from Tetuan. A swim was the one thing on board that the old man seemed really fond of.

No help there, thought French. Even if he had suspected William, William had not been ashore, and even if he had been in league with the Dugdales, French was satisfied he could never have pulled the body up single-handed. Mant was a big and heavy man and William was an invalid, and sick into the bargain. Nor could the Dugdales have gone to William's cabin on their arrival and pulled up the body. The porthole was closed when the steward was sent to call the doctor.

No, French was further from the truth than ever. Discouraged and very tired, he went up to try to find someone sufficiently inured to the sea to join him at deck quoits.

Play on the heaving deck involved such concentration that for the time being French forgot all about his case. He played three games before lunch – draws, as neither side scored anything – and then, French's table mates still being *hors de combat*, his partner kept him company during the meal. It was not till after it was over and French was going up on deck to have another look at the sea that his thoughts turned back to the real object of his trip.

Then an idea struck him which brought him up, as it were, all standing. He moved on like an automaton to the rail and stood gazing outwards, but in reality seeing nothing but the implications of this new conception.

The more he did so, the more his excitement grew. Wonderingly, tremulously, he asked himself the question: Had he got his solution? Wondering, tremulously, he became more and more convinced that he had. Yes, truly he believed he had! As he considered it, detail after detail fell into line and the whole affair took on a coherence which would permit of no explanation other than that it was the truth.

Yes, he could see now what had happened on that deserted wharf at Ceuta. At last it was plain how the body had reached the point at which it was picked up. No longer did the question of the closed portholes present a difficulty. All was now clear as day. And not what happened at Ceuta only. French was equally satisfied that he knew just what had taken place in the old house in Bromsley. He was not investigating two cases, but one. He had at least been right in assuming that the second attempt to murder Mant Carrington had taken place only because the first had failed.

He was more delighted than he could have said. Here once again was success. It had been a problem of enormous difficulty. So much the better: his success was correspondingly greater. Once again he had vindicated himself and upheld the prestige of the Yard.

But, as so often happens, second thoughts were less rosy. It was true he had guessed what had happened, and this was of course splendid. But, from another point of view, he was not so much further on. It was little use to know what had taken place, unless he could prove it in a court of law. And he couldn't prove it even to himself. No, however satisfied he might be as to its truth, his new theory still remained pure surmise.

He saw that he had been a little too quick in his self-congratulations. He was doing well: but he had not done. More work was needed to reach a conclusion. And he didn't quite see what that work was to consist of.

Presently his first reactions to the idea passed away, and he settled down to think the matter out in detail. Then he saw that there was one enquiry which he could make without further delay. He drew a pad towards him and wrote a message to the chief of the Sydney police. Would that officer kindly wireless to him a précis of Mant Carrington's history, as far as this could be learnt. The answer, he believed, would not only finally confirm or refute his theory, but if the former, would constitute an invaluable piece of evidence for the future trial.

Believing that he could do nothing more until he received his reply, French tried to banish the case from his mind and give himself up to the pleasure of the trip. He saw with growing regret that if he were right in his new ideas, the cruise had for him very nearly reached an end.

The wind by this time had dropped and the sea was already falling, and *Patricia* was moving along in a much more sober gait. After tea deck quoits became a practical proposition, and he had the satisfaction of beating his former opponent. By dinner time only a slow roll remained and once again they had a full complement of diners.

Next morning French received at once a thrill and a disappointment. He went on deck to find *Patricia* lying in a large harbour dotted with shipping, mostly of the smaller types. Her bow pointed to a wide street which ran along its shoreward side. The houses in this street were built in isolated square blocks, and there was a slight suggestion of untidiness in their irregular distribution. Somehow it looked to French as if a fine modern city had been begun, and that the builders had grown tired when half way through. But the street was busy and there were evidences of a moderate prosperity.

French's thrill was due to this being his first sight of Greece; his disappointment to the picture not being more imposing. Piraeus, the port of Athens! What history had been staged upon these waters and this shore and those overlooking hills! Two thousand five hundred years ago this was one of the centres of world life, and never from then till now had it ceased to be a place of importance. French did not exactly know what he had expected to see, but somehow the reality did not quite come up to his vague expectations.

He had booked for the day excursion to Athens, and presently the party went ashore to find rows of cars parked in the side street across the waterfront. A short drive through the town and along the coast, and they came to a magnificent new boulevard stretching straight as an arrow from Phalerum Bay to Athens, some three miles away. Building was in progress all along it; small and apparently admirable dwelling houses, but unfinished as to sites. Even those which were complete and occupied seemed to have been left surrounded by debris, as if they were samples erected in a builder's yard.

With the older part of Athens French was lost in wonder and admiration. Though his knowledge of the classics was sketchy in the extreme, he appreciated what he saw as much as anyone in the party. Always he was in the front rank when talks were given. He was not afraid of exhibiting his ignorance, and asked the guide conductor what he wanted to know. The temples staggered him by their size and beauty, and he was left marvelling at the details of perspective design which the lecturer explained. The Areopagus, or Mars' Hill, he had read about in his Bible, and he gazed with a thrill at the place where St Paul had preached.

On the whole he had a gorgeous day, returning to the ship with a keenly whetted appetite for Grecian exploration.

That evening after dinner, he encountered the Carrington group in the smoke room. Though in a technical sense they might have looked upon him as an enemy, actually he got on with them very well. They had also enjoyed their day, and they were comparing notes as to their experiences, when a wireless message was handed French. With a muttered apology he opened it, saw that it was from the chief of police of Sydney, and thrust it into his pocket. A few moments later he drifted away from the others and retired to his cabin to read it.

Though it was not a long message, he saw as he read it that the Australian police had done him very well indeed. It read:

> YOUR MESSAGE RE MANT CARRINGTON STOP SON OF ENGLISHMAN GEORGE CARRINGTON ASSISTANT ENGINEER CORPORATION ELECTRICAL DEPARTMENT DRINKER AND BAD LOT DIED AUGUST OF LAST YEAR STOP MANT WELL EDUCATED AS ELECTRICAL ENGINEER GOOD JOB WITH STEVENS AND PENTLAND STOP DISMISSED TWO YEARS AGO FOR FRAUD NARROWLY ESCAPED PRISON SINCE THEN LIVING ON WITS STOP LAST APRIL SOLD UP SUDDENLY AND LEFT FOR ENGLAND STOP.

French rubbed his hands in high satisfaction. This was just the kind of reply he had hoped for, and though it did not exactly establish his theory, it so strongly supported it that the last lingering doubt of its truth was removed from his mind. Yes, beyond the slightest question he now knew what had happened in this troublesome case. But still he had no proof. This information, useful as it was, would not be accepted as such in a court. He must do better still. There must surely be plenty of evidence, if only he could obtain it.

Once again he took from his case the dossier handed to him by Inspector Kirby. Knowing what he knew now, there must surely be in this some indication of his next line of research. Lying on his berth, he began for the nth time to reread it

It started with a history of the Carrington family, and a précis of the careers of all the members in any way concerned with the poisoning affair. In this history it mentioned Mant's father, George. French read all there was about him.

It appeared that on completing his education George had been taken into the firm. He had been trained as an electrical engineer and had done the machine assembly in connection with the firm's various jobs. This had involved visiting various parts of Europe and Africa, not infrequently with William, his younger brother, who did the site work, buildings and foundations. He had left the business on the completion of a job at Akkondi on the Gold Coast. In this he had been associated with William, and from the Gold Coast he had gone to Australia without returning to England. On his reaching Australia, Kirby's information came to an end.

From the report of the Sydney police George had turned out badly in Australia. Character seldom deteriorated suddenly, therefore did it not look as if the seeds of decay must have been present before he reached that country? It was not unlikely. French wondered why he had broken adrift from the firm. There had been some trouble at Akkondi between the brothers. What exactly had been its nature?

There would at all events be no harm in asking the question. French drew a pad towards him and wrote a message to the chief of police at Akkondi, asking if he could look up old records – and tell him anything he could about the Carrington brothers, who had been connected with the erection of an electrical plant in that town many years previously.

French continued wading through the dossier. Then suddenly he came to an item which completely puzzled him. An error apparently in the dates.

Old William Carrington's breakdown began early in June. He had attempted to carry on, and it was not till some time later that he admitted his inability to do so. He had then wired to Mant to ask him if he would take over the works, and it was after receipt of that wire that Mant had come by air to England. He had arrived at the Grey House on July 17th, and presumably had reached England on that or the previous day. Therefore according to Kirby's information, he had not left Australia till early in July.

But now the Sydney police wirelessed that he had left in April. There was here surely some mistake. It did not seem a matter of great importance, but discrepancies in the details of a case were always worth following up, as experience showed that they frequently led to unexpected discoveries. French wrote another message, this time to

Scotland Yard. He would be glad if they would try to trace the cables which had passed between William and Mant, as well as to check up the dates on which Mant had used the Australia-England air service. Then as an afterthought he added a number of questions which he wished them to put to Messrs Cunn, the cruise agents. The answers to these he suddenly saw might prove decisive.

He went on deck to hand the messages in to the wireless operator. It was a magnificent night with a brilliant moon, and the ship and harbour were illuminated almost as if it were day. He remembered that a party had left the ship after dinner for Athens, so that they might see the Acropolis and Parthenon by moonlight. He regretted not having gone with them. However, he thought with keen anticipation, tomorrow was a day, and he had booked upon the optional excursions to Eleusis and Marathon.

As he reached the boat deck he saw a figure strolling along it. It was William Carrington. French stopped and spoke to him.

"A lovely night, Mr Carrington."

"Yes, isn't it," the old man answered. "I came up for a breath of air before going to bed. The others have gone to Athens."

"I was just wishing I had gone too," French admitted. "They say the Parthenon by moonlight is a sight you never forget."

"So I've heard, but to go in again would have been too much for me."

For a moment they chatted, then French passed on along the deck. The wireless operator happened to be in his office and French handed in his messages. Then after a short stroll he went down to bed. William Carrington had already disappeared.

French was down early at breakfast next morning, eager for his excursion. Eleusis, he had heard, was one of the most wonderful places to be visited, and the lecture which was always delivered made the old ruins glow with life and filled them with the shades of people who had been dead for thousands of years. His quoit friend was going, and French had arranged that they should sit together on the drive.

He had already joined this man in the crowd at the head of the ladder when Jellicoe came up to him and touched his arm. The doctor was looking very grave, and he beckoned French aside.

"I'm afraid there's more trouble, chief inspector," he said in a low tone. "Something dreadful has happened. Old Mr Carrington is dead."

The news was like a blow in the face to French. He stared at Jellicoe, for once speechless from astonishment.

He could scarcely be blamed that the thought which leaped to his mind was not regret for the passing of the old gentleman nor yet awe at the presence of death, but concern for his case. This was utterly unforeseen. Was he entirely wrong after all? He thought he had known the criminal, but this development suggested that he had done nothing of the kind, that his suspect was innocent and that the murderer was someone as yet unthought of.

"Good God!" he said at last in shaky tones. "How did it happen?"

They were walking towards the cabin, meeting a stream of people dressed for going ashore. Till they had passed them Jellicoe did not reply. Then he answered: "Medically I don't know. It looks like poison, but I couldn't be sure without a post-mortem. But there's an empty bottle of prussic acid on the shelf beside him and a note addressed to you."

French groaned. So the man had known! But *how*? French had kept his ideas absolutely to himself. He had confided in no one. William *couldn't* have known.

A nice mess he, French, had made of things at all events! He had been put in charge of the case and he had bungled it like the merest beginner. He swore bitterly as he thought of his failure and the resultant cold looks of his superiors and of his loss of prestige.

However, nothing could now be done. He turned to Jellicoe.

"It was suicide all right," he said grimly. "And it was best for himself. You must prepare yourself for a shock, doctor. He was guilty both of the poisoning and of the murder."

– 21 –

THE EXPOSITION OF FRENCH

These last days, during which French had reached forward to the climax of his case, had been eventful also for Katherine Shirley. During them she also had suffered a continuous nervous strain. Though her fears for Jim had largely evaporated as a result of the finding of the body in the Straits, and its resulting suggestion that a boat must have been used, she remained dreadfully apprehensive of what French might discover.

With French himself she was agreeably surprised. She had pictured an official of Scotland Yard as aggressive and overbearing, suspicious of all with whom he came in contact, and taking little trouble to hide his disbelief in the statements made him. But French was just the opposite. He was quiet and polite in manner, approachable at all times, and seemed kindly in disposition and anxious to give everyone concerned as little annoyance as possible. Indeed, she felt that he was to be trusted: one in whom she might almost confide in a difficulty.

This impression of French's personality, and the slow passage of the days, quite uneventful so far as the tragedy was concerned, tended gradually to restore her peace of mind. Every hour that passed without some new development made it more likely that the hideous episode was over. The longer French took to clear the affair up, the more likely it became that the explanation did not lie aboard *Patricia*. Her belief that until he made enquiries at Ceuta nothing further would be discovered, grew stronger. The hope that none of the Carrington party were involved became gradually more tenable, though she had bad moments when she remembered that no native of Northern Africa could have arranged the poisoning at Bromsley.

To her horror and shame she found herself actually glad that Mant was dead. Now that she looked back dispassionately on the months during which he had lived with them, she began to realise how intensely she had disliked him. His presence in the house had been like a physical weight upon her spirits. Even when he was at the works the knowledge that he was there and that he would soon be returning was on her mind, as a slight toothache, forgotten in the distractions of everyday life, is still there as a subconscious worry. And she was sure that the others felt similarly about him, even her Uncle William, though, as he had brought Mant from Australia, he would hear nothing against him.

How much pleasanter, she thought again with shame, it would be at Bromsley without Mant. She wondered what would be done about the works. Would Jim at last get his chance? Or would Denman Beecher, the manager, be promoted? Or again would her uncle, who seemed so much better recently, take charge once more?

In the meantime there was this perfectly gorgeous trip – with Runciman. How she loved him! And what a splendid time was coming! The wedding need not be unduly postponed because of what had happened. Though it would be quiet, it might be soon. But she would not go to Runciman's house. It was dark and old-fashioned, with a basement kitchen and no modern conveniences. With unexpected difficulty – she was surprised at the opposition he put up – she had got him to agree to moving to a charming cottage which happened to be for sale. Unhappily it would have to be bought with her money, and that was Runciman's objection. It wasn't till she accused him of thinking more of his pride than of her happiness that he agreed that in this case their resources might be pooled.

But though the return to Bromsley would be the precursor of all this happiness, there was an entirely delightful interlude still to be enjoyed. Nearly four weeks of the cruise remained, and the places that they had still to visit were perhaps even more interesting than those they had already seen. What more, Katherine thought thankfully, could anyone desire?

Then just as they were about to go ashore on the second day at Piraeus, this appalling fresh blow fell. The steward, on going into her Uncle William's cabin to see whether the old man was getting up for breakfast, had found him dead. He had at once reported the matter and Runciman had been called. When he came back from the cabin he had told her the news, and she had gone at once with it to the others.

Katherine was overcome with horror: such horror as she had not believed was possible. Another tragedy, and, more dreadful than either of the earlier two! It was this recurrence of tragedy that seemed so unutterably terrible. Directly they were beginning to recover from one blow, another fell. It seemed as if some hideous and relentless fate was brooding over them.

But when she heard that William had committed suicide, and the reason, she was completely prostrated. Though she had never been actually attached to the old man, he had in his way been kind to her. Now that he was gone she saw that he had been kinder and more self-sacrificing than she had realised. What awful madness could have come over him to allow him to commit these terrible crimes? And how ghastly for him to have known that his secret was no longer his own and that he would have to pay the dreadful penalty! The whole thing just didn't bear thinking about.

Katherine, indeed, was stunned and moved about as if in some evil dream. Even Jellicoe, who had taken the earlier tragedy calmly enough, was deeply moved. So was Jim. So were they all.

But they could not continue for long in a dazed condition. Action must needs be taken. There would be an inquest or some equivalent enquiry, and arrangements would be required about the funeral. Also their own plans had to be discussed. Should they continue with the cruise or go ashore here in Greece?

Eventually it was Runciman Jellicoe who took the lead. Largely on his advice it was decided that the interment should take place in Athens, and that the party should leave the ship in order to attend it. They would then go home, either overland all the way, or via Marseilles.

But before they could carry out this programme French asked for a meeting of the whole party. Apart from the necessary routine enquiries into the suicide he had, he said, a special duty to perform, for which their presence was necessary. The captain had kindly put a small private saloon at their disposal, and he would be grateful if they would meet him there at noon.

A trifle resentful that they could not be left alone even in the first shock of this new tragedy, Katherine joined the others in the saloon. French was looking worried, but he spoke sympathetically and, she thought, with even more than his usual kindliness. He thanked them briefly for attending and then went on at once to business.

"I have asked you to meet me, ladies and gentlemen," he said, "for two reasons. Firstly, because I think it is due to you to know what really happened in this very unhappy case; and secondly, because the late Mr William Carrington left a letter addressed to me, and in it he stated that he wished all of you to hear it. I therefore propose to read it to you. I'm afraid it will cause you a good deal of pain, but there is just one message of comfort that I can give you. That is that this unhappy series of tragedies is now at an end. None of you need fear any further troubles from this source. You have had to meet three blows: the poisoning at Bromsley, the death of Mr Mant Carrington, and now this. As you probably know, all three were connected, and Mr William's death ends the series. I deeply regret that the letter will have to be read at the inquest, but that is a matter outside the control of any of us here."

French paused for a moment, glanced round, and then without waiting for comment, went on with the letter.

"I am addressing this letter to you, Chief Inspector French," wrote William, "because no matter to whom it was sent, you would have to see it. But I wish it to be read to all the members of my party, and if they wish for a copy, I should like them to have it.

"To my unutterable amazement I find that you know, or are just about to learn, the part I played in the death of my nephew, Mant Carrington. How you discovered what I thought would never be known by any individual except myself passes my comprehension. But I see that my time is short. Either I shall have to face early arrest and what must inevitably follow, or I must take the coward's way to avoid it. And that is what I am going to do. When you read these words I shall be dead.

"In my opinion it is due to those I leave behind me that I should tell the full circumstances of my crime. Partly for such relief as a confession of this kind may give my mind, but principally lest anyone else should be suspected. I have sinned all through my life, but I should be even worse than I am if I did not guard against that possibility.

"I am not going to take up my time and yours with expressions of sorrow for what I have done. I regret it more deeply than I can say, but that is a matter for myself. Besides, I have much to explain and the time is short.

"And now for my unhappy story.

"The trouble goes back more than thirty-six years, when I was a lad of twenty-two and my brother George was twenty-eight. As you may have heard, the firm did a lot of work abroad, mostly in building and equipping electric power plants. George was an electrical engineer and I a civil, and we were sent together to carry out such jobs. When the trouble came we had done a good deal of this sort of work jointly.

"But though we made a good enough team from the technical point of view, we did not hit it off personally. In this last hour I want to be just, but I honestly think it was George's fault more than mine. However, I need not go into that; it does not affect what happened.

"One of the jobs we had was a large electric power plant for the city of Akkondi on the Gold Coast. George and I were sent out. It wasn't a bad job. The work was straightforward, the people pleasant to us, and the climate not so vile as we had been led to believe.

"It happened that living in the town were two English people, a man named Ryder and his wife Beatrice. Ryder was a bad lot; a sot and a bully, and when he was drunk, as he was most days, he used to ill-treat his wife. He made her life an absolute hell, and she would have left him only that she had neither friends nor money.

"Beatrice Ryder was pretty and charming, and evidently feared and hated her husband. George and I used to go to the house a fair amount, and like the fool I was, I fell head over ears in love with her. She did not encourage me, and that, I think, made me all the worse. At all events I grew infuriated about her treatment. I was careful and my feelings were not generally known, though George was well aware of them.

"One evening George and I had been to call at a house in a deserted spot some little way from the town. It happened that on our way back we met Ryder. He was drunk and I think hardly responsible for what he said. He began to accuse me of making love to his wife. I denied it, and indeed with justice. I loved her, but I had not made love to her. Ryder was very coarse in his remarks, and one thing led to another till we quarrelled. Then Ryder said something very foul about his wife. This was more than I could stand, knowing what she was like and what she had put up with from him. I saw red suddenly and I sprang at the man and hit him with all my strength on the point of the chin.

"He went down like a ninepin and never moved again. When George and I looked we found that he was dead. His head had struck a stone and his skull was fractured.

"I needn't say how terribly upset I was; indeed we both were. I lost my head and wanted to inform the police. But George asked me was I mad? The thing was an accident to me, but it would be no accident to the law. He made it very clear to me that if it was discovered I would hang. He was also afraid, of course, of being thought an accomplice. He therefore suggested hiding the body and denying all knowledge of the incident.

"It happened that we were not far from the town rubbish dump. Work for the day was over and we carried the body there, pushed it in behind some old boards, and hurried to our rooms to put up the best alibi we could. But we hadn't hidden the body properly and we had to do something about it. I was useless from horror and fright, but George thought everything out.

"During that night we slipped out, and after getting a shovel from the works, went back to the dump. There we dug a grave in the front of the tip, where our marks would not be noticed and where the whole thing would be filled over next day. We worked in turns. Then we carried the body over and laid it in the grave. It was my turn to fill, and I began to do so. George called, 'Look here!' I looked up and I saw a flash. George had taken my photograph with the camera we used for works records. As we saw afterwards, the print showed my face, my position of work with the shovel, the hole and the body. It was absolute proof of my guilt. But George had not taken it with any idea of its immediate use. It was his character to take advantage of any circumstances which offered, and he had simply acted on general grounds to get me into his power for the future. Admittedly I didn't see how he could use it without giving himself away, but George was very ingenious, and I could not but realise that he might find a way.

"At all events that night we filled in the hole, replaced the spade, and slipped back to our rooms unseen.

"There was, of course, a police enquiry. We were suspected, I know, but nothing could be proved against us.

I kept away from Beatrice Ryder, and as soon as she could she left the country and I never saw her again.

"Fortunately for both George and myself, the job was nearly done, and we both left the place with overwhelming relief. But George had had enough of the old connections. He said he couldn't stand going back to England, and he left the firm and went to Australia. He sent us his address, but though we knew where he was, there was no real correspondence between us. When our father died, we both got a legacy, I the works and some money, George money only.

"You know my history from that time on. I never heard the Ryder incident referred to, and believed it was buried in the past.

"You can imagine my horror, therefore, when at the end of last May I received a letter from Mant, saying he had come to England and wanted to see me on business. He advised me not to mention his return, and suggested my meeting him secretly in London. He went on to say that his father had just died, and that on going through his papers he had found a certain photograph of a scene in Akkondi, and a note stating how it came to be taken. It was about this photograph that he wished to see me.

"I was, as I say, horrified at this letter, but I realised I must see Mant and hear what he had to say. I accordingly met him in Town. As I had feared, he was out for blackmail. He said that up to the present I had had all the luck. I was rich, while his people and himself had been poor. He now wanted some reasonable adjustment, and the photograph gave him the power to demand it. He trusted I would see that and agree to his proposals pleasantly.

"Of course, I tried to argue. I needn't go into it. I explained that his father had had his share of the family money, just as I had, and could have made as good use of it. He brushed this aside. Then I argued that he could not use the photograph without dirtying his father's name and getting himself into trouble as a blackmailer and accessory after the fact. To this he answered that he was not worrying about his father's reputation and that he had thought out a plan to safeguard himself. If I would not agree to his terms he would have the remainder of his things sent from Australia, and he would pretend to find the photograph and account of the Akkondi affair in some papers of his father's which he would declare he hadn't known existed.

"As I say, I needn't go into our conversation. It is enough to admit that he made his threat so plausible that I felt compelled to agree to his proposal.

"In brief, he wanted the works. He made me an offer of complete freedom from trouble if I would hand over the works to him with sufficient capital to keep them going. He said he knew how to run them and could make good with them. But apart from that one outrageous demand, he was reasonable enough. I could take out with me the greater proportion of my money. He didn't wish to inconvenience me and I should have plenty for everything I wanted. As a matter of fact, he pointed out, I should have to retire shortly in any case, and all he asked was an anticipation of this and a favourable notice in my will. It was wholly proper, he declared, that I should retire in favour of my elder brother's son. No one would think it strange or suspect that anything sinister lay behind it. He ended by repeating his threat. If I met his wishes I should have no further trouble; if not, the police would receive conclusive evidence that I had murdered Ryder. There was my choice, and what did I propose to do?

"Whether I am to be blamed or not, I couldn't face this latter alternative. But, equally, I couldn't face giving up and retiring just as things were. I saw that if I did so, no one would believe there had not been compulsion. I therefore looked about for some way to make my retirement plausible. I thought of feigning a breakdown in health. This would not only meet the immediate case, but I could recover at any time in the future, should the circumstances change.

"I put this to Mant, and I must admit that again he was reasonable. He agreed on two conditions: that my illness should develop before a certain date, and that I would make him an allowance during the interval, as he had no money of his own. To those I consented, and the matter was settled.

"It was easy to simulate the breakdown. I am a good actor. The doctor could find nothing wrong with me, and therefore said 'overwork'. That suited my purpose all right.

"I needn't relate what then occurred. I expect you know, or if you do not, my relatives can tell you. Mant arrived and took over the works. Things seemed to settle down, and no one had any suspicion of the truth.

"But to me life grew more and more insupportable. When I found Mant at the works and myself excluded, and even worse, when I had to have him living in the house with me, I felt I simply could not bear it.

"Then I saw further trouble arising. Mant was a bad lot: from every point of view. He was making trouble with certain customers; he was making trouble with my nephew Jim, who though we hadn't always seen eye to eye about things, was a good fellow. Then the climax came. I happened to discover Mant was making himself objectionable to my niece, Eva Dugdale. This was the last straw. A wave of fierce hatred swelled up in me. From that moment I began to plot Mant's death.

"I needn't tell you of my first attempt and its failure. You know it all. The idea was suggested to me by my discovering one evening at dinner that my glass had not been washed and a little liquid lay at the bottom. I saw that liquid could lie at the bottom of these goblet-shaped glasses with their blue tint, absolutely hidden from casual observation. I obtained arsenic from the weed-killer in the garden and made a saturated solution. I had intended to drop one drop into each glass except Mant's and six drops into his, so that all six of us would be ill with the symptoms of food poisoning, but that only Mant would die. Then I found that six drops would not be enough to kill him, and that if I put enough arsenic in his glass to do so, he would almost certainly discover it.

"At first I thought my scheme had broken down. Then the eserine occurred to me. I read up its action and came to the conclusion that a dose of the tiny pellets would be fatal. I would give Mant the same amount of arsenic as the others, so that the symptoms of all six would be similar, but I would give Mant the eserine as well. Experiment showed me that the pellets would dissolve in the arsenic.

"I carried out this plan, and before dinner dropped four drops of arsenic into each glass and in addition a number of pellets of eserine into Mant's. I thought when I had done so that my niece, Katherine Shirley, had discovered me. But I pretended to be looking for the cigars and she suspected nothing. And here I wish most earnestly to ask the forgiveness of my relatives for the pain and trouble I gave them in this attempt.

"I was astonished beyond measure when I found that my plan had failed and that Mant was recovering. But having come to a decision I did not give up my design. I had failed once: I would not fail again. I began to consider other plans.

"I had been on part of an Olympic cruise in the previous spring, and the incident of a man falling into the harbour at Ceuta, while the ship lay there, recurred to me. I had thought at the time how easy it would be during darkness to get rid of someone by knocking him on the head and throwing his body into the water from that deserted wharf. I began to consider getting Mant to Ceuta on the grounds that what we all wanted to set us up after our illness was a cruise. But I soon saw that nothing so crude as to knock him on the head and drop his body into the harbour would suit, and I began to consider other methods.

"I needn't explain the various plans I worked out and rejected. It is enough to say that at last I devised one which seemed absolutely watertight. It seems so to me still, and one of the smaller drawbacks of what I am about to do is that I shall now never know how you discovered it.

"From one point of view it does not matter how I killed Mant, so long as I admit I did so. But it has occurred to me that I must give the details, lest by some chance my statements should not be believed, and I should be thought to be shielding someone else. What I did then was this.

"I had considered acting at many places, but decided in the end that Ceuta was the most convenient. My plan might not come off there: it depended on certain things which I could not foresee. However, I knew in detail what had been done on the visit on the previous spring, and I counted on the same programme being followed. As it chanced, things worked out perfectly for me. Had they not done so I should have made another attempt at Piraeus, another at Istanbul, and so on till I succeeded.

"I began my preparations by asking the Olympic people to send me a booklet of their cruises, and I contrived to have this in my hand, as if it had just come, when the doctor was visiting us. He saw it, as I had intended he should, and said, as I had hoped he would, that this was the very thing that we all wanted. I pretended to have been so much delighted with the cruise of the previous spring that I wanted to complete the itinerary, and so it worked out that we should go without suspicion devolving on me.

"But my scheme would only work if we could get certain cabins. I wanted, firstly, an outside cabin to myself on the starboard side: starboard because I expected the ship would moor at Ceuta with the port side to the wharf. Secondly, I wanted it on B Deck, so as to be reasonably near the water and yet high enough to ensure the possibility of being able to open the porthole irrespective of the weather. Thirdly, I wanted it to be fairly near the stern, so as to be well away from the bridge.

"I went to Town with my niece, Katherine Shirley, and when she had gone out to shop, I phoned for some of the cruise people to come to the hotel. I saw what cabins were available, and was able by some rearrangement to get what I wanted.

"The affair now seemed a possibility, and I went on with my preparations. I designed and had made in light brass a special bracket. It was a curved bar about fourteen inches long with a hook turned sideways at each end. I told the manufacturers that it was for a special link in a pump I was making, but it was really to hook on a porthole from the outside. The two hooks were so small and so much the colour of the porthole rim, that from the inside only a careful inspection would reveal them, and the curve in the cross-bar was to keep this out of sight below the bottom of the porthole. I also had a ladder made of the best light rope I could find. There were rings on the bracket to which to fasten the ropes of the ladder, and I was sure that with this apparatus I could hang a practically invisible ladder from the porthole to the sea. I also made for myself a sort of veil or headdress of thin black material, which could be worn over evening dress, and which would hide the white face and shirt-front. I got rubber pads for my cheeks, internal heels for my shoes, and a short length of heavy lead piping.

"With these articles in my suitcase we left Glasgow. Still there was no possible suspicion attaching to me. The next stage was three days before we reached Ceuta. I then took a small quantity of arsenic. It knocked me up slightly, and I got the doctor to see me, so as to establish my symptoms. I had recovered when we reached Ceuta, but I pretended to be ill in the hotel at Tetuan. I was perfectly well that evening, though of course I was all the time continuing to act as if I had had a bad breakdown.

"That evening I asked Mant if he would come ashore with me for a walk after dinner. It was to be short, and I asked him in the presence of others, so that the arrangement would be known, and so that he could scarcely refuse. He said he wanted to leave some films in the A Deck lounge before starting, but would join me in my cabin immediately afterwards.

"This suited me exactly. When I reached my cabin I hung my rope ladder out of the porthole, put my hood and other articles ready to my hand, and got out my piece of lead piping. This latter I wrapped in some pairs of socks, to make a soft surface. I hid it under my pillow and sat down and waited.

"Presently Mant came in. He was dressed in a thin black overcoat and carried his hat. I said, 'What are those brass lugs on the porthole rim?' He turned his back to me to examine them. I slipped the lead piping out from under my pillow and struck him on the back of the head. He fell like a log. His skull was fractured, but the soft wool prevented the skin being broken and there was no blood.

"Immediately I tried to make myself up as like Mant as possible. I took the clothes off the body and put them on, slipping my black veil into the pocket. The internal heels in my shoes brought me up to Mant's height, and while there was a strong family resemblance between us, the rubber pads in my cheeks made my face even more the shape of his. In artificial light our colouring was not dissimilar, and by copying his carriage and mimicking his voice I thought I could impersonate him sufficiently well to deceive strangers.

"I pushed the body beneath my berth, putting my suitcases and shoes in front of it. No sign of what had taken place remained in the cabin, and there was nothing out of the ordinary except the two tiny brass lugs on the porthole. But there was nothing to bring the steward in at that time, and if he did look in, it was a thousand to one he would not see the lugs.

"Having pulled down the brim of the hat and turned up the collar of the coat, I now decided I must risk it. I crossed the ship to the port alleyway, which, as you know, is not really intended for passengers. It was off this alleyway that the embarkation room to the shore ladder opened, and as I thought that by this time everyone would have gone ashore, I was sure I would get off the ship unseen by other passengers. But I had bad luck. As I came opposite the main staircase Mr and Miss Rodgers joined me. I pretended to have forgotten my landing card, and turned back till they had gone on.

"I had no difficulty in getting down the ladder as Mant. His landing card was in his pocket, and the officer never suspected. I walked along the pier for some way, finding it deserted, as I had expected. Then I slipped into a doorway, put on my hood and fastened the hat under my buttoned coat. I crept across the pier and lowered myself into the water. I am a first-rate swimmer, and even with all the clothes on, I had no difficulty in swimming round the *Patricia*, and climbing up my ladder. I managed to swarm in through the porthole, unseen in the darkness.

"As quickly as I could I undressed, wrung out the wet clothes down the basin, and hid them with the rope ladder behind the body. In spite of covering my berth with my waterproof I had dropped sea water on the bedclothes, and I covered these with the extra blanket. All the same I had prepared a story to account for the damp. I then closed my porthole, took another dose of the arsenic, went to bed, and sent for Dr Jellicoe.

"I now received a bad fright. I found I had taken too much arsenic, and I grew really ill. I was terrified lest I should be unable to complete my plan. But I succeeded in doing so. When I judged we were about half way to Malaga, I got the body out, redressed it in its clothes and tied the rope ladder and lead pipe to one of its ankles. I judged that the weight would sink it. I found the wristwatch had stopped about nine thirty, owing to its being in the clothes during my swim, but of course this did not matter. With a great effort I managed to lift the body out of the porthole. It fell into the sea and I was satisfied it would never be heard of again.

"But, as you know, the weight was not sufficient to take it down quickly enough to miss the screws. It was struck, and as bad luck would have it, the weight was cut off. The body floated and was picked up.

"And now I have just learnt that all my plotting and scheming has gone for nothing, and that you know, or are about to learn, my secret. This evening, when we were talking after dinner, you received a wireless message. I felt I must know what it was, and I hung about the wireless room in the hope that if the operator left it, I might slip in and see a copy. I was waiting about on the deck when you came up, and when you left me I saw that you were sending a reply. I hid, but remained watching. Presently the operator did go out, leaving the door unlocked. I crept in and saw the messages you were sending. It was obvious to me that when you received the answers, my fate would be sealed.

"And now I think I have told everything essential. As I said, I am not going to indulge in regrets. My sorrow for what I have done is a matter for myself. But once again I ask the forgiveness of my relatives for the distress and suffering my actions have given them. I thank them for what they have done for me. In the case of my niece, Katherine Shirley, nothing that I could say would express my feelings.

"I may add that I made a new will before coming away, and this letter will remove any possible question that I was of sound mind when I did so.

"To you, chief inspector, I add my thanks for doing your disagreeable job as considerately as you could.

"Yours faithfully,

"WILLIAM CARRINGTON."

Little remains to be told. The replies to French's messages gave him complete proof against William, even had the old man's confession never been made.

From the Gold Coast police he learnt of the death of Ryder and the strong suspicion which had fallen on the

Carringtons, and among Mant's papers was the photograph of William burying the body, and George's note giving the circumstances. Scotland Yard told him that Mant had not come to England by air in July, but by boat, leaving Sydney the 10th of April; that William had written to Cunns' for the tour prospectus, and that he had insisted on getting the cabins he wanted, though this meant transferring other passengers, and though there were similar cabins available on the port side. Finally French was able to trace William's purchase of the brass hook and the rope ladder which he had attached to it. This, added to the traces of sea water found by the steward on William's bed, was held to be convincing evidence of what had taken place.

The party went ashore at Athens, and after waiting till after William's funeral, returned to England. In his will the dead man had divided his property between the members of the family, saying in an accompanying letter that it was his suggestion that the firm be turned into a company with each member of the family, Runciman Jellicoe, and the manager, Denman Beecher, as directors.

This was agreed to and arrangements for having it carried out were put in hand. In the meantime Katherine and Runciman were quietly married. As a result of his improved circumstances, Runciman dropped general practitioner's work and took up the original research he had so long wished for.

As for French, though he had let his man slip through his fingers, he had at least cleared up a perplexing case. Moreover, he had visited Greece, not to mention a lot of other foreign places which for years and years had been to him a lovely but impossible dream. All, therefore, even for him, was not lost!

Freeman Wills Crofts

The Box Office Murders

A girl employed in the box office of a London cinema falls into the power of a mysterious trio of crooks. A helpful solicitor sends her to Scotland Yard. There she tells Inspector French the story of the Purple Sickle. Her body is found floating in Southampton Water the next day. French discovers that similar murders have taken place. After gathering evidence he learns the trio's secret and runs them to ground.

The Hog's Back Mystery

The Hog's Back is a ridge in Surrey and the setting for the disappearance of several locals. A doctor vanishes, followed by a nurse with whom he was acquainted, then a third person. Inspector French deduces murder, but there are no bodies. Eventually he is able to prove his theory and show that a fourth murder has been committed.

'As pretty a piece of work as Inspector French has done...on the level of Mr Crofts' very best; which is saying something.'

E C Bentley in the *Daily Telegraph*

Freeman Wills Crofts

Inspector French's Greatest Case

We are here introduced for the first time to the famous Inspector French. A head clerk's corpse is discovered beside the empty safe of a Hatton Garden diamond merchant. There are many suspects and many false clues to be followed before French is able to solve the crime.

Man Overboard!

In the course of a ship's passage from Belfast to Liverpool a man disappears. His body is picked up by Irish fishermen. Although the coroner's verdict is suicide, murder is suspected. Inspector French co-operates with Superintendent Rainey and Sergeant M'Clung once more to determine the truth.

Freeman Wills Crofts

Mystery in the Channel

The cross-channel steamer *Chichester* stops half way to France. A motionless yacht lies in her path. When a party clambers aboard they find a trail of blood and two dead men. Chief Constable Turnbill has to call on Inspector French for help in solving the mystery of the *Nymph*.

Mystery on Southampton Water

The Joymount Rapid Hardening Cement Manufacturing Company is in serious financial trouble. Two young company employees hatch a plot to break in to a rival works, Chayle on the Isle of Wight, to find out Chayle's secret for underselling them. But the scheme does not go according to plan. The death of the night watchman, theft and fire are the result. Inspector French is brought in to solve the mystery.

OTHER TITLES BY FREEMAN WILLS CROFTS AVAILABLE DIRECT FROM HOUSE OF STRATUS

Quantity		£	$(US)	$(CAN)	€
☐	Inspector French and the Starvel Tragedy	6.99	11.50	15.99	11.50
☐	Inspector French's Greatest Case	6.99	11.50	15.99	11.50
☐	James Tarrant, Adventurer	6.99	11.50	15.99	11.50
☐	The Losing Game	6.99	11.50	15.99	11.50
☐	The Loss of the Jane Vosper	6.99	11.50	15.99	11.50
☐	Man Overboard!	6.99	11.50	15.99	11.50
☐	Many a Slip	6.99	11.50	15.99	11.50
☐	Mystery in the Channel	6.99	11.50	15.99	11.50
☐	Murderers Make Mistakes	6.99	11.50	15.99	11.50
☐	Mystery of the Sleeping Car Express	6.99	11.50	15.99	11.50
☐	Mystery on Southampton Water	6.99	11.50	15.99	11.50
☐	The Pit-Prop Syndicate	6.99	11.50	15.99	11.50
☐	The Ponson Case	6.99	11.50	15.99	11.50
☐	The Sea Mystery	6.99	11.50	15.99	11.50
☐	Silence for the Murderer	6.99	11.50	15.99	11.50
☐	Sir John Magill's Last Journey	6.99	11.50	15.99	11.50
☐	Sudden Death	6.99	11.50	15.99	11.50

ALL HOUSE OF STRATUS BOOKS ARE AVAILABLE FROM GOOD BOOKSHOPS OR DIRECT FROM THE PUBLISHER:

Hotline: UK ONLY: **0800 169 1780**, please quote author, title and credit card details.
INTERNATIONAL: **+44 (0) 20 7494 6400**, please quote author, title, and credit card details.

Send to: **House of Stratus**
24c Old Burlington Street
London
W1X 1RL
UK

Please allow following carriage costs per ORDER
(For goods up to free carriage limits shown)

	£(Sterling)	$(US)	$(CAN)	€(Euros)
UK	1.95	3.20	4.29	3.00
Europe	2.95	4.99	6.49	5.00
North America	2.95	4.99	6.49	5.00
Rest of World	2.95	5.99	7.75	6.00
Free carriage for goods value over:	50	75	100	75

PLEASE SEND CHEQUE, POSTAL ORDER (STERLING ONLY), EUROCHEQUE, OR INTERNATIONAL MONEY ORDER (PLEASE CIRCLE METHOD OF PAYMENT YOU WISH TO USE)

MAKE PAYABLE TO: STRATUS HOLDINGS plc

Order total including postage:______Please tick currency you wish to use and add total amount of order:

☐ £ (Sterling) ☐ $ (US) ☐ $ (CAN) ☐ € (EUROS)

VISA, MASTERCARD, SWITCH, AMEX, SOLO, JCB:

☐☐☐☐☐☐☐☐☐☐☐☐☐☐☐☐☐☐☐☐

Issue number (Switch only):

☐☐☐

Start Date: ☐☐/☐☐ **Expiry Date:** ☐☐/☐☐

Signature: ____________________

NAME: ____

ADDRESS: ____

____

POSTCODE: __________

Please allow 28 days for delivery.

Prices subject to change without notice.
Please tick box if you do not wish to receive any additional information. ☐

House of Stratus publishes many other titles in this genre; please check our website (**www.houseofstratus.com**) for more details